# Between hatred and desire . . .

He looked at the ugly, pink claw lines across his wrists. He lifted his arms and saw his torn shirt. And he remembered how she had fought—standing in his bedroom doorway, flushed and radiant, daring him with her eyes, tempting him with her mouth . . .

**Raw-nerved and starkly real, here is a violent story of an ex-convict who couldn't break free from the criminal world that made him—or the corrupt women who wanted his love.**

**for my wife**
**Jeanette Arnold Friedman**

# EX-CON

(FREE ARE THE DEAD)

by STUART FRIEDMAN

**WILDSIDE PRESS**

**EX-CON**
(Free are the Dead)

# 1

CHARLES GARRELL was disappointed when he stepped off the train and his wife wasn't there to meet him. But he'd learned control in prison, so he didn't let himself imagine things.

He stood clear of the crowd, so that Nora would be able to see him, and scanned the upper-level platform, sure he would see her little figure threading among the moving groups. The slow clang of a bell sounded gloomily through the cold, acrid air of the vast train shed, and the animation gradually left his face. The sight of other men greeting their women began to antagonize him. For three and a half years, for one thousand two hundred and seventy-eight damned days he'd lived for this minute! It was empty. Freedom didn't have any meaning without Nora.

When the crowd cleared, he carried his suitcase to the lighted stairwell and went down to the landing. On the lower flight he held the center rail and moved down, a slow step at a time, searching for her among the boarding passengers.

The clock showed seven twenty-four when he reached the middle of the big station. His train had been late. But Nora knew it had been due at seven-five. They'd talked about it last prison visiting day and mentioned it in every letter since. He asked at the Information Desk and was assured that his name would have been called if anyone had left a message for Charles Garrell. He went to the main entrance and looked out. But in a few seconds he went back where he could watch the side entrances too.

He caught himself glancing over at the clock twice a minute. He lit a cigarette, telling himself she'd come before he finished it. He puffed just often enough to keep it burning and when it was too short to drag, he still held it, pinched between his finger-tips. He had to drop it finally. He took a long time mashing it out and looked down so that when he looked up again she'd be only steps away. When he looked up and she wasn't in sight, he got that lost feeling he'd had the day he'd pawned his suit four years ago.

Everything else had gone. For months he and Nora had been scraping bottom. Pawning his suit had seemed to strip away not only his last hope but his very manhood. In the pawnshop a freak circumstance had given him the chance to steal a gun. He'd been desperate. He thought back cynically that the struggle he'd put himself through had really been cold feet instead of conscience. Anyhow, he'd stolen the gun and used it for the liquor-store holdup that had sent him to prison.

The first few months had been grim. One of the beatings by the screws had put him in the hospital for six weeks. It was the loss of mail and visitor privileges, cutting him off completely from Nora, that had tamed him; not the beatings, not the solitary. Or sometimes he told himself it had been that way, when he was trying to hang onto at least one illusion about himself. But he knew he'd have had to come to heel anyway.

They had been very close, and he had not only left a terrible emptiness in her life, he'd left her broke, in debt, and she'd had to get a job as a waitress. Yet she'd managed the fees to fight for his parole, money for his cigarettes and incidentals, train fares every visitors' day after she was permitted to see him. She always brought some little gift, too, even though she needed things for herself. Sometimes he'd tell her how he'd enjoyed a Sunday dinner or movie or ball game, touting the place like a resort. She'd try to outdo him, prattling along eagerly about her great joys, but she'd fizzle out and he'd see an off-guard forlornness in those deep, gentle eyes that would tear him to pieces.

Throughout everything, Nora had shown him in a hundred ways that he was no less for what had happened, that nothing could shake her love. Even the hat he wore now was her sure understanding of his need for confidence at a time like this. She couldn't afford much, and it wasn't a very good hat, but she had wanted him to have something more than the clothes allowed by the State, something personal from her. He put his hands up and reset it with painstaking care, feeling somehow reassured by simply touching the hat.

He went to the station newsstand and bought cigarettes in order to break the ten-dollar bill he'd got with his release papers and train ticket. He took change and went to a phone booth, dialed the number of her cousin Jerry. There was no answer. He tried looking up the number of the restaurant where Nora worked but his hands were clumsy with nervous impatience and he had to get it from Information. The girl he talked to said they hadn't seen her since last night's closing. She seemed to be a friend, knew Nora had planned a big meal, and she was sure Nora would show up soon. The girl urged him to wait a while longer as it would be a shame for them to pass one another.

He waited. For minutes he was so soothed by the soft persuasion of her voice that he let his attention wander, feeling some of his former amiable attitude toward people. Then, suddenly, he hated the sight of them and withdrew his attention with an icy contempt. Maybe it was true that the man who went into prison never came out: a stranger came out. He couldn't help it. When a man's pride was rammed down his throat it turned to acid in his guts and it never stopped burning. Never.

Just before eight he went to a phone booth again. Jerry's number still didn't answer. The girl at the restaurant had held out a hope that Nora might call and explain the delay. She hadn't, and the girl's effort at a light tone only emphasized that she was worried. Charles's face was drawn as he left the booth.

He went out and got a cab, gave their home address. He rode in a relaxed slump, a willed torpor over his senses. Twenty-five minutes later he stood on the curb looking at the dismal old building. The windows of both upper apartments were dark, and he could barely control the sudden gritty harshness of his mood.

This was where they had moved after they'd lost the home they'd been buying. Here the detectives had come to arrest him. The ugly, two-story wood box sat deep on the lot, its front porches on a line with the backs of most of the doubles and bungalows along the street. Alternating patches of bare ground and sooty snow made the yard look like an abandoned jigsaw puzzle, and the walk was cracked and tilted. There was a rising sense of urgency in him, but he went up the walk with a brittle deliberation, hating and now fearing the place.

He reached the porch, crossed, and went inside. A cacophony from two radio programs in the lower apartments filled the small, square hall as he crossed to the stairs. He went up. At the landing, midway, he twisted around and craned upward with the momentary conviction that she was looking over the banister at him or smiling out from the open doorway. But the door was shut, the transom dark. He tried the knob, and it was locked, of course.

He put his suitcase down and rapped several times, lightly, hesitantly even, as if he didn't want to find out for certain that she wasn't inside. He waited, looking down at the worn floor, his head tilted at a slight listening angle, hearing nothing. He got out a cigarette, lit it, knocked again, more loudly. He must not get panicky! Maybe the meal and the excitement of today had exhausted her and she'd lain down to nap so she would be at her freshest and prettiest, and the alarm hadn't gone off. He knocked again. What he was forgetting was her capacity for idiocy. She was an angel, yes, but first of all a jerk and just silly enough to be in there playing a joke. And if she was, so help him, the minute he'd finished holding her tight to him and kissing her mouth and her eyes and cheeks and forehead and throat, and as soon as he'd filled his eyes and his heart with the sight and touch and sound of her, he would turn her over his knee and lay it on.

He stood listening intently, breathing silently through open lips. All he could hear were the downstairs radios. On one a girl with an orchestra was singing a blues song in a poignant and haunting voice; on the other a super-bright, rapid-fire comic triggered off explosions of gravelly laughter. It was like a plea answered with coarse mockery, and his fist suddenly banged on the door, raising a hollow, thunderous sound. He stopped. He shot a nervous glance across the dim hall to the closed door of the other apartment as if he might be at the wrong door. He frowned and put his cigarette in his mouth with a jerky motion, and dragged hard. He strode to the door which opened onto the upper porch and went outside.

He heard the clack of a woman's high heels and stood at the flimsy wood railing looking toward the street. Through a welter of auto noise, teen-age shoutings, the surge and dimming of a radio, he studied the woman's sound. It was slower and heavier than the quick, sharp, and somehow delicate rhythm of Nora's walk. He waited, nonetheless, on the chance that she was slowed, burdened with packages. It was someone else.

He went to both of their high front-room windows, tried them, and found them locked. He stood before the end window, frowning down, searching his pockets for matches. He found them and raised his head. Suddenly the muscles of his heart cramped. For a split second he saw a feeble stain of light, showing the outlines, planes, and deep shadow clefts of a man's long, broad face. He muttered. It was his own face, reflected on the glass by the glow of his cigarette. He struck a match, held it aloft, and squinted through the window. He could make out only a bare expanse of floor. He tried the other window and several more matches. The place looked vacant.

It couldn't be! He went inside and downstairs. He looked at the mailboxes and saw the reassuring Charles and Nora Garrell card in #4. All the other tenants were new to him. Charles crossed to #2, the apartment below his, and knocked. The radio comic's voice faded, steps crossed the room, and the door opened.

" 'Evening." The balding, middle-aged man's forehead wrinkled, trying to focus attention on Charles, but a grin hung onto a corner of his mouth, and he held his head cocked, reserving an ear for the radio.

"You George Shadd?" Nod. "Custodian?" Grunt. "I'm Charles Garrell from Four. I just got in town. Mrs. Garrell didn't meet my train and I'm afraid she might be sick upstairs. Will you let me in?"

Shadd puckered, fumbled in his sweater pockets, then peered helplessly into the front half of the room. In a moment a hawkish gray-haired woman was beside him, and while Shadd explained, her gaze scoured Charles from head to foot.

"You don't have a key," she told Shadd. "It's a Yale lock."

"I know. I bought it myself," Charles said. "But you have a key to the back, don't you?"

"Well . . . uh . . ." Shadd shifted, looked at his wife.

"Will you let me in?" Charles said, with heavy patience. "I'm worried about my wife, and I'd rather not break a window. I can identify myself."

"She wasn't sick this afternoon." Mrs. Shadd spoke to him directly for the first time, and she made the statement sound like an accusation. He retaliated with elaborate politeness.

"I am glad to hear that," Charles said. "Do you know when she left?"

"I do not!" she announced righteously.

"But you do know, of course, that she did leave?" A boy with a yo-yo and a gum-chewing bobbysoxer had eased into the middle of the room to gape at him, and he couldn't make out if it was fascination, horror, or simple stupor that gave them the distinctive half-witted look.

"I do not know if she left; I don't spend my time . . ."

He cut her off. "Then you don't know if she's sick up there or not. *Mr.* Shadd, I'm going into my apartment one way or another . . . Do I get a key?"

Shadd took the plunge alone. "Yes. I'll get it and meet you up at your back door."

Charles went out, fuming inwardly. The old hag only guessed the state of Nora's health in the afternoon, probably hearing her move around. It was a cinch Nora wouldn't have discussed anything with that type, and he'd bet his last dime Nora had sniffed her out at once and beat her to the snub going away! Charles went around the building and up the outside back steps to the small crowded porch. The door was locked. He looked in their icebox and saw that Nora had made his favorite whipped-cream banana pie. He clapped the box shut, waited for Shadd.

Eventually he came trudging up in overcoat and stocking cap, feeling ahead with a flashlight. Shadd worried aloud that the door might be bolt-locked inside, but it opened. There was a gush of hot air and an odor of roast beef that would have been mouth-watering any other time. Shadd's flashbeam darted around the kitchen as Charles went in. He groped out overhead till the light cord feathered against his hand, then he lighted the kitchen.

The oven was on low and he turned it off with a pass of the hand and went on between the pair of built-in cupboards to the dining room. He switched on a lamp. The table was set. He glimpsed the place cards Nora had made with goofy crayon drawings and lines of writing that he knew would be delicious nonsense poetry. He entered the narrow hall which led along the wall of the bedroom to the front room. He heard Shadd behind him and stopped, turning abruptly.

"Please don't dog me, Mr. Shadd."

"Nervous, huh?"

He went on without answering. "Dark ahead," Shadd said, following. "Hadn't you better take this?" He offered the flashlight. Charles grasped it without stopping, snicked it on.

The bedroom door, set at an angle off the doorless front-room entrance, was shut. He twisted the knob, thrust it inward, setting the thin curtains swaying in the draft. A rake of the flashlight showed the room was empty, except for furniture. He turned the light on over the foot of the bed, then went in and lighted the front room.

He saw why it had looked vacant from the windows. The furniture had been repossessed his first year in prison. Now, a kitchen chair and an occasional chair—a paid-for wedding gift—faced each other across a clean bath mat. There were two crates skirted with creamy curtain material. There was a little lamp and ash tray on one, books and magazines in library binders on the other. The group, by the hot-air register at the back wall, formed a desolate little island on the expanse of dark, bare floor. The shadow of the ancient chandelier hovered on the ceiling like an enormous crippled spider. In a front corner of the ceiling was a big stain from old leaks with scores of wavy concentric lines like old boundaries of a dry lake. Part of one wall leaned inward with a plaster bulge. A crack, like an imbedded, burned-out stroke of lightning, slashed in a jagged line down the dirty buff paper, cutting through dreary vines of print flowers.

The lonely barrenness of that room didn't hit him fully until he went back into the bedroom and looked at her picture facing his in the double frame atop the bureau. A slow, heavy ache rose in his chest and tightened his throat. He felt a crawling warmth high in his nostrils and in the corners of his eyes. He would have cried, he sure as hell would have, but Shadd was there gawping and he wanted him the hell out of Nora's bedroom.

He got Shadd out of the apartment, almost in a bum's rush, then when he was alone he was ashamed. The poor devil looked as if his whole life was one big pushing around. It really bothered Charles, because he'd recognized that the guy had some pull on his sympathies from the start, but he hadn't even acted civil. It was almost as if he'd wanted to hurt the fellow *because* he thought he was weak. Was it possible that prison had changed him that much? He shook his head nervously.

He went back through the apartment to see if Shadd had left the key. He had. He looked wonderingly at the stove, then got a dish towel and opened the oven. He pulled out the tray and roasting pan, lifted the lid. The meat looked about done; she'd put in vegetables and potatoes. To the best of his memory, she cooked the potatoes and vegetables separate and only put them in the meat juices within an hour or so before she expected to serve. He looked into the bathroom, felt the two bath towels. One of them was still moist over most of its surface. Then he saw the slender imprint of her naked foot in a film of powder by the tub. There was a sudden sharp twinge in his belly and a tingling heat like a current of electricity through him. The same craving for her exciting little body that had damned near driven him crazy in prison surged alive, kicking up the beat of his heart, quickening his breath. He swung around agitatedly, went through the kitchen and dining room, forcing his mind away from the fiery barrage of sensual images.

He swept aside the curtain at the doorway of a long pantry. A triangle of light from the dining room showed a cardboard clothes hamper, cleaning paraphernalia, and in the dim back half were boxes and cartons. Among them were journals, notebooks, technical books from courses he'd taken years ago on the way up, and countless things they hadn't been able to sell nor quite bring themselves to throw away. It depressed him just to look at the dusty remnants of the old days. He let the curtain fall, then stood indecisively beside the dining-room table. He took up one and then the other of the place cards, looked at the comic drawings without smiling, read the light and zestful lines without any lift.

A flurry of sound like the sharp signaling of a fingernail on a windowpane yanked his attention to a one-legged alarm clock on a shelf in the cupboard. Its tick dulled out inaudibly as he looked. He went over and picked it up to see if it was still running. It was. It showed eight-forty. Nora kept clocks five minutes or so fast. Hell, it wasn't so late after all. The volume of the ticking rose again for several ticks, as if the works were lopsided. He grinned wryly, put it back, thinking it wasn't the only thing running around this apartment off balance. The huge mystery of Nora's absence could have been cleared up minutes ago by a fairly promising imbecile. He went through to the front door, opened it, set his suitcase inside, and went down to the mailbox. She hadn't been able to get to the station and had left her message there. There was no message. If her mother had had an attack, she might have had to go across town to her. Her mother had no phone. Her cousin Jerry and his wife might have taken her in their car. Still, she'd have left a message. He asked the tenants in #1, but they knew nothing about her. He went out to the corner drugstore.

He phoned Jerry. He got no answer. He phoned City Hospital, and then the Police Emergency. There had been one young woman accident victim since midafternoon, and that one hadn't been Nora. When he returned to the apartment, he carried his suitcase into the bedroom, uncertain what to do.

Something was wrong. He knew something was wrong. He couldn't identify it. It had signaled one of his senses and vanished. He had smelled, seen, touched, or heard something he hadn't wanted to know. It was gone from his conscious mind now, buried like a thorn.

He went searching through the apartment from front room to back porch. He moved with a muscular looseness, sensing that his body must be fluid, free to launch in any direction. He returned to the bedroom, his nerves keen. His sight sharpened so that the lines of walls, floors, furniture all had the stark clarity of figures under a magnifying glass. He looked at his wife's photograph facing his in the double frame on the bureau. It was a soft and lovely face, and the eyes looked out at him with such a depth of tenderness that for a moment the picture was Nora herself. Then the illusion was gone, as she herself was gone. He didn't know why; he didn't know where . . . Then he could feel his gaze being pulled down and away from the sweetness of her picture. He saw the glittering liquid thread.

This was what he had seen, but hadn't dared remember. He stood paralyzed, staring down at it until his unblinking eyes were raw. It ran out for an inch from the edge of the closet door in a crack between two floorboards. It was near the hot-air register where the floor was warm. It hadn't congealed, but remained liquid, as though still in an artery.

He didn't know how he could open that door. He didn't know how he could get his arm up even to touch the knob.

He shut his eyes. He had never known such profound dread. He loved her . . . her body, her mind, her spirit; she was every-thing! If she was in there, badly injured, or . . . He couldn't face it! He bit his inner lip savagely. He had to.

He opened the door.

His breath went out in a long, exhausted sigh. He reached tremblingly back of him, found her dressing-table bench, and pulled it close. He sank down on it. He just sat, his features slack, his dark blue eyes blank.

Charles felt like the lifer he'd known in prison. That cynical old con would roll his eyes devoutly and offer thanks to heaven, because, when he was in so much agony that he had to groan aloud, he was lucky enough to be deaf.

Charles felt that he had wonderful luck like that. It wasn't Nora in there.

Just a man's corpse.

Charles sat suddenly bolt upright, his face going deathly pale. Somebody was knocking, and knocking hard, at the front door.

# 2

THE KNOCKING HAD the iron-fist officiousness of a prison screw. It was some species of cop. He was an ex-con and that spelled guilty. He stood up, poised on the balls of his feet, leg muscles flexed. If they knew about the dead man, the back door would be covered. Flight was out. He felt trapped. Every second counted. He got his handkerchief out, spread it over the closet doorknob, eased the door shut, wiped the knob. He looked down at the rivulet of blood, bit his lip, shook his head. He couldn't do anything about it. The dresser bench pointed at the closet like an arrow; he replaced it. He started out of the room, reaching instinctively for the light cord. He yanked his hand away. It would be better to leave the room lighted and open.

He knew he was visible from the back door and front windows when he left the bedroom. He tried to loosen his gait, smooth the sharp, nervous edge from his manner. He hadn't taken off his hat and overcoat, because that would fit with the fact his suitcase wasn't open yet. It might convince them he hadn't looked in the closet yet. It *might*. Charles answered the knocking.

It was Gobi and Elton, the detectives who had arrested him four years ago. Homicide would have come if they had known about the dead man. Charles wasn't relieved. If they gave the place a rough toss just for the sport of tearing up the joint, they'd find the body. In prison Charles had learned that the cops in this town were rough on parolees, unless a guy was a professional criminal working at his trade and paying off, or stooling, or belonged to an organization that paid off at the top. Charles intended to go straight.

They moved in slowly, like a wedge entering thick end first. Gobi oozed his mass forward as if Charles weren't there. Charles stepped back and back, retreating from his advancing gut till he was in the middle of the room. Gobi stopped, backed off, and looked down at Charles's shoes as if he had just noticed an obstruction in his path. Gobi's thick-jowled face lifted and his watery little eyes studied Charles's face dully. Compressed yellow lines slanted down through the red flesh from the corners of his mouth as Gobi pinched his lips into an inverted curve no wider than his squashy nose. Charles waited, watching in wary silence broken only by the faint snore of Gobi's breathing and the click of Elton shutting the door behind him.

Elton moved to the windows in a languid sag, an expression of sad weariness on his long, sallow face. In his rakish snap-brim and topcoat, open and loose on his slender figure, he affected the manner of a tired collegian. He managed to get an arm up high enough to grip the edge of the blind. He lowered it, and the other one. Then he strolled out of the room, into the bedroom. Charles's neck muscles turned to steel and he listened without breathing. Elton's step left the bedroom, went slowly back through the place. Charles listened to his return, waiting for a pause and re-entry to the bedroom. But Elton came back into the front room, leaned back tiredly against the door. He'd just checked to know they were alone. Neither of them said a word.

Charles knew these silent tactics. But even so he had to fight the temptation to break the silence. His teeth were set and he realized he was slowly clamping and relaxing his jaws, bulging the muscles below his ears in a nervous pulse. Gobi caught the motion and his snout lifted and tightened slightly as if catching the fear scent. Gobi roused and walked in a slow, tight circle around him. Charles locked his neck muscles against the almost unbearable compulsion to turn his head. He couldn't keep his eyes from tailing. He jerked his gaze forward. Elton, watching him from the door, saw the nervous flick of his eyes. Charles felt a flush rise, and knew that that, too, was visible. It gave him a sense of bitterness, stirring raw, painful memories, and he tried to fight off a tortured premonition of defeat. In a second he would blurt out something, anything. Damned if he'd break the silence! He felt as if the edge of a razor blade were scraping across all the nerve ends in his chest; in a second he'd be wheezing like Gobi.

Gobi finished his circling and looked over at Elton. Elton bumped his tail back against the door, jarring himself erect. He sauntered over to Charles and stood looking at him insolently.

"Hi, Charles."

*They'd* broken the silence. He'd won! "Hello, Elton." His voice was cold, and almost steady, but fuzzed a little. It wasn't good to win even a little from a cop, not good. Gobi had moved around in back of him, and he said:

"Whud he say, Don?"

Elton dragged at his cigarette, then snicked a thumbnail against the mouth end, spilling ash. "He said: 'Hello, Elton.'"

"Whutsa matter," Gobi grunted, "don't he like me?"

Charles watched Elton, said nothing. Elton was looking at him thoughtfully. Elton lifted his hand lazily, put the cigarette between his lips, held it there. He started to lower his freed hand, then abruptly slashed out. Charles felt the palm crack the side of his face sharply. His eyes leaped wide with shock. Involuntarily his fists clenched. Suddenly his right forearm was numbed by a hard, down-chopping blow from the edge of Gobi's hand.

"Don't you know no better than to try hitting an officer?" Gobi growled. "I thought you just got back from college."

Charles watched Elton, said nothing. Elton was looking at breath came in quick, shallow draughts. He glared at Elton, his face intensely drawn, his eyes deadly. His throat was ash dry and for moments he couldn't speak. A slap was a calculated humiliation. It denied a man's dignity, his honor.

*"If you ever . . ."* he began hoarsely, cleared his throat.

"Cap asked you a question," Elton said, ignoring his words. "He asked what was the matter, didn't you like him. You didn't answer. Answer when you're talked to." Sometimes the screws couldn't keep their joy from brimming over when they started punching a man around. They'd grin, Charles remembered, or twist the grins into grimaces. Elton did neither. His eyes just brightened up as if he'd come alive.

Charles said in a low, furious voice: "Never slap my face again or I'll . . ."

Elton shifted hands, slapped the other side of his face. Hard. It stunned him. Then he felt a shock of pain in his skull. His head pitched forward, his teeth clicking, his chin mashing down into the knot of his tie. His hands pawed out disjointedly for his falling hat, then everything was a gray blur.

"Stand up straight, you son of a bitch!" Elton's voice slashed at him with thin, grating contempt.

Elton's face bleared in front of him. His eyes hurt. He squinted, trying to focus. He realized dazedly that Gobi had crashed a fist or the heel of a hand up against the base of his skull. His eyes cleared, but there was a heavy pain above them. There was a nausea in his stomach and he kept swallowing down a sour fluid that rose at the base of his tongue.

Elton was saying easily, "Didn't they teach you to read time up in college?"

Charles pushed his hair off his forehead. He saw his hat getting dirty on the floor, the hat Nora had bought to try to help him feel like a human being again.

"I said," Elton repeated with heavy patience, "didn't they teach you to read time up in college? You're being talked to."

He barely heard. All he could think about was his hat. He had to get his hat. He felt unsteady and he tried to concentrate and pull himself together so he wouldn't topple when he bent down. Elton might drive his knee up into his face or club the back of his head if he bent. Charles winced, straightened, strangling a cry of pain in his throat as Gobi jolted a kidney punch into his back and threatened: "Answer, you bastard!"

Charles clenched his teeth, and stared at the hat till tears burned his eyes. His whole being concentrated on one thing, one thing only. Everything seemed to depend on getting his hat. He planned to bend and sweep it up in a lightning motion. He tried to co-ordinate all his senses and made the plunge, but he'd signaled his intention. His reach was awkward and his fingers were far short of it when the toe of Elton's shoe punted it across the room. An inarticulate sound of desperation burst from him and he started blindly after the hat. Gobi yanked him back by the collar; a moment later Gobi's arm was around his neck, the forearm bone crushing into his windpipe. Charles dug his chin down against the choking arm and hooked his own arm back to get a lock on Gobi's head. Elton mashed his body tight to him, stomped a heel into Charles's instep. He pulled his foot away, tried to kick back into Gobi's knee and slug the side of Elton's head at the same time. Gobi's stranglehold tightened till Charles gagged. Elton had the opening he wanted. He drove a knee viciously up into his groin.

For an instant the agony was so great he thought he would pass out, then he wanted to retch. Finally he was standing free, but so weak he thought he'd sink down. He tried to lift himself with a deep breath. He stood breathing painfully aloud, massaging his throat. His legs and arms trembled, his lips quivered. Elton stood panting, wetting his lips, his face menacing.

"Are you gonna stand up and answer when you're talked to, or not?"

He tried to get some flint in his eyes to meet Elton's gaze. The underlid of his left eye began to twitch as if a fishhook was tugging the muscle. He just wanted to lie down and pull his legs up against the pain in his stomach. He felt faintheaded. The thought of getting hit again, anywhere, sent terror through him. The blow could come any instant. "Yes," he whispered.

"Whud he say, Don?"

"I didn't hear him say nothing."

He had to answer louder. He couldn't. He wouldn't. Oh, God damn them, God damn them! The pressure in his chest threatened to burst out in a sob. "Yes!" His voice lashed the word at Elton's face savagely, as if his obedience were defiance. He heard Gobi's chuckle of satisfaction. He was a whipped cur, and the mock defiance made him ridiculous. He couldn't take it, he couldn't! "I just want my hat first, see? Get it?" he said, half-incoherently. "Sure I can read time, but it's a new hat, I got to watch expenses. Have to get it cleaned. I'll just get the hat and then we'll talk it over. Sure I can read time. First, though . . ." It was a stupid try; Elton shook his head with cool amusement, let him know he wasn't making conditions. In prison the beatings had been so rough that he'd been degraded till he thought he could never hold up his head again. But he'd thought all that was in the past. He looked desolately at his hat, knowing with what love and hope and pride Nora had bought it. He was filled with a sick and lonely despair. He was shamed again. Shamed.

Elton glanced at his watch. "Time you got, Cap?"

"Nine-oh-seven, Don," Gobi answered.

Charles saw that Elton was leading to something, but stalling, not as a tactic but to regain composure. He was glad of the breather, glad to be curious over what they wanted; it relieved the sense of shame. But not much. Elton finished mashing out a cigarette on the floor, lighting another, re-pocketing the lighter.

"Now lemme figure back to seven-five, the time your train

arrived. About two hours, h'm?" Elton said with an insinuating purr.

"About," Charles said carefully. "The train was a few minutes late." The question "Why?" stopped unspoken in his throat, automatically. It would sound as if he was daring to put questions. The pain in his body was dulling, but there had been just enough of it to alert all his senses and give a relentless clarity to his mind. He couldn't help seeing the full extent of his intimidation.

"Why didn't you get your ass over to Headquarters to register as a convicted felon?" Elton said.

"I planned to go there from the station. But I thought I could register any time this evening."

"We got a clean town and don't want punks sliming around unaccounted for. You register *immediately,* not two hours later, or three. *Immediately.*"

If that was why they'd come, it wasn't cause enough for the rough stuff. If they were doing this without reason, they wouldn't want the reasonable facts. Nothing had so infuriated the screws when they were bent on kicking the hell out of a man so much as a good excuse from him. The type took a thing like that as an offense that was meant to spoil their fun. If he told this pair of bastards that his instructions from the warden had not mentioned 'immediate" police registration, but simply "day of arrival," they wouldn't like it. If he told them he had been too concerned about his wife to think about rushing to Headquarters, they might make some obscene remark. Then he would have to hit them or, worse, not have the guts to. For the first time he was glad she wasn't here, and instantly he despised himself and said in a tone edged with self-accusation:

"I just didn't hear the orders right. I thought it would be all right to wait for my wife to meet me . . . I worried about her. I don't know where she is, even yet." He had apologized for her to them, as if there'd been something wrong with her for not being there and causing them this trouble . . . and more contemptible yet, he'd managed to appeal for their sympathy. *Their sympathy.* He couldn't stand seeing himself like this. It was something that had never happened during or after any beating in stir. He wasn't hating them; he'd whiplashed the hate back on himself, and it was so potent that it was making him act contemptibly, cravenly, as if he must prove that he was hateful. This was all new; he'd never known himself to be like this.

"Listen, tough boy, we've got a line on you. A baby with a lot of lip, a guy thinks he can use his mitts on cops, a real troublemaker," Elton said, and Charles liked the sound of it; he wished it was still true. "But we can soon take the juice out of you, and one more nose-thumb at the cops out of you and we'll take you in and forget to book you. Get it?"

He got it. He'd heard in stir that it had happened more than once. Unbooked meant a solid working over, and if the thing got out of hand and the prisoner died, there was no record. Sometimes the body was found crushed in a railroad yard; sometimes on a road, just one of those never-solved hit-and-run cases.

"I get it," Charles said.

"Or we can send you right back to college on that old gun-theft charge."

"*What* gun-theft charge?" he blurted in real surprise.

"You stole the gun you used in the holdup. The statute of limitations during which you can be charged still has three years to go."

"But that charge was packaged in with the other, wasn't it? Didn't the lawyer deal?"

"You had a great lawyer, that court appointee. Just the match for an incompetent stickup punk. If you're going to steal, steal enough at least to get a lawyer. He just *thought* he had a deal. But no charge was brought for gun theft, so how the hell could it be quashed?"

He didn't think. He said: "I got a good lawyer since then. He wouldn't let you get by with that. And by God I don't think you can get by with this kind of crap either, coming in here and shoving me around. . . ."

Elton slapped both his cheeks, with palm and back of hand, delivered so fast it was like a single blow. The sting watered his eyes. He flattened his lips against his teeth and his hands flexed at his sides, the fingers set in rigid curves like claws.

Gobi had been standing for the last few minutes at his side, but he vanished from the earth. The intensity of his hatred was so violent, so concentrated, that there was only one other man in the world: Elton. There was a feverish acceleration to his thoughts, and in a split second he knew the whole sequence of action to come. He was past planning whether he dared attack, he was only deciding exactly how he was going to kill Elton.

His eyes had narrowed, screening the cold, dark, killer depths. His body concealed its intent from his victim with a cunning appearance of relaxation. The motion of his right hand closing was so cautious that it failed to catch even a flicker of Elton's attention. He left his other hand as it was, a claw, for he was going to seize the throat with it. The fist would drive into the lower gut, then club the head until it was sense-less while the claw held the windpipe, and then both hands would lock into the throat, and hold on and on until death . . . Elton's or his, or both . . . but until death!

And then something very strange happened. The mask stripped away from his face, showing it distorted and menacing, and the murderous violence in his eyes unveiled. The impact was so powerful, the deadliness so awesome that Elton moved back as if sprung. Gobi felt it, and launched the weight of his body against Charles's arm, pushing him sideward and digging into a lining pocket of his coat for his gun. He brought it out and held it threateningly by the barrel, ready to club him with the butt. Charles hadn't moved before he was bumped, and yet both of these men had been caught by the scruff of the neck and shaken, because he had made them feel death. He had not even moved  He had only revealed himself, and they had known death! Not only they had been shaken . . . not only they . . . Charles had been closest to it, far the closest, for it was in him.

He subsided, but it was still there. He heard Gobi saying over and over: "Take it easy, take it easy," but it was still there. Gobi said: "You're a real actor." Gobi said that, and he had not made a move. But Gobi knew.

It was then that the revelation came. Elton took up the attack, in words, again, and Charles answered, but they were unimportant. It was the revelation that was important. It came almost like a white light and he felt that a miracle had taken place, and although he had not used the word "soul" since childhood, he thought that this revelation, this miracle had saved his soul.

"Whattaya say, Don?" Gobi said. "Wanta slap the bracelets on him?"

"Not this time," Elton said coldly. "But if this smart son of a bitch thinks we can't make a court case, we'll show him. We'll have that hock-shop owner bring that charge."

"It wouldn't go with a jury," Charles said, "and you know it." He argued like that, in the spirit of a game, since it was unimportant in the face of the new thing within him.

"As it stands, no. A slobbery jury might think it was just not nicety-nice of the bad ole policemans to hold a dirty stick over a poor little ole parolee. But if the parolee is a dangerous man, if he goes in and threatens, and even tries· to kill that hock-shop owner, and if he feels it's his civic duty to press all available charges against a character who can be proved to have been living a secret criminal life all the period he was on parole . . . whatta *you* think?"

"I think I'll go straight, and I think I won't threaten his life."

"You *are* stupid," Elton sneered. "It'll be your word against his whether or not you tried to kill him, and *he* will have corroborating witnesses. The details of when and how you broke parole by consorting with hardened criminals, gambling, drinking, spending money in dives which you couldn't possibly earn on your legitimate job . . . the details will come easy. Savvy?"

"You'd pull that? And the hock-shop owner would?"

"Give us some trouble, and you'll find out, you bastard. Now, if you're not registered by ten-thirty, that'll be trouble."

"I'll register," Charles said. They made as if to go, so he knew it was time to tell them of the miracle in him, his sudden awareness of himself. For they must know that he finally saw that evil had dominated his life until that moment. He saw it clearly, and he saw clearly that even if some of his apparently good characteristics had fooled him, he knew they had been only sly tools of the dominant evil. This, he now saw, had really applied to every relationship. He had risen from a foundry

ladle carrier to a junior executive in a good corporation, but no
real merit nor character had been involved, only a cunning
mask of personality in the service of his evil intent. He had
been as clever as sin to employ devices of pretended innocence,
and human traits, knowing the value of these in winning favors and advantages. But his basic self had shown when he had
defied an edict of a superior and justly he had been thrown
out, seen for what he was. Scheming, evil, contriving, basically
ruthless in seeking selfish ends. All of the jobs he hadn't got
after getting jolted off his perch had been because he had not
been able to compose a good enough new mask, and always he
had stood revealed for what he was. And even his love, as
he had called it, for Nora, had been a shrewd pretense so that he
could enjoy the advantages of her love. In the showdown he had
not applied for public relief, but had become an outlaw and
put her in disgrace and at the mercy of the world.

To know finally one's true self was the first step toward
rehabilitation. He knew that every beating he had had, and
now this one, had been deserved. Because these were just men,
they had experience with evil, and dealt with it as it should
have been dealt with. To be abused by them was no more than
acceptance of due punishment, and he must show the courage
to accept it, yes, and to find joy in it. He must never think ill
of them, but he must trust them. As a first step he would tell
them of the dead man in the closet, for they would help him
when they saw that a miracle had occurred in him.

"Before you go," Charles said, "I have something to tell you.
Something important."

Gobi's face wore a coarse expression, as if he were looking
at dung. And well it should, Charles thought, for that coarse-
ness had been stamped on him by the soul-wearing labors
against evil, so that his ugliness was a badge of honor. And the
face of Elton! That genuine depth of weariness, as though his
sensitive soul had been injured, and deeply injured, to have seen
so much of wickedness. These men, forced to demean their basic
goodness for the sake of resisting the viciousness which might,
without such as they, have polluted all mankind. Elton, whom
he had hated, before he had understood, was a victim. These
men he could trust. He would tell them honestly about the

dead man, and they would be his friends. *But what if Nora had killed him!*

"Whattaya got to say that's so goddam important?"

"I'll be there to register."

"Damn right you will. And damn right it's important."

They left. His mind had snapped back. It was healthy again. He hated them.

It was always insidious. He'd got the confidences of other men about that sickening mental trick. It always seemed you were thinking at your best. It happened when the point was reached where you could not take any more and then you wanted to murder, and that always made you more scared. And you didn't let yourself be degraded another notch; you took over the degrading with your own mind and turned brutes into saints, and justified them so you would not have to believe you were at their mercy, but undergoing justice . . . and so you wouldn't be forced to know that human beings could be such monsters.

# 3

HE LOCKED THE DOOR, shut off the light, and stood motionless, listening until they had gone down and out. Then he went to the windows and raised one of the blinds. He located their moving figures and watched until they had reached the car at the curb, got in, and drove away. He found his hat by one of Nora's skirted crates on the floor, then hurried through the apartment to the back. He turned off the light, bolted the back door. He peered intently out at the alley, his mind trailing them in the car as it circled around into the alley. He kept thinking he would see it pull up in the back. He waited by the door until he was sure they'd have had time to do it. They didn't come.

He turned and moved cautiously into the dining room, found a chair, and sat down. The dark and the quiet soothed him and he leaned forward and put his face in his hands and rested that way with his elbows on his knees. He felt little physical pain and no emotional stress, just an awful weariness. He felt so drained that he couldn't imagine ever being replenished. He let his mouth hang open and he could hear himself breathing. A slow, languorous numbness began to move through him, and in the darkness and quiet he had a sense of refuge and of deep, deep peace. He felt himself drift away into a healing sleep. There was a moment's uneasy consciousness that he must get down to register at Headquarters, but the warning lost itself; he was too exhausted to move.

It couldn't have been more than a minute before he roused, his heart hammering. His head turned sharply toward the mouth of the narrow hallway leading to the front room. A grayish light showed from the distant front window, and into the edge of it moved the black silhouette of a figure. It was outlined clearly a moment later, and he saw that it was a woman, and she came silently back through the hall. She came into the dining room and around the table with the effortless glide of shadow, and he knew it was Nora.

"Nora!" he whispered, and then he saw the faint paleness of her hand and felt her fingers on his lips, as though stopping the sound. A moment later her lips fastened to his, and he could feel the warmth of her palm, soft on one cheek while her other hand opened the buttons of her coat. She parted the coat, and pulling her lips from his she caught his head to her breast and held it there fiercely, and he whispered her name and shut his eyes and there was not a word between them, just the bliss. He could feel the beat of her heart and the soft rise and fall of her breast, and the warmth and fragrance of her was in his nostrils like balm, and there was the nervous, gentle play of her fingers in his hair and stroking his neck and ears and soothing his cheek. His arms circled her body and he moved his hands over her, fitting his palms and fingers to her. And then he had the terrifying thought that she had been on the front porch and had, through a crack in the blind, seen all that had happened to him. And she seemed to know his thought, for she eased his face away from the solace of her breast, and cupped her hands like spread flowers below his chin, lifting his chin, lifting his head erect again, as though she was saying that he could not be shamed in her eyes. And he wanted to speak and tell her that he was the one who must uplift her, that he had planned it that way. And she knew the thought be-

fore it reached his lips, and she put her fingers on his mouth
again.

And then she did a curious thing, but he didn't wonder at
it, but sat, passive as a sick child, trusting that it was a right
thing. She loosened his tie and unbuttoned his overcoat, suit
coat, and the upper buttons of his shirt and she put her hands
in against his bare chest and held them over his heart. And it
was as though she held it in her caressing hands and quieted
its beat. Then her cheek was like velvet on his and he could
feel the tickling of her lips and warm breath on his ear as
she whispered something. He could not make out the words,
and he strained to hear, and she said them again, and still he
could not hear. But he knew what she was saying, because
there had been many nights during that jobless, hopeless period
before prison when she had whispered the words just like this;
and she wrote the words in letters to him in prison; they had
never been spoken aloud, because they came from the deepest
and softest and most intimate part of her. He pressed his hands
around her precious head and whispered those words into her
ear, the same ones she was whispering and he could not hear:
*The beat of thy heart is the pulse in my veins.*

He woke sharply. He sat erect, and his hands flew to his
chest. His coats and shirt were buttoned. It had all been a
dream; she had not come. He got to his feet, cold. He suddenly
knew it must be after the ten-thirty deadline Gobi and Elton
had set. The darkness of the apartment had lost its feel of
refuge, and in the depth of emptiness was only the feel of
death, spreading from that bedroom closet. He clutched out
overhead frantically in search of the light cord. He couldn't
locate it. He dug into his pockets and got matches, scuffed one
aflame. He found the light and turned it on, wincing against
its sharp glare. He looked at the clock on the cupboard shelf.
It showed only nine-thirty . . . he'd slept only five minutes.

He had a half-hour before he'd have to leave. He had to do
something about the dead man; he didn't know what. He stood
smoothing and cleaning the smudge from his hat, working with
tender concentration, the while scowling. When it was fairly
well restored, he put it on a chair. He looked into the percolator,
saw there was coffee, lit a burner under it. He went into the

bathroom, watching his step in order to keep the graceful out-line of her foot in the powder film by the tub intact. He saw the marks of Elton's slaps in the bleary medicine chest mirror and ground his teeth. He set cold water hissing into the bowl, bent and filled his cupped hands, and sloshed his face repeatedly until the flesh was almost numb. He scrubbed on the dry towel until the rest of his skin was as pink as those brands on his face . . . but *he* knew they were there. He felt fresher, but not clean by a damned sight. An acid of fury churned in his guts and climbed his gorge like a column of fire down the center of his chest. He tightened his abdominal muscles and forced up several belches that left his breath like gall. He found some mouthwash and squished it around in his mouth, then spat it out violently.

In the kitchen he poured a cup of coffee and drank it off black, but tepid. He drank a second, hotter cup in two gulps. He'd have to find out if the man was dead for sure, and who he was. It might be a grisly, messy job. He went back into the bathroom, wet an end of the towel, rolled it loosely, and carried it into the bedroom. He put it on the dresser bench, lowered the blinds. He took off his overcoat and suit coat, looking at the bed. A faint depression, marking where she usually lay, showed in light shadow on the glossy peach-colored satin bed-spread. It roused unwelcome memories of intimacy. He tossed his coats on the bed, loosened his tie, and rolled up his sleeves. But his glance caught the array of dime-size creams and lotions on the lacy dresser runner, and he began to remember the sinuous and serpentine grace of her hands as she creamed them and her exquisite legs and graceful, high-arched feet. His thoughts rebelled at the memory of her soft thighs, her de-licious warm little belly and pert, beautiful breasts. It was loath-some to let himself get sexually excited at a time like this in the same room with death. He began rummaging through the scented feminine things in the dresser drawers, searching for a small mirror and a pin, and his sexual desires became even stronger. He was disgusted at letting them get the better of him at such a time.

Then, quite suddenly, he remembered that it was at just such a time as this that such things *did* happen. And it happened in spite of the nearness of death. It had always happened in prison as soon as he'd recuperated from a beating . . . if that beating had included a kick in the groin. A man didn't have to articulate a question about something like that, but he had to answer it somehow as soon as possible. He had no trouble controlling his sex thoughts, knowing that Elton's knee hadn't crippled him.

He got the little mirror from an old purse and settled for a small safety pin since he couldn't find a straight one. He got matches from his coat and opened the closet. Men died hard; he must find out if there was even a flicker of life.

The man, who was stout and looked around fifty, lay chest down, and the upper back of his overcoat was a bloody mess. Charles eased down into a crouch, studying his face which rested on one side. Glasses hanging from his ear down along his left jaw and magnifying a hairy wart through one lens made the profile uncertain, but Charles didn't think he'd ever seen him. He felt for pulse in the left wrist, but there was only the tiny vibration of a ticking watch. Reluctantly, holding his mouth and nostrils tight, he pressed a finger into the clammy neck flesh to find a jugular beat. His eyes flinched at sight of the depression remaining in the flesh as his finger withdrew. In strained silence he held a mirror over the gaped mouth for fully half a minute without raising a cloud of breath. He knew it was useless after that, but he felt grimly committed to see it through. He jabbed the pin point lightly, then sharply into the skin without getting a tremor. Finally he held a lighted match near the flesh at several points. The man was dead.

Charles reached back, got the partly wet towel, and put it beside him. If he had to get into a breast pocket of the suit it would mean turning the body. But first he explored the dry part of the overcoat below the waist. He made out the contour of a billfold in a hip pocket. He stretched an arm in and pulled the bottom of the overcoat as far up as it would come. It wasn't far enough. He would have to go into the closet and grope and struggle to get to that pocket. He looked at the blood, dark and drying in an ugly cratered scab over the punctured upper back of the overcoat. The man's one visible eye was slightly open and it had rolled down to the inner corner so that he could see only a blind, milky slit. He drew back, swept by a powerful revulsion. It was one thing to reach across the threshold; to go in there with death in that confinement was something else.

He stood up, stretched his cramped muscles, took a long breath. He balanced himself with a hand grasped to the doorframe and stepped widely across the dead man's upper legs. He put his foot down, then brought the other leg in and stood facing the wrong way into the dim end of the closet, his upper body at a strained side bend to avoid the hanger rod down the center. The hangers, with old dresses, sweaters, raincoats, and coats, had been pushed back to the end wall, and shoes, including some old sneakers and house slippers of his, and galoshes were in a jumbled heap on the floor around the corpse's shoes. Charles turned around carefully, compelled by some acute sense of animal stealth to move with absolute silence.

He bent over the body and began to work. He grasped the seam that ran lengthwise down the back of the coat and pulled up. There was almost no looseness. He had to use both hands and pull up with all his force. Finally he got the cloth stretched enough to form a taut, shallow tent. He held the pressure with one fist and lowering himself in an awkward, strained crouch he managed to burrow under with the other hand and forearm. He had no trouble getting below the jacket of the suit but the hip pocket was buttoned. With his arm and hand pinioned by the cloth, he began to work with the button. It was tedious. The sweat began to crawl on his scalp around the roots of his hair with a maddening itch. At last the button was free and he got his bent fingers in a pincer grip on the billfold. Even his hands had begun to sweat, and the tension needed to maintain the grip on the leather in that unnatural position felt like embers imbedded in the muscles of his hand. He worked the billfold free of the pocket. He let it lie a moment on the suspender buttons. Some of the sweat blisters on his forehead had run together and into his eyebrows. He worked them up and down, trying to stop the itchy discomfort, and some of the sweat ran salty and stinging into his eyes. He blinked and looked ahead and to the left at the open doorway and the visible part of the open door. The appalling idea of that door being slammed shut struck him with the sensation of nightmare. He almost yanked his pinioned arm free without the billfold, as if he had to save himself from a lunatic skulking about plotting to lock him in a horror chamber. Soothing syrup, Charles thought coldly! Hell, he was already locked in, and not in any simple, cozy few cubic yards of space with definite walls and a door. Maybe there wasn't any door.

He got the billfold out without haste. He got into the open space of the bedroom with a feeling of very slight relief. He lifted one arm and the other and wiped at the sweat with his sleeve. He looked at the billfold. Taking it had put him over the line. Not reporting the fact of a dead man had been right on the line, just a delay. He could have believed that he would find justice within the law and reported the body. Not, of course, to cops like Gobi and Elton, but to Homicide. That would have been thinking straight; if he'd been determined to really go straight he'd automatically have reported the body. Years ago he'd have done it without a second thought. No matter if the circumstances looked damning, he'd have felt that truth would inevitably triumph. He really would have been fool enough to trust cops when, even then, he'd known in a painless, detached, intellectual way about the police-political-crime tie-in. He'd really thought of himself as sophisticated because he hadn't been prudishly shocked by corruption; it had been the easiest, cheapest thing in the world to be worldly about something he couldn't imagine touching him. He'd thought then that there were a few rat cops; he thought now that there *might* be a few decent ones.

It was only sensible, he told himself, to line himself up against the cops in this. What bothered him was the way he felt about doing it, even if he believed he must. He liked it. It excited and stimulated him. It was like lifting a dreary, suffocating weight from his spirit. He had renounced the gritty compulsion to somehow strike back at all species of cops because of Nora . . . and because of himself, too. He'd known that if he let himself think like a criminal it could go beyond hardness to brutality and from cunning to total falseness . . . and his victims would be only substitutes, means of defeating and outwitting cops. It would be vital to deceive Nora about a

major part of himself; it would be necessary to close out
thoughts of the suffering he might cause, and it could not be
done without strangling his sympathies, his imagination, his
sensibilities. He thought Nora would stick anyhow, even after
she realized that he couldn't love her or anything; she'd live
in fear and he wouldn't be able to see it without hating himself . . . and her, too, finally. Oh, he had seen the thing clear
in all its potentialities of horror, and yet, now, even before looking for the identification in the billfold, he took out the seventy
dollars cash, counted it, and put it in his pocket with a sense
of satisfaction. He shrugged: he could go down any road he
chose and turn back any time he pleased. He wasn't a shivering
sheep, and if his immortal soul was so damned fragile, it had
cracked long ago anyhow. It was damned good to have a few
spare bucks . . . he'd be able to use them much more handily
than the bloody stiff.

A photo-identification card showed the man was E. V. Brattsford. The name itself was vaguely familiar. He remembered.
The man was a fence for stolen goods, he'd heard in stir. He
took out one of the business cards. His lips flattened against his
teeth and he looked at the corpse with loathing. Brattsford was
proprietor of the Beacon Loan Company where Charles had
stolen the gun. This was the hock-shop owner who'd have
been willing to help Gobi and Elton railroad him back into
prison!

Obviously Gobi and Elton would have enough on a fence
to send him away any time. And Brattsford would know
enough about them to return the favor if it came to it. None
of them would be likely to incriminate the other and be equally
involved in the ordinary course of things. But it wasn't hard to
imagine that Brattsford could be a threat to them under pressure. Gobi and Elton would kill if they had to and could get
by with it. With Charles for a fall guy they might get by with
it.

Brattsford had been stabbed fifteen or twenty times. As
though in blind rage by someone of a violent nature. The sort
of man who hadn't had sense enough not to fight the prison
screws. They'd testify that he'd been a troublemaker. Gobi and
Elton might swear that Brattsford had been afraid of Charles.

The motive would seem to be fear of being sent back to prison. It wasn't reasonable to kill the victim in his own home, but that would only prove the insensate violence that had made him stab so many times.

But why hadn't Gobi and Elton "discovered" the body if they'd really known about it? Maybe because it would have been too obvious. If they had a motive, they would keep clear of discovering the body after they'd gone to the trouble of pointing the motive away from themselves.

Charles had a hunch they would see to it that other cops found the body . . . maybe while they were sure he would be accounted for, going downtown to register.

Of course there was another, more obvious reason for the number of stabs. The killing might really have been blind rage. Or hysteria . . . temporary insanity. Nora, even, might have killed if she'd been in a state like that. Yet, if for some reason, Brattsford had come here and told her he was going to put Charles back in prison, she'd have seen their lawyer. Unless she had been under stress for days and had exhausted all possibilities. But under such stress could she have cooked the meal and made such lighthearted place cards? Yes. It was possible . . . it wasn't likely, but it was *possible*. He put on his suit coat slowly, his eyes dark and withdrawn. He hoped her mind had blacked out temporarily and that she had done this and was now safe, moving about of her own will, and would come to her senses and come home . . . alive.

When he picked up his overcoat to put it on, the satin spread fluttered and settled back. He realized that the depression her body had made in the mattress showed more clearly than it should have with sheets and blankets below the spread. She was not heavy, and besides she would frequently turn the mattress. He finished shrugging into his overcoat and pulled the spread up from the foot of the bed. He whistled tonelessly. There were no blankets and sheets; just mattress and pillows. He picked up an end of the mattress until he could see more than half the underside. He did the same at the head of the bed, looking for blood. He didn't see any.

He went to the closet and studied it. He pulled the clothes forward on the hangers, looked at them one by one. There weren't any bloodstains. He went in and inspected the shoes and galoshes. No blood. None on the closet wallpaper. It would have gushed, spurted, sprayed, and splattered in a bloody horror. Yet the only blood to be found—and he'd have seen it if it had been in another part of the apartment—was on the upper back and side of the overcoat. There wasn't even a spot on Brattsford's face, hat, or sleeves. It had all been absorbed—by their bedclothes! He noticed the knife for the first time. It was wedged between Brattsford's right arm and the back baseboard. He reached across and pried the black bone handle up with a hooked finger. He let it fall back; the surface was too rough to hold prints. He went into the dining room, got the box of their old carving set from the cupboard. As he thought, the matching sharpener and fork were there but the knife was in the closet.

It was a quarter of ten. It would be begging the cops to come and shake this place apart if he didn't make that ten-thirty deadline. They might come anyhow. If Nora hadn't done this, the killer—or killers—would manage to tip off the police and complete the frame. Meanwhile, if he could find those blankets, he might have a chance. With no blood on the walls, it might look as if Brattsford had been killed somewhere else.

He went into the curtained pantry, looked hastily through the laundry hamper. Then he moved deeper into the long pantry, going slowly, lighting matches, his brows bunched, his eyes sharp for sign of disturbance among the boxes and cartons. Then he saw faint smudges in the light dust on three cartons stacked in back. He seized them, went through the top ones. It was in the bottom one that he found the bloody bedclothes. There were the telltale punctures from the knife showing in the outer blanket. He carried the carton out to the light. The bottom was soggy, stained. He couldn't carry them in it.

He got sections of newspaper spread out, wrapped the bedclothes in one bundle. He crushed the bloodstained carton flat and wrapped it. He took two sheets from the dirty clothes in the laundry hamper, carried them into the bedroom at eight minutes to ten. He yanked off the spread, laid the sheets. He got one of the worn cloth coats from the closet, laid it on the top sheet. Still, it wasn't enough, not for winter. He went back and got several newspapers, laid them over the coat. Then he got the bath mat serving as a rug in the little group in the front room. There would be his overcoat, too, and it should give a clear enough picture of the state of their finances that blankets wouldn't be missed.

It was just ten when he finished the bed. Then he remembered she always kept the clock fast. He took a good look at everything in the bedroom, straightening it, removed the towel. He put his suitcase on the dresser bench, opened it. He threw a pair of shorts in a bureau drawer, left it open. He shut the closet door, wiped the knob. He got his bulky bundles and went out the back door.

He went stealthily down the back steps, past the lighted kitchen of the Shadds. The woman was busy giving her daughter hell and he wasn't noticed. He made the alley and moved at a fast walk to the corner. He planned to take a trackless trolley before he remembered having Brattsford's seventy dollars. He got to the corner of the through street and spotting a town-bound cab hailed it.

On the ride downtown he kept thinking about the murder. Brattsford had been laid out, carefully covered, and stabbed to death through the bedclothes. Afterward, the murderer had put the spread over the mattress. Or maybe—and the possibility was gruesome—the killer had fixed the spread while his victim lay unconscious, waiting to be killed. The spread had been laid meticulously, smoothed over the pillows, tucked neatly under, and Charles remembered that it had hung perfectly even at the sides. It was chilling to imagine a murderer making deliberate preparations, keeping his clothes fastidious, hiding the ugliness under blankets as if it was a beautiful ritual. A few stabs through to heart and lungs would have killed. Not fifteen or twenty! Each of those powerful knife thrusts would have had to be precisely controlled to keep from breaking the blade or jamming it crosswise between rib bones. The killer's elaborate care with the spread, the unnecessary and time-consuming number of extra stabs, the terrible deliberate calm showed a tendency to prolong the thing. He had attended to details as if enjoying everything connected with the job, and no more anxious to be done than a man making love.

Nora certainly couldn't have killed in that manner . . . nor
in any other. He'd imagined she could give way to hysteria
because he didn't want to think of her being in the hands of
a killer. And there was a particularly menacing quality about
Brattsford's killer. But there was no avoiding it: Nora's disappearance at this time was tied directly to the murder.

He paid off his cab in the zone outside one end of an arcade
which ran through the big downtown office building at the
busy Point. The driver gave him a dollar's worth of dimes. He
carried his bundles into the arcade which was lighted softly
by the window displays of the closed shops and almost deserted. He put the bundles and Brattsford's billfold in three
separate lockers in the middle of the arcade. He walked on
through to the next street into the dazzle of light from the
Point, the three keys clenched in his fist, afraid of them, not
knowing what to do with them. A cafeteria clock showed ten-
twenty-three, giving him seven minutes for the three blocks to
Headquarters. The unfamiliar crowds, lights, sounds, movement of cabs, cars, trolleys at the big, five-point intersection con-
fused him after the years of grim, orderly quiet. He veered
around a group at a big newsstand, threaded his way into traffic against the light into the chaos of the street. If the cops
already knew about Brattsford when he walked into Headquarters, these keys and almost seventy extra dollars would send
him to the chair. A cab whizzed around the corner, barely
missing his heels; a trolley horn bawled at him. He ran for
a safety island, stood shakily alert watching for a hole in the
moving lines of traffic. He found a tight one and dashed for
the curb. A sewer grating looked so tempting that his fist almost
opened to drop the keys. Sweat prickled his face. That would
have been brilliant! In twenty-four hours the lockers would be
opened, the stuff found. If not laundry marks on the sheets .
there would probably be cleaners' stencils on the blankets.

He walked close to the store fronts, looking frantically for
a temporary hiding place as he came closer to Headquarters.
It must be some place from which he could be sure of retrieving the stuff, because those bundles would have to be removed.
He came to a cross street, scanned it. He saw an outdoor laundry drop. He cut down that street to it, wrapping keys, billfold,

and money into his handkerchief as he went. He thrust the handkerchief down into the box, returned to the street he had been on.

He was a minute before the deadline as he went up the old steps of the Headquarters building and went in. He went inside and started toward the desk, wondering feverishly if he was going to walk out again. Suddenly it occurred to him that he had stripped away part of the murderer's protection by removing those blankets. He'd put a hole in the frame, and left it wide open for Homicide to look for another motive. And if they looked in the right direction, the murderer would get jittery, and if he was holding Nora for a good reason, he might kill her. His step faltered. Gobi and Elton were lounging at the desk; the desk lieutenant was eying him. He couldn't turn back.

# 4

CHARLES FORCED an icy calm over his mind and nerves. Emotion or tension at a time like this could ruin his chances. He was able to glance at Gobi and Elton with genuine indifference. *First things first,* he thought, moving toward the desk, and then *one step at a time.*

"I'm Charles Garrell," he said in a firm, quiet voice. He stopped before the desk and handed his release papers to the lieutenant in charge. "Registering as a convicted felon. I got out of State Prison on parole today."

The lieutenant nodded impersonally, looked at the release papers, and began to write slowly on a form he'd evidently had right at hand. Gobi and Elton smoked and watched him write. If they had arranged to have the body discovered after he left the apartment, a report would have been radioed in by now, Charles thought. The desk lieutenant revealed nothing except that he was a man of composure and routine who would attend to the details of registration whether or not he would book him for murder a minute later.

. If Nora was being held, it was because she knew who had killed Brattsford. If he, Charles, confessed, the killer would be safe; therefore Nora would be. All he had to do now was open his mouth and prove that he really would give his life for hers. He lighted a cigarette. This was no time for games, and that's all it was. Even if Charles went to the chair, the killer would never give her a chance to talk. He had to do something else. Provide a false motive for the killing which would fit neither him nor the killer. That at least would stalemate things. The killer would not feel there was any immediate threat or urgency. He would hesitate to kill again if it wasn't necessary. Meanwhile, Charles would find him—would *try* to find him. Then, if he had Nora, he would either make a deal or kill him. The first step would be to move Brattsford's body. Just like that, he thought ironically. The lieutenant's voice cut into his thoughts.

"All right, Garrell. This is the regulation governing your conduct." He pushed his release papers back to him and began to read in a drone. Charles pocketed the papers and when the lieutenant finished reading and glanced at him he nodded to indicate he understood. "That's all, Garrell."

So they didn't know about the body. It was over. Gobi and Elton moved off without a word and vanished into a hallway leading to offices in back. He watched them go and something happened that seemed good, very good—at the time. He had a feeling about them that he couldn't explain and which certainly didn't make sense, but there it was and it seemed good, very good. The feeling was satisfaction, a deep satisfaction, as he would have had from solving a hard problem. At the same time he felt that they had no real meaning any more, that nothing they might do or not do from that moment forward could have the slightest significance. They were a settled issue . . . his reason told him that it couldn't be true . . . but it *was* true. He didn't know why, he just knew that it was true, and it seemed good, very good—at the time.

He went down the steps of Headquarters, turning his collar up against the cold wind, his thoughts shifting easily away from them. He reached the street where he had hidden the locker keys and Brattsford's money, turned down toward the laundry deposit box. He took some coins from his pocket as he walked and let one of them drop so he would have an obvious reason for taking a good look around. He chased the coin, retrieved it. Then he went into a doorway, lighted a smoke, completed his scan of street and walk. When he was reasonably sure no one had tailed him from Headquarters, he went to the laundry box. He located the handkerchief-wrapped money and keys easily, pocketed them, and went on.

He didn't want the keys on him till he was ready to dispose of the bedclothes. He went to an all-night cafeteria near the Point to put the keys in a safer hiding place. While he was getting his tray and silver, he noted the location of the phone booths in an alcove of the wall opposite the counters. The place wasn't crowded and the tables weren't filled that far over. There were four booths and they faced one another, rather than the restaurant, two on each side of the alcove. He got coffee and carried it to a table near the booths. A girl was using one of the phones and he wanted all the privacy he could get so he sat drinking the coffee and spirited the table knife off his tray and up his sleeve. Sleeving the knife gave him a big kick. It was damned childish of him, he thought, but it was so. The girl from the phone booth passed him, gesticulating toward someone at the counter on the other side. He waited to make sure the pair settled down to eat and then entered one of the booths.

He made sure the ceiling light worked so it wouldn't attract a repairman. Then he eased open the folding door until the light was out. He took the table knife and removed the two screws holding the fixture to the ceiling. He worked standing, facing out so that he could see anyone approach. He put the keys into the circular saucer of frosted glass within the metal fixture. He replaced the fixture, got the screws in. He shut the door and the light went on. It was dimmer, but the frosted glass diffused the bulb's rays so that there was no well-defined outline of the keys. He thought he might as well give Jerry's number another try. He dialed it and sat waiting with a sense of ease and competence, feeling that he'd handled the detail of the keys with a craft worthy of a pro. He'd picked up a lot of tips, tricks, general rules from various cons. He hadn't recognized himself as "belonging" but they'd recognized him, ironically enough. The rule seemed to be: "Ask not and ye shall receive." He'd made a good start by battling the screws, but that hadn't proved that he was right. But during the months after he'd learned to accept what he had to without making useless trouble for himself, he'd been on trial with the other prisoners without knowing it. If he'd shot off his mouth about hating the screws and tried to chum up with the other cons as if he was trying to gain their trust, he'd have been suspected of stooling. He said almost nothing, volunteered nothing, invited no confidences. It made no difference once they trusted him fully and talked freely that he talked about going straight. The line zigzagged on both sides of the law; a man could be against the coppers and still have rat blood; he could go straight if he didn't have rat blood and he would still "belong."

Jerry's number had rung several times when Charles was dumbfounded to see Jerry himself. Jerry, carrying a tray, was within his angle of vision only a second, but the sight was startling. And it had nothing to do with the coincidence of seeing him while he was phoning him. Charles left the booth and went out into the aisle, thinking he might have been wrong. But unmistakably it was Jerry. Charles stood and watched him take a back table and set a roll and coffee off the tray. Jerry's profile was toward Charles so he didn't see him. He sat and began to eat, and even that was different. He was pudgy and had a love for food that used to animate him and set his whole body bouncing until he was fairly chuckling. Now he sat stiffly, his jaws working stolidly as a machine, and he stared fixedly at nothing. Charles approached him slowly, even warily. It wasn't the old, cheerful, likable nitwit Jerry. This wasn't the guy who made a deliberate buffoon of himself, the guy that nobody—least of all Jerry—took seriously. Charles had sometimes wondered if there wasn't a core in Jerry that had nothing to do with his clownish surface personality, a core that refused to take Jerry in any way seriously. There was a core, and it was visible now.

Charles reached the table, pulled out a chair at one side, and sat down. Jerry looked at him sharply.

"Hi, Jerry," Charles said, his mouth shaping a smile, his eyes penetrating.

"Charley!" Jerry howled in delight. There was a transformation of his features as sudden as in the old slip-paper toys. The down-curving gloom lines lifted into a smile with lines like bowls brimming with joy. The fat in his cheeks climbed and rounded like apples under his eyes, and his jowls and chins trembled with happy excitement. "How's the boy, Charley? Jeez, I'm glad to see you, old boy, old boy. How you doing, guy?" Jerry grabbed his hand and shook it and clapped him on the shoulder. For a moment Charles thought that what he had seen before had been only a normal slump of mood. Yet, although he found himself grinning and putting in a word here and there as Jerry greeted him with a steady gush of happy talk, Charles felt detached and his eyes continued to probe.

Suddenly he knew Jerry was aware of the scrutiny and Jerry's own eyes were magnetized to his and reading the doubt. Jerry talked louder, happier, the smile grew bigger. Maybe, Charles thought, Jerry had always tried to make himself ridiculous and poke fun at himself just to beat others to the punch because the punch hurt. Probably he'd never enjoyed being laughed at; it hadn't been fun but something he feared and hated.

"Where's Syl?" Charles said.

"God knows—I *hope.*" He shut his eyes and churned with laughter. Then he opened his eyes and got up busily, saying: "I'm going to get you coffee and stuff, Charley old boy." Jerry moved off to the counter in a bouncy rush. Charles watched him go, coldly. It hadn't occurred to Jerry to wonder where Nora was, what Charles might be doing alone in a cafeteria on his homecoming night. Of course if Jerry didn't know where his own wife was, that would explain. When Jerry came back with two orders of doughnuts and coffee and began the same laughing line, Charles said coolly:

"You're not that happy."

Jerry's face suddenly puckered like a miserable infant and he looked down at the table.

"No. It's Syl. She changed, Charley. She never thought I was much, but she kinda loved me or felt sorry for me—or something. There was something there. You know"—he looked at Charles and down again—"a little feeling. I guess you thought she was all ice. But she wasn't. She's high-class and proud and she was ashamed of a dumb, fat slob like me—in public. See?

But in private she was warm—lots of times. Honest, Charley!"

"I didn't say she wasn't."

"Well, she was. But that's all done. I don't know where she goes or who with, but . . ." He let one hand roll over, palm up on the table, and looked at it, falling silent.

Charles shifted uncomfortably. "Well, I'm sorry, guy. I didn't know."

Jerry's mouth twisted bitterly and he stared desperately at Charles. "I just ain't got guts, Charley," he said hoarsely. "I can't walk out. I just got to have Syl. I just keep hanging on. I keep thinking maybe, down underneath it all, she cares. Charley, you understand things. You know her, too. You and her used to argue politics and philosophy and stuff way over my head, and you were one guy that could back her down and make her like it. You'd really bring her to life; she really did admire you. You know her better than anybody I know of, Charley, so whattaya think? You think right down deep she probably cares for me?"

Charles looked away, touched. He started to say Syl did care; that's what Jerry needed to hear. The words wouldn't come.

"She always treated you with contempt."

"Always. She'd show people she didn't think I had any brains or manhood. And she's right. Sixteen years I been with that insurance company and not yet head of my department; and four men with less seniority passed me. In her job, though, nobody passes her. She makes more than I do. She shows me up in everything," Jerry said with a rising enthusiasm that made him sit more erect, livened his features, and made his eyes shine. "Why shouldn't she despise me?"

"You took it for years," Charles said slowly. He disliked saying the rest of it; he wanted to hold to the notion that Jerry had sympathy coming and that it was tough when a man loved so deeply that he had to take it from the woman in spite of the fact she was a bitch. But Jerry loved her because she was a bitch, not in spite of. "You took it for years," he repeated. "You liked it."

"She calls me a masochist."

"She's right."

Charles leaned close to him, his face stony. He forced Jerry's eyes to meet and hold to his, and said in a low, commanding voice, "How bad was it? Physical?"

"Awful," Jerry whispered, wide-eyed. "She'd hit me. And kick. And once at a fair I bought one of those little whips and some toy spurs and a cowgirl hat, and joked that next thing I knew she'd ride me and spur me and beat me like a horse. You know—a *gag*. But, Jeez, you wouldn't believe it, Charley, she—"

Charles cut him off with a biting "I believe. Save the details. Horrible for you, eh?"

"Well, Jeez, you can imagine. One night, in the middle of the night, when I was fast asleep and *helpless,* Charley, she woke me violently, and she was savage. She was naked, and she started in with that little whip, and I tried to plead and reason and she was without mercy, Charley. You wouldn't believe what I went through."

"Happen a second time?" Charles asked coolly.

"Second?" He rolled back his head and gave one short laugh, then sobered. "It happened time and time again; you can't imagine the horror I lived."

"You're drooling, pal."

Jerry started guiltily, began to blink. "Of course that doesn't happen any more—not for a couple years, maybe," he said. "That's one good thing."

"Good?"

"Sure, good! Whattaya mean?" he said indignantly. Charles kept looking at him, silent. Jerry frowned with the effort to meet the gaze. "I didn't like it, if that's what you mean. I *hated* it."

"If she stopped being cold to you, came back to you—"

"She still lives with me."

"If she came back in spirit, put it that way, it would be on her terms, and that would mean what you call 'horror'?"

"I guess."

"And you want her back. So who are you kidding? Not that I would give a damn how you take your pleasures, ordinarily . . ." Charles changed pace swiftly. He leaned forward, harsh-featured, and said in a low, coarse, rapid tone, "Where I was the last few years the psychologists know all about masochism.

There's something funny, if you like that word, in a man masochist. The male is aggressive, he'd rather hit than be hit. When he likes being hurt too much, there's something wrong. One of the things that can be wrong is having too much aggression, hostility, savagery. One of the reasons he wants punishment is to guard against a monster-sized desire, not to be hurt, but to inflict pain. Get it? He doesn't *dare* let that underside come to the surface, because if it got free in *some* men it might show itself as nothing less than a killer."

He stopped abruptly, watched Jerry's face closely. Jerry's coloring ebbed and he looked slightly pale. He blinked his eyes and swallowed several times. "No crap, Charley?" he breathed. His eyes bugged. "No crap?"

"There's one rule that they say always holds. Wherever there's a pronounced masochism there's sadism. The two of them are Siamese twins—one in plain view, the other buried, out of sight, deep down in the dark. But alive. And sometimes the balance is upset. Know what happens then?"

"What, Charley?"

"The hidden twin takes over. The masochist is deprived of his dose of pain, so the sadist takes over." He reached out and gripped Jerry's arm painfully. "Then a man could inflict pain —even the final pain, death. He could kill—with pleasure. *Where's Nora!*"

"What are you talking about?"

"Where's Nora?"

Jerry was shocked; he showed guilt, clear guilt. Charles tightened his grip on his arm and threatened: "Look at me, Jerry. See if I'm lying to you. I'll get the man if it's the last thing I do, if she's hurt."

"Let go my arm, fercrissakes. I don't know what you're talking about. I don't. So help me God! I drove her down to the station to meet you. I left her there at six-thirty."

"Jerry, don't lie to me. You haven't noticed the fact she's not with me."

"But I thought . . . I thought she was in the restroom . . . I mean I didn't think anything about her, just about Syl."

"Syl looked at me like she'd look at a man, and at you like a kid; don't tell me you didn't hate me for it."

"I never gave it a thought. You're one type and I'm my own type. To hell with your type. I get as much as I like out of my life the way I like it, taking it easy. I don't want to be like you, never did. I, at least, stayed out of jail, even if I ain't a goddam superman."

"Superman, huh? So you thought like that about me."

"Let go my arm or I'll yell for the cops, you jailbird, and they'll know what to do with you."

"That's right. But if you've got Nora, Jerry, I'll fix you. If she's all right, I won't do a thing. I'll fix the matter of the hock-shop owner; I'll take him away from my place and I'll be off the spot and so will you. I'll guarantee Nora will never incriminate you. Is she alive?"

"Charley," Jerry pleaded earnestly. He raised his right hand. "I don't know anything about her. You're out of your mind; I don't know what you're talking about."

Charles released his arm and sat back. Jerry had shown guilt, all right. But Charles was suddenly certain that it had had to do with the things he'd said about masochism and sadism. There was truth enough in it for Jerry to have recognized things about himself, maybe remembering some small cruelties and fleeting hostile thoughts. The guilt he'd shown was of a guy exposed. Maybe only that.

"You're right: I'm half out of my mind. Sorry if I got tough; probably I had no right to. But Nora is missing, Jerry. I think her very life is in danger. Was she all right when you left her —I mean, she acted natural?"

"Giddy. She was all souped up. Happy. Listen, Charley, maybe all you told me is good to know. I can't hardly think of nothing else, but fercrissakes you know I love Nora, not the same way, but nearly as much as I do Syl. I want to help find her if she's in trouble. You ought to know that about me. Sure I got lousy parts to my character, but you know me, Charley, don't you?"

I hope so, he thought. Aloud he said: "I think so. I may ask your help, Jerry. Now, I've got things to do, people to see." It occurred to him that he wanted to go through Jerry's apartment. "Say, you driving home?"

"Syl comes in here. I sometimes wait and she comes for coffee, then we go home together. I haven't seen her since morning, and if she comes I wouldn't want to miss her."

"I'll see you later, then." Charles left the cafeteria. He stopped in the entryway of an office building next door from which, in concealment, he could see into the cafeteria. If Jerry was leveling, he'd stay where he was. He wouldn't use the phone; he wouldn't feel any urgency to get to his apartment. Jerry had told him a lot about himself, and there could be a shrewdness about that very fact, for it gave an appearance of revealing everything . . . it might all be a pack of lies and it might simply be a cover. Jerry didn't stir from the table. If Jerry was a man capable of murder, he was also capable of realizing that Charles might be watching him.

Rightly or wrongly he'd told Jerry all he wanted Brattsford's killer to know. If Jerry had done the killing, Charles's message was clear. Charles had offered an out. Now, he couldn't waste time. He'd have to make good on providing a motive for the murder which fit neither the killer nor Charles, by moving the body. First he'd have to check the apartment and see if that was still possible. He got a cab at the curb. He gave an address a few houses beyond his.

He looked for signs of a cop in front of the apartment as the cab, slowing, passed it. Then, the address he'd given being dark, he had the cab take him through the alley, ostensibly to see if the people at the address were in the kitchen. There was no sign of police car or waiting detectives in the back. Charles then told the driver to find the first open drugstore where he could use a phone. They found one. He went in and called a number given to him by a confidence man in prison. It was a number he never had intended to use, and he got a sort of sinking feeling. He was really in it now; no turning back.

# 5

"YES?" A man's deep, dry voice came over the phone. "Who's calling?"

"Is this Grig Proctor?"

"If you don't know my voice," he said, a little amused, "how do you happen to have my private number?"

"Si Dawson gave it to me," Charles said.

"The name doesn't quite register," Proctor said regretfully, then continued without pause, his voice serious: "I asked how you knew the private number because a lot of people have got hold of it lately somehow. I meet hundreds of people, and it's entirely possible that this—uh, Hi Dalton??—was one of them." Proctor chuckled, as if he might be shaking his head in bafflement. "On the other hand, I've found that not a few of the people I meet have one name one week and another the next. I've been getting a lot of phone calls recently from people claiming to be a friend or a friend of a friend." Proctor became exaggeratedly gruff, as if trying to hide the true sweetness of his nature. "The trouble with me—" he sighed as if bracing himself for the manly confession—"I'm just too soft-hearted. People know that if they can get to me personally I'm what's known as a pushover. I'm apt to take their various claims at face value instead of exercising my better judgment. Right now I'm just a bit cagey about getting involved with people who may turn out to be . . . Lord knows what."

"I imagine all sorts try to impose on you," Charles said. Si Dawson, The Bargain Day Kid, was almost as fabulous as The Yellow Kid in the crime stratosphere where big-time confidence men operated. The cheapest carny grifter knew the name Si Dawson. Something was queer when Grig Proctor, boss of the state gambling rackets, pretended not to know. Charles went on, deadpan, "But it's said that the Lord tempers the wind for the shorn lamb."

Proctor laughed appreciatively. "Well, I don't exactly claim to be defenseless. And I'm going to take a chance on your really being a friend of this Hi Dalton. Wasn't he connected with Alec Graham?"

Charles quickened. Alec Graham was a code warning, standing for Alexander Graham Bell, and it meant the phone was tapped. Proctor's talk was for a tape-recorder audience.

"Yes. He mentioned that name. I'd like to talk to you in person. I'm Joe Bell."

"Fine, Joe. Can you drop out to the club?"

"I'll come right out."

"Fine. Fine. Just give the doorman your name: Joe Bell. Good-by."

Proctor's place was beyond city limits. Charles tried to rest during the half-hour cab ride. He couldn't. If Proctor was having snoop trouble, he would be suspicious. Even if he loaned Charles one of his fleet of panel trucks, he might have him followed, in which case Charles couldn't risk using the truck to move Brattsford's body.

The flashing colored signs of the Merry Land Club burst against the night like colliding rockets. A doorman in a clown costume opened the cab door, thrust a huge pistol at Charles, and held out a dishpan painted with skull and crossbones and the words: "You don't *have* to tip!"

"Ha ha!" Charles said sourly, getting out. "How jolly. I'm here to see Proctor on business. My name's Joe Bell."

"C'mon, pal, if you don't kick through, the gorilla watching us from inside will knock me to the boss."

Charles tossed a quarter in the pan. "I'll bet they sew up your pockets."

"Pal, you miss the spirit. Not only pockets sewed, but they stomach-pump me so's I won't swallow a nickel. Boss expecting you?"

Charles nodded. "Joe Bell."

"Go on in. See the floor manager in the casino. I'll phone him."

Charles went inside. The small, dim foyer was warm and musky with perfume. A cuddly little redhead with a soft and sulky mouth confronted him.

"Check your coat and hat, sir?" She purred it like an invitation to bed and began to unbutton his coat. He started past her, shaking his head. A thick mass in a tux with a smile like a wrestler trying to break a stranglehold blocked the door.

"Club rule to check your things, sir."

"I'm here to see Mr. Proctor on business."

"Yeah, I know, but club rule to check your things, sir."

"But, I'm only—"

"Club rule to check your things, sir." There was no threat or any other expression to his voice, just a dull repetition, and the same strangled smile. Charles shrugged irritably, gave the redhead his things. Instead of giving him a check she held out a tray on which were glued silver dollars and halves.

"Take a half," he said resignedly, giving her a dollar bill. She gave him his check and vanished into the cloakroom at one side. The gorilla held the door open suggestively, smiling as if the stranglehold were tightening. Charles abandoned the wild hope of getting change from the buck. It didn't cost him a cent to walk through the cocktail lounge.

He went through a pyramid door marked Circus Room into a high, gaudily bright room with a circus décor. Twenty-five and fifty-cent and dollar slot machines lined the walls and formed a double line down the middle of the long room. Only a few devotees were at the levers. He walked toward the glass doors at the far end where a luscious cluster of girls in brief, tight panties and bras stood watching something in a room beyond.

"Change!" He was startled by the screech of an old crone in a strapless gown playing a quarter machine with an air of dedication. Two of the scantily clad girls turned with trays of silver coin and came down the room. One, a fluffy blonde, went to the woman who had shouted. The other, a slim, pretty little thing with a piquant face and low, straight, sexy black bangs shining like black silk, came directly toward Charles. There was a lazy, sensual grace about her motion that keened his senses. He slowed and stopped as she reached him.

"May I give you change, sir?"

She lowered her eyes slowly, drawing his gaze down her white body to the tray of coins resting against her bare stomach. She held her frail, sloping shoulders slightly forward to form triangular hollows back of the fine ridges of her clavicle and to emphasize her breasts. The flesh surged out, rich and soft, above the low, narrow bra. She stood with her hips tilted, one knee bent provocatively to show off the long, lovely line of her leg in the high-cut, snug panties. There was an ultra-feminine look of submissiveness about her which excited him. Then her vivid, dark purple eyes opened wide and he felt guilty, as if she'd caught him.

"I don't want change," he said. He cleared his throat and

searched busily for cigarettes. "I'm looking for the casino . . . the floor manager." He realized his tone was conversational, although he'd meant to convey a certain urgency. He looked past the match as he lighted up, as if searching for the casino, but his glance strayed back.

"Straight ahead into the main clubroom. Turn right just as you leave the Circus Room here; you'll see the entrance."

"Thanks." He let his eyes go over her casually again and moved, without undue haste, as though to bypass her. She sidestepped with the effortless delicacy of a dancer, blocking him. The sound of her voice came as a surprise because, although he was looking directly at her face, he didn't see her lips move.

"I'll split with you if you'll play the number six dollar-machine," she said secretively, a faintly husky warmth in her quiet tone. "It's due to jackpot. It's fixed, and I know!"

"Back in stir," he said, grinning wryly, "you not only had to keep your lips dead when you talked, but you had to duck your chin to cover your throat. I saw your throat move."

She slid her eyes up and down over him wonderingly. "Well, how do you like this apple?" she said softly, and grinned.

"You ought to be ashamed trying to grift me with that 'fixed-machine' racket. Do I look like a mark?"

"Sure not, hon. I just follow orders. It boosts the take."

"Rope many?"

"Could I miss?" She tossed her head contemptuously. "Show me an Honest John who can pass up a chance to steal! Oh, sometimes a freak that wouldn't even steal if your back was turned wanders in." She shrugged, and his glance darted to the brief dimple in the round of her shoulder. "When *that* happens, I get him pondering on how remarkable it would be to meet a raggle like me privately to split the take. So if the larceny don't get 'em they're caught in the five-seven bracket."

In grifter lingo the number bracketed by five and seven was spelled s-e-x. Charles said, banteringly casual: "It's like The Bargain Day Kid says: If you'd take the larceny out of the marks, all the grifters would starve to death."

"You know *him?*" She was impressed. He'd meant for her

to be, he realized with sudden self-contempt. "Don't con me, hon."

"Why the hell should I?" He suddenly tried to tear her to pieces, noting the unreal, exaggerated curve of raw red lipstick laid on in a thick paste and the blue grease on her eyelids. Artificial! But it boomeranged. The artifice didn't detract; it added, just as it was supposed to do. Her build, the lines of her body, the texture of her skin were so much like Nora's that he was pulled and repelled equally.

"Why! the man asks!" She rolled her eyes, laid her outspread hand on her bosom. "Oh, the shame of it all!"

He grinned in spite of himself. "Whatever you think, I'm here to see Proctor on business."

"I notice the way you are straightarming me out of your path and moving on about your business," she said, lightly mocking him. "But as to that question you've been putting to me with the eyes . . . it's not impossible, hon!"

"I already run as an entry. I married her. So don't get me wrong. You're first-class scenery but I'm just a tourist."

"Don't you think I know the difference between a simple drool and that wild-bull look? It pleasures me to have a man want me that damn bad. Hon, it really pleasures me."

He didn't answer, but started past her. She caught his arm. "Wait!" she whispered. She reached under her change tray, brought out a little gadget. "Here's a counter. One of the boys in Service Repair downstairs has got heaves over me. He fixed the #5 machine to jackpot on the 427th play." She showed him the counter in her cupped palm. It read 423. "Four plays does it. That #6 machine is for the marks, but the #5 is the goods." She looked up at him and let her eyes melt and her lips part; even her body seemed to go limp as though rendered helpless with passion. "Hon," she breathed, "I'm leveling."

"I'm not a mark! Turn off the sex."

"Oh, hell," she said resignedly. She felt in beside him as he went on toward the glass doors. The three other change girls were watching them with catty smiles. Charles glanced at the little brunette beside him. She was scowling at the others. She'd fail to rope him and they were laughing at her.

"Relax," he whispered impulsively, "I'll take you off the

spot." Then, as they approached the other girls, he said in a low, carrying voice: "Remember, don't let anybody else play it. I'll be back as quick as possible."

She squeezed his hand intimately. "Count on me, hon! Hurry, though. My name's Cleo. Remember, now!" Cleo scampered ahead, pulled open one of the glass doors, and with a lithe turn, twist, and shift caught the door on her hip. She stood, trim little legs braced apart, holding the door open for him with one hip, and gave him an impish smile as he went through into the main clubroom. He walked across the raised platform along the end of the room, ignoring the floor show in progress, to the doors of the casino.

The big casino, lighted like an operating-room, was nearly deserted. There was a player at one of the roulette wheels, two at a chuck-a-luck table, one playing blackjack against a dealer, and a strident, rangy girl talking drunkenly to the dice at a crap table. Most of the croupiers, dealers, and housemen were idling, smoking, talking, drinking coffee at one of the big poker tables near the cashier's cage at the back. Charles went down the center aisle toward them. One of them, a compact, medium-tall man in a well-cut tux, got up briskly and came to meet Charles. He was in his forties. He had clipped, sandy hair and there was an air of alert competence about him, although his broad, unlined, tanned face was bland.

"Are you the floor manager?" Charles said.

He nodded and waited.

"I'm Joe Bell," Charles said. "The doorman said he'd phone you. Mr. Proctor is expecting me."

"Oh?" the floor manager said doubtfully. "The doorman called, yes. But Mr. Proctor didn't mention you."

"I talked to him just a half-hour ago, and he said to come on out," Charles said. "Will you let him know I'm here? Or tell me where his office is?" Charles had wondered why Proctor hadn't sent word out front that he was coming if he intended to be friendly. As the floor manager shook his head now it occurred to Charles that he might not get to Proctor, much less borrow a truck.

"Mr. Proctor is somewhere in the main clubroom watching the show right now." He glanced at his watch. "It won't be over for twenty to twenty-five minutes. He won't be in his office till afterward."

Charles nodded toward a door beside the cashier's cage. "Is that his office?"

"Yes, but I'm not authorized to admit anyone. I'll check with him as soon as he comes back in here. Meanwhile, if you'd care to try your luck . . . ?"

Charles shook his head. He felt he was getting a brushoff. The men idling at the poker table in back seemed to be showing no interest in him. Yet, none of them were talking. If they were really indifferent, some of them would talk and banter while they relaxed.

"Why not go in and take in the show?" the floor manager suggested. "Then, afterward, see me and I'll check with Mr. Proctor."

"All right," Charles said, "I'll do that. Thanks."

They exchanged smiling nods and Charles walked to the front of the casino. He felt edgy, frustrated. Rigor mortis had probably begun in Brattsford's body already. Every minute counted. Maybe this whole trip to the Merry Land Club was a waste. An extra twenty-five-minute wait with no certainty that he'd get what he wanted seemed unendurable. He chain-lighted a new smoke nervously, choked the old one in a sand container. He went out of the casino and stood indecisively there on the raised platform running along the end of the main clubroom to the Circus Room. He glanced across and saw Cleo there behind the glass doors among the other change girls watching the show. He looked away from her.

He had the uneasy sense that he'd been deliberately blocked from the moment he'd stepped out of the cab. Maybe Proctor *had* sent word out front to expect Joe Bell. Maybe instructions *had* gone along the line to slow him down in order to give Proctor's people a good chance to look him over. Naturally Proctor wanted to know all he could find out about anyone unknown to him at a time when his phone was being tapped. Charles didn't think he had anything to lose, and if any of Proctor's people had known him in prison it would be an advantage to be fingered. Still, the idea that he might be under secret scrutiny made him damned uncomfortable. Most of the audience watched the floor show, but he felt conspicuous.

"Table, sir?" Charles started at the sound of the headwaiter's voice beside him. The man had an air of polished suavity that was almost satanic. He looked at Charles with one eye squinted, as if inspecting him through a jeweler's glass with secret amusement.

"No," Charles began. He was on the point of asking where Proctor was sitting, thinking he could gain precious time. He realized it would be poor psychology to intrude, a stranger asking a favor, while he was watching the show . . . if that's what Proctor was doing. "No, I'm just waiting. I'm here to see Mr. Proctor when he gets back to his office. I can go back to the casino if I'm blocking the passage."

"But that is not necessary. Feel free to remain, by all means." He moved off.

Charles thought he was going to snap if he didn't relax. He let the bawdy, jazzy mood of the show bombard his senses. There was a frenzy of racing music, a breathless, brittle beat of drums and dancing cleats, a blare of trumpets like stabs of raw flame against his nerves. A dazzle of light caught fire from sequins on the breasts and hips of the girls dancing to the fevered beat. They kicked and spun and bent and arched, flinging themselves into the rhythm with a driving urgency as if their bare bodies were being lashed. Charles felt the intensity of it cut down to the naked, wild cravings in him. He shifted his glance, roaming it across the audience at the tables. There were scores of exquisitely gowned, perfumed, bare-shouldered women. Their ornaments winked when they turned their pretty heads or moved their hands, and now and then he could hear a tangy-sweet peal of laughter above the music. He looked compulsively back at the dancers. He realized he had been stroking his thumb across the palm of his left hand as if to caress or to wipe away the feel of Cleo's hand. He eased around so that he could watch Cleo over there in the Circus Room without being too conspicuous about it.

She stood in place, but the rhythm of the dance she was watching vibrated through her slim, exciting body like an exultant pulse. Her shoulders shook slightly, and there was a short, quick movement like a crackle of electricity in her sexy little legs. Her black-banged, piquant little face had a look of radiant delight. She was the best of them, Charles thought; a cheat, a grifter, a cheap little tramp, all of that, but she was the best of them. He was starved for a woman. He craved her. He'd given her a triumph over the other girls and displayed himself as a sucker doing it. Now he wanted to go back for more. The craving was so blind and intense that he thought nothing less than complete surrender of his pride to her would do. He told himself it was degrading, loathsome! It didn't help. He couldn't shame himself. He called himself a yellow dog who wanted to grovel at the feet of a little bitch instead of standing up and fighting at a time when his very life was at stake. And Nora's life. He was suddenly sick at his stomach. He watched Cleo begin to spank her palms together and hop around like a giddy two-year-old, laughing and babbling to the girls beside her. He turned away, coldly disgusted by her silliness, and looked stonily over the applauding crowd.

He was aware, casually at first, that a man and woman at a table near the dance floor were peering in his direction. An old man and a young, very attractive woman. Then, with a shock, he recognized the woman. It was Jerry's wife, Syl. The old man was a stranger to him. She rose and made her way between tables to the aisle by herself. Charles turned his head, muttering, hoping she was headed for the casino. But she'd seen him.

She wore a dark blue gown which shimmered with light to the faint undulation of her hips and molded sinuously to her long thighs with each step. The gown was strapless, displaying her bosom, shoulders, throat, and blonde head like a marble sculpture. In fact she carried her upper body as erect and motionless as if it were the mission of her lower body to bear a precious work of art. She wore no ornaments, and her hair was drawn over the crown of her head in tight regal braids. Her finely chiseled, severe, and haughty features were expressionless, and her pale blue eyes were wide open in a stare of cool insolence. She came along as though in rehearsal for her coronation. Charles guessed Syl was in one of her detestable phases where her natural dignity decayed into arrogance.

"Charles," she said, reaching him. Her voice was barely

audible, one of the tricks of Syl in this phase, the idea being
to force him to bend down to her. He caught the scent of her
perfume mingled with liquor on her breath.

"Hello, Syl. Come on down out of the castle if you want to
talk to me. I'm in a lousy mood and I've got important business
to take care of, so if you want anything, spit it out. Nietzsche's
dead and the psychiatrists are handling all the current supermen, so don't irritate me with that high-tail stuff."

"I only wanted to say hello and to tell you I'm glad to see
you, Charles," she said distinctly, "and I have gone out of
my way to do it. I don't remember that you were rude."

"Since then I've had a taste of the slave society à la Nietzsche.
Prison. I've got no stomach for anybody who likes that stuff.
And if I wasn't rude to you before, I'm sorry. I used to try
to tell you what that philosophy amounted to: a glorification
of brutality and the killer instinct, and a worship of force. I
thought you didn't understand it, so I didn't quite despise you.
Now, I think you understood perfectly."

"Well!" she breathed. Her staring eyes moved up and down
over him, then rested searchingly on his face. A smile flickered
briefly around her lips. "Darling, do you know the state should
always make your clothes. That suit brings out a certain rough-
cut crudeness. You used to be so well-tailored that a woman
couldn't be sure there was a nice primitive you underneath."

"There's one woman who could have relieved your doubt,"
he said coolly. He glanced frowningly to the side, watched a
busboy close heavy drapes across the doors of the casino. He
watched him go across to the doors of the Circus Room and
pull the drapes there, shutting off Cleo. Lights began to dim
through the main clubroom, and the emcee at a mike on the
dance floor was announcing an act. He looked again at Syl,
standing before him, and got out cigarettes. "Why don't you
go back to your table, Syl?"

"Come with me and meet my friend and have a drink."

"Have you gotten stupid or are you drunk, or what? I've
made myself damned clear, Syl. You and I are at opposite ends
of the world."

"Really?" she said with light mockery.

"You sound like you don't believe it," he said in annoyance.

She didn't answer for some time, but lifted her hand, indicating his cigarettes. Grudgingly he shook one from the pack for her, then lighted for them both. She stepped so close that her breast touched him.

"Of course I don't believe you," she said very softly, her face lifted, her eyes watching him steadily. "You ought to know by now that we're the same kind."

"I admit nothing of the sort," he said with quiet contempt.

"Merciful Jesus! where's that icy-precise logic you used to have? I should say *word* logic to distinguish it from action logic." He knew her comparing his word logic with his action of committing armed robbery in a crisis was mockery, but it was gentle, closer to pride than disapproval. "At least be accurate. I didn't say you admitted we were the same kind; I said you knew."

He shrugged and moved a few steps away from her. She came along. The clubroom was very dark, the only illumination on the now empty dance floor was a hazy column glowing downward as faint as starlight penetrating a jungle clearing. From somewhere out of the dark a drum began to beat, slow and heavy. The voice murmer began to drain out of the crowd and through its shadowy mass there was a nervous shifting. Here and there a match or lighter flared, a glass clinked, but in a few moments the silence was complete but for the slow and somehow awesome beat of the invisible drum. A girl's laugh rose thin and sharp with hysteria, then choked away.

Charles had the sensation of being enclosed in a huge decompression chamber from which most of the air had been removed. And with the lowered pressure against him it was as if his vital organs accelerated, as though expanding in a sudden vacuum. The faceless, unknown crowd seemed to be suspended like some primitive creature, crouched and waiting, caught by the sultry, lawless pulse of the drumbeat. He saw Syl's face, obscure in the half-light from a fire exit. She was staring at him and he remembered she used to do that when no one else was watching. He'd wondered if she was inviting or challenging him. He had thought she was frigid; he had believed that was why she was attracted to the ideal of a superior being, stripped of compassion. He had believed

that if she ever got him to try seducing her it would be for
the sake of scoring a triumph over Nora. Now, in these clothes,
in this setting, she emerged in another aspect, freer. She gave
less the impression of frigidity than of carefully wrapped lava.
There was a concealed intensity about her, he realized. He had
never dreamed her capable of unbending and showing any
sort of passion. An image of her using a whip on Jerry leaped
into his mind. Then he remembered the fable of a tiger which
tasted blood, and the taste had been good, and it called for
more and more. . . .

A figure emerged soundlessly from the shadow into the hazy
column of light on the dance floor. It was a woman with a
body of dusky bronze and she was naked except for a long,
transparent skirt hung low on her hips. She extended her arms
above her head. A boneless serpentine motion began at the
tips of her fingers and rolled as effortlessly as a slow wave
down her arms and supple torso and lean, animal thighs. And
then the motion flowed sensually upward from her bare feet
to her finger tips, shivering in her hips and belly and voluptuous breasts. She was a beautiful creature, like powerful music, dark and passionate and savage, to which the slow, heavy
drum throbbed. She held the crowd like a drug. Charles felt
the slight pressure and warmth of Syl's body against his arm,
and in the dark her fingers crept into his hand and laced with
his.

"Charles," she said, her voice faint and hushed, "take me
with you when you leave here."

He started to free his hand, but her fingers locked convulsively. "Damn it," he muttered, "get away from me! I mean
it."

"We're the same kind," she whispered. "You proved it! I
used to wonder about you, if those ideals you spouted could
be true, if you really believed. I thought you were genuine,
and if somebody genuine really believed the way you talked
then maybe I'd always been wrong about everything. But then
in the showdown you got a gun and showed you knew might
was right. . . ."

"You fool. What I did once doesn't prove anything." He

wrenched his hand free. "I'm not going to take the trouble to argue, Syl."

She went on urgently: "It proved to me that I'd always been right, and I stopped being miserable trying to conform and began to take what I could get out of life."

He frowned in astonishment, and said in a low voice: "You don't mean you're blaming me for not setting you a good example. Is that why you think you've got a claim on me—why we're the same kind?" He frowned, gestured vaguely. "You can't be serious, Syl."

"Certainly not! I'd give you credit, not blame, if you'd been responsible for setting me free. I'm happier, much! And you can't shake me off."

"You leave me cold, Syl; you always did. So cut that stuff!"

"I don't leave you cold. I *enrage* you! Wouldn't you love to cut me down and prove I'm not a naturally superior person! But you don't dare try. You know better. You always sensed that I was of the elite; you could sense it because you were, too. We were never made to conform to a slave morality. You *tried,* because if you had let yourself believe what your instincts told you, that superiority is inborn, you'd have had to see that you had married beneath you."

"That makes us both better than Nora, huh? Well, I concede that you're better than her at breaking in a pair of size-twelve shoes."

Her wide-open eyes narrowed, and the thin flanges of her nostrils tightened. She dragged deeply from her cigarette, exhaled slowly, managed a grin, and looked down. "Seven, please." She extended a sandaled foot free of the hem of her gown, then looked up. "You really can get absurd, can't you, darling? But facts remain. As I remember my college literature courses, some wise author laid down the rule that action proves character, action *is* character . . ."

"Hold it! First you have to know the forces that cause the action. For instance, if I clipped you on the chin and spilled you on your tail, that wouldn't necessarily prove that you had a character of heaving yourself over backward and landing on your rump. And my taking a gun and committing a robbery didn't necessarily prove . . . Ah, to hell with it! I'm still not your kind. And, if you don't mind, I'm far more interested in watching the gal shaking it up out there than your blah."

When she started in again, he walked away in exasperation. He found the opening in the drapes across the casino doors, slipped through into the bright, sterile light of the big gambling room. Syl followed. She was so pale with anger that her rouge stood out like raw, scraped patches, high on the outside of her cheeks. He looked at her in forbidding silence, but she talked, her voice quiet and hoarse with emotion.

"You did prove character. You could have hung on longer, or borrowed more, or got a laborer's job, or taken charity. And before that, why did you get yourself thrown out of your job? You were a bright young corporation executive and you had the brains and tact to have avoided that trouble. It was a personal feud and you were too proud. That's all. You didn't want to hold onto that position and I'll tell you why."

"I'm breathless."

"Because you didn't want the kind of success approved by the mob. You wouldn't conform to their ideals or abide by a slave morality. It was beneath you." Her eyes glittered and her upper body inclined aggressively forward. Her features were too austere for prettiness and she fell short of beauty, but still there was a striking quality to her, and Charles found something intriguing about her in this mood of intensity. "Then, finally, by choosing to solve your problems by committing a holdup, you did the one thing that you could have done to desert your wife without admitting to her or to yourself that that's what you were doing. Your instinct drove you to break with her and her species. She fit the slave society— not you! But you were softened too much to desert her in an obvious way."

"That's one possibility," he said indifferently. "If you think I didn't really love Nora, though, your case falls. Because if I hadn't loved her I wouldn't have found it so tough to break with her. I sure as hell wouldn't have taken the prison way."

"Love! It's what we give to inferiors. Or, if it's given to superiors, it's a form of worship. That kind licks the feet that trample it, and there's nothing more degrading. Either way, it binds and chains and prevents the assertion of our wills and makes us knuckle under to slave morality instead of rising as free spirits."

"Free spirits above good or evil. It prevents us from being supermen, all right. It's sure soft, contemptible stuff; it makes it hard to be a son of a bitch without being ashamed."

"You really could kill me for telling the truth. And it's good, isn't it, to have someone like me that you can hate, and know at the same time that you're satisfying yourself with one of your own kind. You and I know that love isn't the only joy, don't we?"

"You think you can get me involved so I'll like fighting with you, then I'll like you, and . . . ho hum . . . to bed. You still leave me cold."

"Oh, I do, do I? I could give you *real* joy, and I'm not cheap. You seem to prefer it cheap. Nora!" She said it with withering contempt.

He felt a searing rage. "You phony, vicious slut, you!" He shut himself up, forcibly, stood clenching and unclenching his teeth. Finally he got his voice. "Leave her alone. You know how I feel about Nora. How dare you talk like that?"

"You think she's so-o-o good. But she's so human, darling; oh, so very human, after all."

"Meaning?" he said, his voice low and controlled.

"Fifteen minutes before the happy, loving, loyal little wife was meeting her long-lost cherished husband she met a man. Young, good-looking and, believe me, a wolf. Oh, you think I'm lying, but I'm not. I'd spit on myself before I'd use a thing like that to take a man, but I hate your smugness."

"Who's the man?"

"Ask your darling."

"I'm asking you!" he said threatingly.

She swallowed, unsettled by the look on his face.

"I wouldn't tell you . . . even if I knew. I might have . . ."

"Listen to me. Nora didn't meet me. I don't know where she is. It's serious. She's missing. Now what do you *know?*"

"If you please me I'll tell you."

"What do you mean?" He stopped, gaped incredulously. "You mean . . . knowing how I feel about you . . . *no!*"

Abruptly she moved close, gripped his hand. "You fool, do

you think I'd give a damn about you if you didn't loathe me?
That way it has an extra dimension. It excites me! Doesn't it
do something to you to think of making love to a woman you
hate?"

He stared at her. There was a horror about it; a tinge of
depravity. "It's like a nightmare," he said slowly.

"That's just it. It's the nightmares that grip, not the sweet,
shallow daydreams. It puts a tension in you, doesn't it? It
twists your insides. You think it's revulsion, and it *is* . . . but
it isn't. It's terrible and wonderful both!" Her fingers tightened
convulsively to his. Her eyes were sharply animated, her voice
urgent, her tone husky. "I'd help you track him down. You'd
find her and win her back. You'd beat him, and maybe kill
him, and it would all be your love for her. But I wouldn't care,
because what you and I had together would be another
world."

"You're lying! You don't know the man."

"I swear. They were together in the lobby of a cheap hotel
next to a burlesque show." She laughed, a curiously animal
sound of exultance, soft and deep in her throat. Her eyes
flashed. "Think of it, your nightmare! Feel it! A twisting in
you. Revulsion . . . but fascinating." Something feverish in
her eyes held his gaze compulsively. "The only way you can
have what you crave is through me. To get the woman you
love you'll have to love *me*. You'll have to spend your joy on
a creature you *hate*."

"You make me feel slimy," he said. "Anyway, you're lying."

The doors from the main clubroom had opened and the
crowd had started to come into the casino.

Syl laughed. "Think that, then. I'll be at my table if you
want me for anything." She turned and walked away. A man's
deep voice beside him said:

"Joe Bell? I'm Proctor."

# 6

CHARLES FELT DULL and lumpish as he shook hands with
Proctor. He was making a bad impression, as if he wasn't all

there. And he wasn't. He kept thinking about Syl. She might
actually know where Nora was. If so, he was wasting time trying to get a truck to move Brattsford's body. Finding Nora
was the first—the only—thing that really counted. If Syl wasn't
lying . . . but she was! Lying to torment him. With sudden
revulsion he realized that his mind was under her whip, just
like Jerry's body had been.

He looked at Proctor and shook his head slightly. "I can't
talk here," he said. He scanned the crowd irritably and looked
back at Proctor, knowing his manner was too abrupt. It was
no way to win friends and influence people; if he wanted a
favor from Grig Proctor, the state gambling boss, he'd better
turn on the old charm of his respectable days.

"Of course," Proctor said imperturbably. "We'll go to my
office."

They started across the casino. Charles saw why Si Dawson, The Bargain Day Kid, had said back in prison that
Proctor could have made the grade in the Big Con. He
looked positively wholesome, and it was looks that counted
among *really* nice people. Big and solid, with venerable gray
hair, abroad, virile, healthily tanned face, there was nothing
sharp or flashy about Proctor. He was well-groomed in his tux,
and his manner was genial and subdued, while his eyes seemed
intelligently aware rather than shrewd. Even his walk inspired
confidence: fast, but too smoothly co-ordinated to suggest
haste. He was like a good shepherd spreading a sense of well-
being through the flock. Some of the lady sheep at the gambling
tables gazed starrily at him, and even the gruff, stout fellas who
read character at a glance nodded, obviously sold on the notion
that Proctor's games were straight. But it wasn't grooming,
manner, nor the fact he probably smelled nice that gave him
his aura. It was what he represented: power, might, force. That
was the heart-warming quality that thrilled 'em, Charles
thought. He himself looked tough, he knew; but not in the
same way. He didn't make any of these nice, smug folks feel
easy. It was a damned satisfying thought.

Proctor opened the door alongside the cashier's cage and
they entered a bright, mirror-walled hall. Nerves or instinct

made Charles glance around as Proctor shut the door behind
him. He saw the terminals of an electric eye set among the
ornamental designs in the walls, and the light beam spanning
the hall. The beam broke when the door opened.

"You're sharp, Joe," Proctor said in an admiring tone. But
Charles saw a brief, swiftly suppressed look of peevishness in
the mirror. It gave him a slight jolt. For all Proctor knew he
could be casing the joint, or getting the layout for whoever was
tapping his phone.

"That gadget is the most gracious touch of hospitality I ever
saw," Charles said lightly as they walked ahead. "When unex-
pected guests drop in, you have advance warning so you can get
things tidy and comfy for them. That *is* the purpose?"

"What else?" Proctor smiled as if genuinely amused. Charles
hoped he'd recovered some of his ground. The hall made two
right-angle turns before reaching the door of the sanctum. All
bright and aboveboard; no sordid characters guarding the approach. He speculated on the probability that the mirror walls
were special two-way glass. He didn't think Proctor would be
delighted to hear his speculations.

They entered a large, pleasant room, thick-carpeted, the
lower walls paneled in dark wood, upper walls and ceiling an
airy blue. There were two cozy lamplighted groups of sofa,
chairs, cocktail tables; another group facing a television set;
an unlit fireplace, a small bar. A desk was the only business
note. Proctor crossed the room, indicated a white-leather straight
chair at one end of the desk, and said:

"Sit down and I'll bring us a drink."

Charles sat fishing out his cigarettes and watching Proctor
who was behind the bar, his back turned.

"Irish, Scotch, rye, bourbon, vodka, rum, tequila, slivovitz,
cognac, brandy?"

"Bourbon, thanks."

"Set up?"

"Straight'll be fine."

"That's fine with me, too. I get goddamn sick of those nyah
nyah little concoctions." Proctor laughed. He came to the desk
with a bottle and two old-fashioned glasses, settled comfortably
in his swivel chair. He slid the desk lighter and an ash tray to

Charles. Charles lighted while he filled the glasses to the brim.

"To our mutual friend, Si Dawson, The Bargain Day Kid." Proctor gave him an easy, friendly smile, raised his glass. Charles nodded and smiled, took up his drink. Proctor let his drink roll down, open-throated, without swallowing. Charles took one good swallow, and put his glass down. For a nauseating moment even that threatened to bounce. It had been a long, long time between drinks. The liquor settled down and began to soothe through him.

"I'm Charles Garrell. I met Si Dawson in prison and he took a sort of fancy to me even though I'm not in his league," Charles said.

"Who is?" Proctor shrugged. "The Big Con is the real aristocracy. And I'm honor-bound to do what I can for you if Si sent you, Garrell. What do you want?"

"I need a panel truck and a crate to move some hot electrical appliances. I just got out on parole tonight. A friend has been keeping the stuff and I have to move it fast, because there's a pair of dicks who want me bad."

"I see." Proctor nodded slowly. Charles took another swallow of his drink. "Can't you grease the dicks? I'd be glad to stake you for that. It'd probably be simpler, and they'd catch up with the goods and stick you good. It'd be cheaper in the long run."

Charles shook his head slowly. "Personal grudge."

"Here's the hell of it," Proctor said, pouring himself more whiskey. "There was a ball team that came to town awhile back for a celebration, and they ran into a fan—fellow called Bates, a canner from Chi. Bates wanted in on the fun so they arranged a picnic and he agreed to provide food. Well, somebody knocked this Bates and a fight started. The park authorities tried to break it up, but Bates was too hot to handle with tin mittens. A free-for-all started and one of the team members fell on a plate of chicken and got all bloody. It sobered them and they got Bates's coat back on him and buttoned up and brushed off. Some of the team came out to the Merry Land here. But some of those open tins of fruit salad they'd had at the picnic drew ants, and the team must've carried some on their clothes, because we got 'em in our linens, on the clothesline, and they spread through our fleet downstairs. A mass of ants!

Kee-rist, you could get bit all to hell. It'll be a couple a days before any of my trucks are fit to use."

Charles edged forward slightly on his chair. He was getting a grifter spiel, and if he was an authentic friend of Si Dawson he could translate it. Otherwise, he'd have to wait a couple of days until Proctor could get word to and from Si and find out if he was safe.

"I told you I wasn't in his league," Charles said. "I've never been on the grift. I know that's con lingo, and I catch some of it, but . . ."

"Si's a wordy bastard. If he liked you, he talked plenty and explained plenty."

"That's so. I know Mr. Bates means mark or sucker. A team would be a con mob. Tin mittens a fixer. Fruit salad—slot machine," Charles said. The hell of it was that con jargon wasn't fixed and static, but continually changing. There were a few sucker words, commonplace to outsiders; but grifter talk was full of switches, ad libs, private slangs, variations of every sort. Anyone who spoke the language could catch the drift— like a Southerner could comprehend a New Englander and vice versa, whereas a Frenchman would be lost. It was a matter of pride with con men to figure out any other grifter's private variations.

"Furthermore," Proctor said, "if Si liked you, you've got some brains—enough to translate my spiel, pal."

"Look," Charles said earnestly, "I'd be well coached on the lingo if I were snooping or posing as his buddy."

"Oh, perish the thought that I mistrust you, Garrell," Proctor said sardonically, "even though you, a parolee, show yourself in a drinking-gambling joint like this . . . as if you could break parole terms with immunity."

"Would I leave myself open to doubts by flaunting parole if I had some underhand reason for trying to get in right with you?" Charles said, looking at him levelly. "Wouldn't I be damned cautious about things like that and not leave myself open? I'm here on an urgent personal matter. It's a chance I took, showing myself publicly here. Maybe a stupid one."

"Si Dawson despises stupid people."

"Nobody's a genius every minute of his life," Charles said

sharply. He suddenly got to his feet. "Thanks for your time."

"Wait. I don't doubt your name's Garrell or that you're on parole, and maybe the mistake in showing yourself publicly here is in your favor from my point of view. And yet again it could be one of those careful-careless kind of things. See? I don't know you. You're on parole, granted. But how'd you get the parole, f'r instance? Make a deal to stool? I don't say yes or no . . . I just don't know. I can get word to Si Dawson and have his anwer in a couple days, and if he says you're a righto, then . . ."

"You're right. What the hell? Two days from now is too late, that's all."

"Sit down and use your head, Garrell. You've got one if Si took any real interest in you. Dig what I told you and I'll trust you . . . now."

It was childish and infuriating. Proctor knew as well as he did that anybody sent to snoop on him would be expert at grifter lingo. Proctor had made up his mind one way or the other already, Charles was positive. Charles chainlighted a new smoke and concentrated, remembering Proctor's spiel.

Proctor had said the phone was tapped when he'd first called him. In the spiel he'd said ants had got in the linens, on the clothesline . . . telephone line? . . . A mass of ants. Ant-uncle. Mass spelled backward was Sam. Uncle Sam. Federal snoops. Must be. Proctor owned local and state law. He'd fear only the Feds. He knew fruit salad could mean slot machines. The Mr. Bates who came from Chi and provided the food for the picnic was the fall guy in a con game if team meant con mob. Somebody had knocked him. That meant an outsider had tipped him off he was being swindled. The reference to tin mittens meant fixer. Too hot to handle with tin mittens. The sucker had squawked too hard and even the local fixer couldn't take care of the thing. If the Feds were involved, it meant the usually bribable local officials couldn't be induced to go along . . . they'd be afraid. The cans of fruit salad were what drew the ants, and the sucker Bates from Chi was the canner. Did he manufacture slot machines, maybe? A fight in the park and a member of the team fell on a plate of chicken and got bloody. Picnic chicken wouldn't be bloody. Cacklebladder!

Charles' eyes flashed. Proctor hadn't used the term cackle-bladder—a too obvious term. But if a team member had fallen on chicken and got bloody it had been a con game all right, and one that had gone wrong. So wrong that in order to get rid of the squawking victims they had resorted to an old-time confidence-game trick. A mock fight had been started. One con man whipped out a gun, shot another con man. The gun had blanks. The supposedly shot man broke a concealed chicken bladder—cacklebladder—against his chest, and pretended to fall dead. The sucker, believing himself a witness to if not an accomplice in a murder, was then only too glad to shut his mouth and leave town—"buttoned up and brushed off."

"I dope it like this," Charles said to Proctor. "A con mob got hold of a sucker from Chicago, a man who manufactures slot machines. They roped him in some sort of a setup . . . you didn't say . . ."

"I didn't know. But go on."

"But somebody tipped him off that he was being taken. He yelled. The local authorities couldn't be bribed, because there were Federal people who knew about it. There's a law against transporting gambling devices across state lines, and a manufacturer of such devices would naturally be under surveillance by Federal authorities. Whoever rigged up the con game bungled, if you ask me, in choosing a mark who was hot that way. But anyhow it got too hot and they pulled out the cackle-bladder and cooled Mr. Bates off—put him on the send. But inasmuch as the con game was played in your territory, and probably some of it was handled right here at the club, and because you have a big interest in slot machines, the Federal officials were sicked on you, too. Now they are trying to get the dope on you to stick you with transporting gambling devices across state lines. And they're watching your operations closely."

"Yes, that's what it must be," Proctor said soberly. "I had no hand in the game at all. They entertained Mr. Bates here and I suppose I met him casually. But the Feds aren't convinced I'm clean. What the hell, if you'd use one of my trucks and they'd happen to seize it while you were hauling hot goods . . ." He shrugged. "It's up to you."

"Yeah," Charles said limply. He shook his head. "I'll risk it . . . if you'll let me."

Proctor nodded and pressed a buzzer. "I'll have Jack come up and take care of you. Want to finish your drink?"

"I sure as hell do." Charles picked up the glass, feeling giddy with relief. He looked suddenly baffled and put the glass down. What the hell was he feeling so high about? It was slightly premature for celebrating, he thought wryly. "Thanks, but I'll pass. It would be just dandy as hell if I started getting that warm, muzzy all's-right-with-the-world feeling."

The door in one of the side walls opened and a dead-eyed, stony-faced hood in a low snapbrim and loose overcoat came in.

"Jack," Proctor said, "this is Garrell. He wants a panel truck and an empty crate. He'll tell you what size he needs. Fix him up."

Jack gave Charles a glance of icy indifference, nodded to Proctor, and without a word started back to the door he had come in.

"Don't mind Jack." Proctor laughed. "Santa's beard fell off in his crib and destroyed his simple faith. Been mad ever since. But a *lovable* guy. Well, good luck, Garrell."

Charles followed Jack out and down the stairway just outside the door. Jack got in a small sedan parked a few feet from the bottom of the stairs and started the motor, leaving the door open for Charles. Charles got in and shut the door, and Jack drove into a long, concrete-floored passageway which was lined solid on both sides with ceiling-high board walls. At intervals there were padlocked doors. It was an open secret among men in stir that the underside of the Merry Land Club was a warehouse, distribution, and service center of Proctor's dominion. Punchboards were stored by the ton, slot machines and pinballs by the hundred. He didn't see them, but there were supposed to be big repair shops where the machines were serviced and gimmicked. Jack said nothing, simply drove, making several turns, familiar with the crypt-like maze of private streets in the vast, gloomy underground area. Charles had never seen Jack before, but he'd seen scores of copies of him in stir: closed-in, harsh men, no longer capable of rousing to anything but hate. A very deadly baby.

They came out into an open garage area. There were a few men in work clothes around a little office and moving about among the machines: panel trucks, electric lift trucks, ordinary cars.

"What size crate?" Jack said, stopping, honking the horn.

"Got anything around five and a half or six feet long, two or three feet wide, and about the same depth?"

A man in overalls and jumper came over and Jack cranked down his window. "Bring an empty from a Number 74 slot. Put it in that Number 19 truck."

When the workman left, Jack got out and crossed to the office. He came back after several minutes with keys, and jerked his head at Charles, who got out and followed to a line of panel trucks. Jack got in #19, swept a flashlight beam around the empty interior. He got out, handed Charles the keys.

"Bring 'er on up near the doors and he'll be coming with the crate."

The crate looked just about right. If anybody thought it was about right for a coffin they didn't say so. The crate was in, the doors opened. Charles drove out, sitting tight and nervous. And cold. He had to get his coat and hat.

He drove around to the entrance, where the clown doorman opened for him without stalling. He got out his check and the little redhead saved the syrup and got his things speedily. The atmosphere was changed, definitely. He started back out and then he remembered Syl.

He had to go to her.

He set out angrily. The garish Circus Room was noisy and crowded with slot-machine players as he went through. Cleo, the sexy, little, black-haired change girl, was busy and didn't see him. But he caught a glimpse of her, her slim, pale body moving with a quick, tantalizingly feminine grace. Her build and movement were so like Nora! But she wasn't Nora by a long shot, yet she roused him . . . or she had not so long ago. Another man could rouse Nora, too. Like Syl had said: Nora was human. Human and healthy, and he'd been gone a long time. The man, according to Syl, that Nora had met fifteen minutes before his train had been due had been handsome and wolfish. Nora loved him. He *knew*. But if she hadn't been able to hold out . . .? A slow agony twisted in him, as if the core were being cut out of him, leaving him hollow and meaningless. At the last minute Nora might have been overwhelmed with shame, unable to face him and lie. *No!* Syl was the liar. There hadn't been a man with Nora in a cheap hotel lobby, or if there had been it wasn't a lover's meeting, but something else —something worse! Nora had *not* disappeared of her own accord!

Syl was alone at her table, her pliant body against the chair in a relaxed, almost languorous curve. She saw him and came slowly erect, lifting her regally coifed blonde head, setting her features into sharp-honed arrogance. She widened her pale blue eyes and followed his movement with a cool, steady gaze as he came and sat down. She didn't speak. Charles stared at her a moment, wondering if she was being deliberately detestable in order to remind him that he was coming to her, hating it and her, but forced to come.

"Who's the man you saw Nora with?" he demanded. "Where were they, and where can I find him?"

Syl didn't seem to hear. Her eyes remained wide and almost blank. He began to realize the torture Jerry must have gone through; the physical pain of her whip must have been a pleasure compared to that icy withdrawal. It was almost a shock when he glanced down, his eye caught by the motion of her breast, half bare in the strapless dark blue gown. She was breathing fast, excited. And her face remained emotionless and hard. She was pitted against him, and she was enjoying it. She hadn't been lying or posing or hysterical when she had talked about the thrill of a bond of hate between them. He couldn't help thinking of some of the prison screws, and of Gobi and Elton with their depraved pleasure in sadism. And he thought of Brattsford's murderer who had seemed to linger in a morbid fascination with the details surrounding his handiwork, after inflicting the final pain.

He looked at Syl with a growing sense of . . . something more than loathing . . . horror. She had beauty, of a kind, and a certain taste and fastidiousness. She was a legal stenographer, and her mind was trained and precise. She would have been just the person to put that bedspread on with such care if she had killed. And she might be just this unconcerned so soon afterward, because her belief in Nietzsche was no pose. He had thought so when he had known her before prison. He had been wrong. She truly believed in herself as a superior being—above good and evil. And she could kill without compunction. Brattsford or Nora.

He leaned toward her and said, barely aloud: "Is she alive?"

"Nora?"

"Of course."

"I don't know why she shouldn't be. He doesn't usually have such a powerful effect on women. He kills 'em—but just figuratively."

"God damn you!" he whispered. "You know she didn't go with a lover."

"You said I was lying. Leave it that way. Why did you come to me?"

"Something happened to a man," he said carefully. "I won't be blamed for it. Neither will the person who did it. I am going to fix that. Neither of us will be blamed. Whoever is holding Nora will be safe, you understand, if nothing happens to her."

"I don't know what you're talking about, Charles," she said levelly. "I told you what I know. You said I lied." She shrugged.

"Maybe," he said uncertainly, "you didn't lie."

"Well then, you're ready to admit she's cheap . . ."

He clenched his fists. "Will you tell me who he is?" he said with forced calm.

"Now?" She lifted her brows. "I thought I made it clear on what terms . . ."

He looked down at his clenched hands. There it was! She was going to require that he make love to her! He couldn't bear to look at her and let her see the intensity of his hate. He thought if he looked at her face he'd smash it. "Listen," he said harshly. "Wait two—no, three hours, I have to leave. It's urgent. But wait."

Her head went up in a terse, insolent motion. "You have the wrong approach. I won't be taken by storm. You are asking me a favor, and you'll do it courteously, very courteously."

He took a long breath. "Will you wait? Please?"

"That's a little better. Yes. I'll wait."

He left her, thinking he'd kill her before he'd make love to her.

He caught himself speeding on the highway back to the city. He got his speed down to the legal limit hurriedly. He couldn't afford needless risks. What a fiasco it would be to get hauled in for speeding. And without a driver's license! he thought with a sort of grim humor.

# 7

EN ROUTE TO THE MIDDLE of the city Charles had pulled down a residential street and parked for a minute. He'd imagined the car holding position a block or so behind him was following. He'd been wrong, but he didn't regret the caution.

He parked downtown near the Point and went into the cafeteria where he'd hidden the locker keys in the phone booth. He scanned the tables for sight of Nora's cousin, Jerry. Jerry said he often waited there for Syl, hoping to reclaim his wife when she was through bitching for the night. He wasn't around.

Charles went into the booth where he'd put the keys and dialed Jerry's number. There was no answer. He left the receiver off, letting Jerry's phone ring, and walked to the mouth of the alcove for a casual look around. Then he went back into the booth. He wadded his handkerchief, pressed it against the overhead light fixture, and broke the glass with his fist. He put keys and shattered glass, wrapped in his handkerchief, into his pocket. He listened to make sure Jerry's phone was still ringing unanswered, then hung up. The sound of his returned coin echoed halfway across the cafeteria. A busboy a dozen feet from Charles caught the sound, glanced at Charles. Charles gave him a bleak stare, wheeled, and went back for his coin. He didn't want the guy going in there and spotting that broken glass, not while he was right there!

He walked down the street, entered the arcade. No one was around as he opened the lockers and retrieved the bundles of bloody bedclothes, stained carton, and the dead pawnbroker Brattsford's billfold. He left the arcade at the opposite end, coming out a few yards from the panel truck. He put the stuff in the truck and started for his apartment without incident.

He could feel it in his neck and shoulder muscles. The tension. From time to time as he drove he shrugged his shoulders and turned his head from side to side and it relaxed. But in the motionless intervals the creeping tightness began again. The muscles running down from the bone at the base of his skull seemed to solidify and lock his head in an unnaturally rigid position, and then he would turn his head slowly from side to side and release the clamp.

He reached his neighborhood. Bone and flesh at the base of his skull, bruised by Gobi's slugging, became intolerably painful. There was a stabbing in his groin where he'd been kicked; the muscles felt sore low in his back where he'd been punched. The blood ran feverishly to his head so that his slapped face felt raw and stinging. A feeling of rage swept him. He suppressed it.

Every house along his street was dark. He was overwhelmed by a sudden sense of futility as he drove past his apartment. From the distance it had seemed reasonable and possible to move that corpse. He was strong. But God, he couldn't handle it alone! He felt completely exhausted. It was fear, nerves, strain, he knew it. Just that, exhausting him. It would be all right. It had to be!

He drove into the alley. He reached the back yard of his apartment. He backed the panel truck up as close as he could to the steps, and got out. He stood there in the cold air a few moments, breathing slowly and deeply. His knees were watery. His thighs literally trembled. He didn't know if he could even get his own body up those steps.

He went up the outside steps to the back porch apprehensively. He went slowly, stealthily, expecting a police trap to spring at any instant. He reached the top, winded, and stood there getting his breath. He got out the key, which he knew to be a key, but which felt utterly shapeless and alien because his fingers were numb, insensitive, sending no impressions whatever to his mind.

He managed to unlock and open the door. He went into the dark apartment and shut the door and stood there listening. The swift drumming of his heartbeat in his ears had the startling sound of someone running toward him. He knew it wasn't so, it was only a feeling, a part of the dark and of his acute sense of death.

He turned on the kitchen light and then the dining-room light; he went through the dark, narrow hall, his shadow massed and then dwindling before him as he reached the front room.

He couldn't see. He stretched out his hand, groping for the light, missing it. A sudden hysteria seized him, and he struck out and spun around, certain that he was being attacked. The sound of his coattails brushing the wall made him turn again, until he felt like a mindless animal, threatened and tormented. The darkness seemed immense. He stood still, realizing that no one had attacked him, and that he had been striking at and fleeing from shadows. He pressed his face in his hands. Maybe it was too much; maybe his mind was shot. Something in him knew there was just no damned use in any of the things he'd done or planned to do; he was beat, he'd never see her alive, never; he *knew*.

He *couldn't* know . . . he *wouldn't* know. He wouldn't quit. Even if Nora was—even if she *were*—dead, he wasn't beat. He would have a purpose then, all right. To kill.

He lighted the front room, raked its emptiness with a glance, went into the bedroom, and turned on the light, opened the closet and looked in at Brattsford's body. Everything was as he had left it, Charles thought. He took off his hat and coat, tossed them on the bed, and moved with swift, muffled steps back through the hall. He set the dining-room table and chairs to one side, making a straight-line clearance for the crate, managing the moves without scraping or bumping, setting the pieces down almost inaudibly, his emotions in control, eyes, nerves, muscles functioning in tight integration. He went out and down the steps, his body lithe and resilient, his sense of timing and balance flawless, his consciousness narrowed and intense, cut off from past and future in an awesome concentration.

He turned the door handle of the rear door of the truck,

applying a slow, silent pressure, and opened the door. He took one end of the crate and slid it out until its weight tipped it. He stood it up-ended on the ground and moved onto the steps and eased it toward him until it rested lengthwise along the edges of the steps. He pulled it to the top, sliding it easily. There was a delay in maneuvering the turn onto the porch, and a close squeeze in angling it past the edge of the ice box and in over the doorsill.

He left the crate in the dining room. He went into the bedroom, removed the drawers from the bureau, putting them on the bed. The bureau frame was light enough to lift, and he put it between dresser and bed, leaving the closet end of the room clear. He got the bath mat from under the bedspread, where he had put it along with a coat and some newspapers to account for the missing blankets, and got another mat from the bathroom, to obliterate the sound of dragging the crate over the rough wood of the hall—over the heads of the custodian Shadd's family.

He took off his coat and shoes. He lay the two bath mats end to end in the hall. He pulled the crate from the dining-room linoleum onto the bath mats. He pulled it carefully beyond the front bath mat, until the crate's rear had cleared the second mat. Then he carried the second mat to the front edge of the crate. It was tedious, but silent, replacing the mats to form a continuous rug under the crate until he had it in position near the closet.

He got in position straddled over the dead man's upper body. The blood from the many stab wounds in the back was dry on the overcoat. Charles rolled up his sleeves, braced himself. He bent and worked his hands down between the upper arms and ribs, then his hands burrowed in under the chest. He could feel some of the skin scraping off the backs of his hands against the floor, but the pain was trivial. He managed to get his hands together, the fingers locked.

Then he lifted. The body came up like a log imbedded in muck. The head didn't sag, the arms didn't drop. He just rose in a solid, unjointed mass, from knees to head. Rigor mortis had worked down past the hips. Luckily it hadn't locked the knee joints, because the crate wasn't long enough for his whole height.

There was no avoiding the sound of those knees dragging, and of the dull, weighted thump of Charles's stockinged feet. He got him out into the room and alongside the crate. The open side of it was at right angles to the floor. Charles stopped to wipe the sweat from his eyes and calculated the next and most difficult job yet. Then he pulled the long, hinged lid of the crate up. It would go only so far, it wouldn't fold back up on the upper side of the crate out of the way. It stuck out like an unsupported roof. If he let go, it would fall shut with a bang! He didn't have enough hands! There was no way, without tools and lines, to tie it up so that it would hold secure.

He let the lid shut, and picked the unwieldy crate up and put it down so that the lid lay open on the floor. He lay it open, and regarded the setup with dismay. The noise would be fearsome at two in the morning. He got the bath mats again. He placed them under the lid. Then he lined the edge of the lid along the edge of Brattsford's body, allowing a couple of inches clearance for his head at one end. The feet stuck out a few inches beyond the other end. The whole thing was getting grisly.

He took the feet and lifted them. He held them up, the legs bent at the knees. By pushing against the legs, he could roll the body. He tried. The leverage wasn't enough. He swore, silently, his face twisting in mingled anger and desperation. He got onto his knees along the side of the body. One of the legs slipped from his grasp and the toe of the shoe hit the floor like a sledge. Charles caught his breath, his face going sick. He let the other leg down easily and began to claw the knot of his tie loose. He pulled it over his head. He maneuvered the loop around Brattsford's ankles, tied them together. Then he lifted the legs again in his right arm. His left hand secured a hold on Brattsford's upper arm. He paused, braced, then with a mighty effort lifted the arm and thrust at the upright lower legs. The body turned, rolling onto the lid, where it settled on its side. The feet were just in the crate, and there was no way now to use those bent legs as levers. The only thing for it now was main force. He pried his hands under the lid edge, got a grip, and heaved. The bent legs prevented the body from rolling.

Charles forced himself to his feet, holding securely to the lid, lifting inch by inch, increasing the angle of the plane on which Brattsford lay. Finally the weight of the upper body responded to gravity and began to slide, slowly, oh, so goddamned slowly, until it was half on the lid, half in the crate. Charles had to trust the hinges from then on; the stress on them would be more than they'd been made for. He lowered himself to his knees, his whole body strained to the breaking point to hold the weighted lid up as he went down. He managed to get seated on the floor, then he reached across and clutched the far edge of the crate and began to force the lid shut with the pressure of his thrusting chest and the pull of his arms. He heard a creaking as the hinge strained. But the body within was moving. At last the lid shut. The corpse was safely inside.

He had to turn the crate over so the lid would be on top and not flopping open. He went and got his shoes and put them in position to catch the edge of the crate as he let it down—he wanted to be able to get his fingers out from underneath. When that was done, he managed to free the shoes. Then he had a smoke. A few drags were all he had patience for.

And then the *real* work began. Placing the bath mats. Pushing the heavy load inch by inch. Changing tactics, pulling from the front, losing his holds, tearing his nails. Guarding against buckling of the mats, fighting against the hellish urge to get the clothesline and try dragging it as fast as possible, damning the tedious replacement of mats, damning the noise. He reached the linoleum of dining room and kitchen and got speedily to the back door.

He was very tired. He smoked again. He must be in top form for the rest of it. He knew precisely how he was going to manage. He visualized the position of the truck in relation to the base of the steps. It was wrong.

He put on his suit coat because his shirt and undershirt were sopping. So was his hair, but he didn't bother with a hat. He went down and got in the truck and crawled it into position so that its open back end was facing the steps directly, a few inches from the last step. He went through the truck and onto the steps and up. He turned off the light and opened the door.

He was afraid of this, damned afraid. Inch by inch, minute by minute . . . that was the only possible way to manage. He must not think of anything beyond the physical labor involved. If he did, his nerves and control would shoot all to hell and this whole thing would collapse on him.

Getting the crate over the sill and onto the flat porch floor was more difficult than he'd anticipated. It threatened to bottle-neck everything. He needed some lengths of pipe for rollers. There was nothing to do. The rear corner came down with a thump that shivered the structure and made some bottles clink in one of the iceboxes. He stood suddenly still, his glance flicking nervously to the back door of the apartment next to his. Then, as nothing happened, he shrugged irritably and continued.

He got the crate to the upper landing at the edge of the porch, and turned toward the steps. He went down a few steps. He pulled the crate forward, slowly, very slowly, watching it narrowly, feeling the balance of weight closely. Then it began to tilt down toward him. He pulled it yet another fraction of an inch. Dangerous. Damned dangerous. Finally he turned about, facing down the steps, his feet braced widely, his body going down in a low, almost a sitting crouch. He reached behind him and edged the crate a little farther. It began to tilt fast, like a teetertotter loaded on one end. He was in position. He grasped both railings in his hands; his bent, braced legs were like spring steel. The crate bore down and his upper back struck flat against it, and he tensed his strength, repelling the momentum, stopping it.

Then he started down, hands and feet continually braced, letting the crate move atilt along the surfaces of the edges of the steps. There was nothing to it, really, he thought, with a flash of his old, slightly perverse humor. All he had to do was keep the crate from going faster than he did. It was an absolute cinch that he and Brattsford would get down; no danger at all that either one of them would be deprived of the protection of the law of gravity and hurtle upward.

He was halfway down when it happened, what he had feared.

A baby began to cry. A light went on upstairs in the apartment beside his. He froze, motionless, dimly silhouetted, in full view of the rear windows of the custodian Shadd's apartment, a few feet to his right. The infant wails above grew lustier, and against that sound he detected the quick, light rhythm of footsteps coming to the back. A woman, he thought, in bedroom slippers. He heard her reach the kitchen and winced as that light went on. He counted her steps—ten—then heard the grind-click of a turning key, the metallic clatter of the door-knob. When the door opened, the light brightened and spread, sweeping out across the snow-patched yard, the three parked cars across the alley, and down the steps. He heard the woman come onto the porch above. If she came out to the landing he was caught. He didn't dare move, or risk the slightest sound. The unrelieved tension of his strained position began to tell. His muscles began to burn, fatigued. He started sweating, and it chilled on his face and in his matted hair. The weight on his back began to press heavily. He was going to have to shift, and get relief. He shut his eyes, and let his jaw fall slack, as he breathed heavily through his open mouth. A quivering and a shuddering started through his body and he began to shut and open his mouth, gasping. He heard the woman open the icebox, and bottles clicked. The baby inside howled. He began to feel light-headed, dizzy. He opened his eyes swiftly; the gaping dark interior of the truck yawned below; its edges blurred a little; his vision swirled.

Abruptly the strength fired through him, as if the sound from the alley had pierced his adrenal glands, sending a flood of raw power to meet the danger. His eyes jerked to the corners, searching the source of that sound. He couldn't see it, but un-mistakably someone was walking very cautiously. The dry snow creaked under the controlled pressure. Someone moving away from the light.

Above, the icebox clipped shut, the woman hurried in, shut and locked the door. In a few seconds the lights went out. There was a final dry-snow creaking of a footstep. Then silence, complete silence, and darkness.

Someone was out there watching him from the alley.

He got the crate down to the floor of the truck, sacrificing caution for speed, and shoved it inside, deaf to the noise it made, knowing only that unseen threat. He moved to the driver's seat without getting back out of the truck, and fired the engine alive, turned the wheels, and started off. He went a few feet, and caught himself. He couldn't barrel out of there with the back end open. He clenched his jaw and locked his fists on the steering wheel. He was losing his head. He had to think cold! Whoever was snooping hadn't made his move yet. Cops would surely have tagged him by now and not played it coy. He let the engine idle, toyed with the light switch while he peered at the parked cars.

Three of them. When he had first come home this evening there had been two. When he had come back with the truck there had been three. He'd assumed it belonged to his upstairs neighbors who hadn't been home earlier, the ones with the baby. Maybe they didn't own a car, and the third one belonged to the snooper. The third car was beside the other two, at the left. It, unlike the others, faced the alley. He flipped on parking lights, peering toward that third car, but the illumination wasn't enough. He switched the headlights on and off, fast, as if it had been accidental, and caught the license. He repeated it over and over, shut off the engine and lights, got out, and closed the truck's back door.

He didn't dare precipitate action with someone probably armed and dangerous. To go searching the alley was out of the question. Charles went rapidly up the stairs and into his apartment. He stood watching intently. Presently a man's figure emerged from the alley, hurried to the car there on the left end. He got in, and closed the door soundlessly. Charles waited. Nothing happened. The car didn't start. The snooper's plan was obvious. His car was in position to take out down the alley after him, whatever direction he went. Charles couldn't let himself be tailed!

He studied the setup below. Somehow he should be able to outmaneuver the guy. He calculated the positions of the three parked cars in relation to the panel truck, a plan shaping in his mind. It might work, too, if, as he thought, the snooper didn't know Charles had spotted him.

Charles watched for another few moments, until he was sure the guy wasn't going to do anything but wait and try following him. The fellow was patient. He'd been there since before Charles had arrived with the truck. He'd wait a while longer; he wasn't immediately dangerous. But it would be dangerous to leave the apartment with things left dangling, just in case Homicide arrived.

He found salt, a pad of steel wool, a paring knife. He took a little water in a cup. He went into the bedroom, located the blood dried there between floorboards near the register. He moistened it, loosened it with the knife point, poured in salt, heaping it all along the furrow. It absorbed the liquid, including parts of the dried blood. Then he cleaned it away, and shaved some of the wood off. He wadded a little of the steel wool into the crack, and scoured back and forth. It left the crack looking raw, pale, and conspicuous. He rubbed his hand over the floor, but scarcely soiled it. He needed dirt. He went outside onto the front porch, scraped lightly along the length of the railing, sifting plenty into his hand. He came back and applied it. He swept up the salt, replaced the bureau, put the drawers back in. He put the bath mat in place under the spread, as part of their poverty-pinched bedcovers, just in case he had to explain about the lack of blankets. He took Nora's picture out of the frame, put it in the inside breast pocket of his overcoat. He took the murder knife, and while he was at it the whole carving set from which it had come. He rechecked the place, and when he went down he was fairly sure he'd done all he could.

He got comfortably settled in the driver's seat, started the engine, and idled it, warming it. He left the lights off. He peered narrowly at the three dark cars parked in the back yard, side by side. His vision adjusted to the dark, and the engine was warm. He raised himself and resettled on the seat, thinking: *Ready to go* . . . and without a tail. He slipped into first gear, his foot balanced on the clutch, and began to thread the power out, crawling the truck forward, the wheels turned at a slight angle so that the left half of his bumper would contact one side of the front bumper of the car on the right. The vision of the man watching him from the car on the left would be blocked by the car in the middle, Charles hoped. His plan was to roll the car on the right out across the alley, and cut off the snooper long enough for a getaway down the alley.

Charles drove forward, very slowly, coming nearer to the bumper he was aiming at. In the dark it would be hard to tell from ahead and off to the side that he was not bypassing the car. There was a click, sounding explosive to Charles's ears. The bumpers were in contact. He applied power; the engine sound rose and the car in front of him didn't budge, and he thought for an instant that its brakes were on. In another moment the watcher would realize what he was up to. Then, suddenly, he felt the inertia break. Charles tensed, knowing the split-second complexity of the maneuver ahead of him. He sat high and forward in the seat and gunned the engine, giving the slow-rolling car a hard shove. He slapped into reverse, barreled back, braked hard, switched on headlights, clashed into first gear, and roared out of the yard in a tight arc. He made the alley, but the force of the speeding takeoff turn slammed the crate over against the side of the truck. Behind him, the car he'd pushed was crosswise of the alley.

He raced toward the next street, his engine thunderous in the narrow alley. In the rearview mirror he saw headlights. The car was maneuvering past the blockade. Charles doused all his lights as he came to the intersection, in order to make the pursuer guess which direction he turned. He turned neither direction, but continued ahead another block up the alley. Then he turned to the right, and parked. The other car had cleared and roared after him. It didn't follow into the second block, but turned when it came to the cross street. Charles rolled down his window and listened to ascertain which direction it had gone. To the right, toward the middle of the city. Charles pulled ahead, going the same direction on a parallel street. The other car would soon discover its mistake and might backtrack. He slowed, listening. He heard its engine sound fade out, knew it was stopping. He heard it roar again, briefly, as if it had backed a short distance; then the sound rose full. The car was going back along the same street it had been on, not circling the block. Charles drove ahead, going in the opposite direction. For several minutes he zigzagged along the streets,

putting distance between them with left and right turns, following a street a block or two, until he was reasonably certain
he'd shaken pursuit.

City Park had a history of muggings, and in the back of
his mind Charles had decided on that location for Brattsford's
body. But as he drove along one of its dark, curving roadways,
the drawbacks became formidable. In the first place, there
was snow—definitely not strolling weather. Then there was the
matter of producing false clues, including necessarily splattered
blood. He definitely was not going to draw blood from the
corpse and fling it about. The grisly thought made him shudder.
A cab or two passed as he cruised along, reminding him that it
would be impossible to unload the crate anywhere except in
one of the secluded areas. To get there would mean leaving
tracks . . . and tire prints were as good as fingerprints in the
clues department these days. Well, not quite, but he couldn't
take a chance on connecting Proctor's vehicle with this murder.
Proctor would be able to explain without any hesitation—
loaned truck, coffin-sized crate, Charles Garrell. Very simple.
He was absorbed in the gloomy setup and wracking his mind
to think of a safe place, and the headlights on his rear-vision
mirror went unnoticed at first.

He watched the beads of light expand, and a few moments
later the car was coming alongside and adjusting its pace to
his instead of passing. His heart began to slam and his mouth
went chalk-dry. The other car edged forward, and then a
spotlight beam raked the panel of the truck and slashed across
his profile briefly. He squinted out and saw the insignia of a
police car and two uniformed cops within.

He saw the near cop crank his window down, and he waited
sickly for the pullover signal. Maybe the light beam had been
the signal. He eased up on the gas. His scalp began to prickle.
He was caught flat-footed. Desperately he stared at the curve
of macadam just ahead, wondering if he dared make a run for
it. He didn't dare. It was idiocy even to consider it. Well, the
crate was shut. If he could hold his head, not get panicky, not
act like he felt, sick with fright.

The cop was shouting something. Then astonishingly, the
police car spurted ahead, gave a couple of beeps of farewell with

its horn, the cop's arm waved jauntily and vanished inside. A second later the car was gone, out of sight around the curve.

Charles pulled over, braked. He just sat there, limp, a look of dull stupor on his face. He shut his eyes and shook the gauze out of his mind. What the hell! What the hell!

Then it was clear, and he thought grimly that if he was somebody else—for instance himself about three years ago—he would laugh like hell. The cops had acted like pals because they knew a Proctor truck when they saw one.

He got the hell out of the park, and out of the city. He rolled along the highway at a steady clip, searching his memory of the area, wanting to get onto a side road. He couldn't think of any place specifically designed to accommodate his purpose. But he certainly had to get off the highway. He turned onto an empty crossroad.

He drove for miles, and seemingly for hours, turning onto lesser and lesser roads. All of them were lined with fenced fields, barns, houses, tilled fields. From afar it seemed a cinch to find a remote road and vast, uninhabited hiding places, but when it came to finding something specific it wasn't so simple. At last he came to a bridge with a gravel road leading down under it. Not a road, actually, just a pair of ruts that had been filled in with gravel, and bare of snow, so that the tire tracks wouldn't show. The ground under the bridge was rocky and frozen.

He worked in concealment, with little stress. He got the crate out, the body removed, took his tie off the ankles. He took off his shoes, socks, and pants and dragged the body out into the icy water. Just before letting it go he remembered the wrist watch! What an absurdity! A robbery motive would be ridiculous if the watch remained. He felt both of Brattsford's wrists. The watch was gone.

He realized with a jolt that somebody, probably the guy who had tried to follow him, had prowled his apartment, had taken the watch. And knew all about the corpse.

So, there it was, and there wasn't a damned thing to be done about it now.

He dressed, put the empty crate back in the truck, and got away. He found another, similar bridge within a mile, and he drove down under it. He put the crate against a bridge pier and ran the car into it several times, making kindling of it. He got out the stained carton and the bloody bedclothes and the billfold. He dipped some of the newspaper wrappings into the gas tank. He started a good fire, and while it was burning he took some stones and managed to break the metal parts of the carving set. The fire was a little conspicuous and he drove a quarter mile away from it, waited there, in case any cars got curious and went under the bridge. He went back, tended the fire until he was sure everything was reduced beyond recognition. Then he headed circuitously along back roads for the Merry Land Club. As he went, he flung out fragments of the broken carving set every mile or so, into a creek or ditch.

It was almost dawn. The parking lot was empty, the club shut down. He'd missed Syl. He turned the truck over to a man in the garage area under the club and phoned for a taxi. When it came, he got in and gave the address, then collapsed into deep sleep.

# 8

"HEY, BUDDY! Wake up!"

Charles got out of the cab, stiff and groggy, thinking a little sleep was worse than none. He mumbled: "Wait for me," and went up the walk and into the foyer of the handsome three-story brick apartment building. He squinted in the gloomy dawn light, found the card Jeremiah Aldrich—Sylvia Aldrich, and rang the bell. He waited, tried the inner door which was locked, then rang again. Jerry's voice came into the foyer, a metallic grumble. Charles spoke into the wall grille.

"Sorry to wake you . . . this's Charles . . ."

"C'mon up." The door-release buzzer hummed and Charles went into the apartment and walked up to the third floor. Jerry was waiting in the open door, his fat face frowsily peevish, his pudgy body in striped pajamas and a screaming red-and-yellow robe.

"Find Nora?"

Charles shook his head and went in. He glanced around the brittle, modern living room with its angular plastic and pale wood pieces, thinking it was just like Syl, a sterile showpiece, not a hair out of place. "Is Syl home?" he said as Jerry shut the door.

"No," Jerry said, his eyes pained. His eyes slid away; he nodded at the room. "This place is beautiful . . . but she's got another apartment."

"Yeah?" Charles frowned in surprise. "Where?"

Jerry turned up his palms. Then he jammed his fists in the pockets of the splashy red-and-yellow robe and blurted: "What good would it do to find out when she don't want me to? What if I'd go and find somebody with her and get beat up? Disgraced in front of her!" He walked agitatedly to the middle of the room, turned around, and thrust his face angrily at Charles. "You think I could *live* after that? I thought about what you said, me being a masochist and taking all kinds of stuff on account I'm really so goddamned mean underneath I don't dare let it come up and out . . ."

"Wait! I didn't say it exactly fit you . . . I said . . ."

"It does fit." He brought his fists out of the pockets and brought them down together in a violent motion. Then he brought them up to his chest slowly. "I think sometimes I want a gun." The fists chopped downward, came up. He talked in rising excitement, in short phrases, emphasizing each one with his fists. "I'd find the place . . . I'd take the gun . . . I'd see him . . . Syl would see me . . . I'd take the gun . . ."

"Who's the man?"

"I don't know," Jerry said impatiently, and went on talking and underlining the words with his fists with an intensity that was formidable in spite of the fact that he looked a little grotesque. "Whoever it is, I'd *look* at him . . . he'd look at the gun. Syl would look at *me* . . . I'd aim the gun." He aimed a forefinger, and then his hand began to jerk. "Bang—like that. Bang! Bang! and he would fall . . . and I'd turn to Syl . . ." His arms fell suddenly limp, his intensity collapsed, his face going dull and flabby. "I don't know if I'd kill her, too."

The display shocked Charles. They looked at each other dully for seconds, then Charles said, very softly, "Why a gun? It's loud, and a bullet's impersonal." He moved up to Jerry. "Not close and satisfying like a knife."

Jerry scowled and shook his head. "Don't you see? He might take the knife away from me. I'd be humiliated worse than ever. If I ever did it, I'd want to be *sure*. Oh, well, I guess I'm all talk. Anyway, Syl's probably just in a phase, and . . ." He shrugged. "Any line on Nora, Charley?"

Jerry didn't react to the mention of a murder knife. But what if Brattsford had been Syl's lover and Jerry had lived with the idea of killing him for a long time? He'd have become familiar with it, conditioned and hardened to it. If he had killed, he might feel that he'd wiped out the guilt of not being a man, and far from being haunted by murder guilt he'd have new confidence. He'd gloat over his ability to conceal himself under a believable surface. Jerry had bared his teeth last night in the cafeteria, called him a jailbird, referred to him with hostile contempt as the superman type that Syl liked.

"I haven't heard anything on Nora . . . past the time when you drove her to the station. Not yet," Charles said. "But for whatever it's worth, I've got a lead. You're in touch with the state auto license bureau in your insurance work, aren't you?"

"Not personally. Why?"

"I've got a license number. Could you find out who owns the car?"

"Sure. Fred Stalmayer can get the dope for me. What's the number?"

Charles said carefully: "T-810-D."

Jerry bobbed his head, turned, and started for a door across the room, calling: "Lemme get a pencil in the bedroom and write it down."

Charles's eyes narrowed. He poised briefly on the balls of his feet. That license might be Jerry's. Maybe Jerry only dreamed about bang-banging, or maybe he had a real gun. Charles didn't want him out of sight.

He followed him quietly. He was several feet behind as Jerry entered the bedroom. Jerry went rapidly past the foot of twin beds, one of them rumpled, heading for a desk in the corner. Charles lengthened his stride, catching up. He was right on top of Jerry as he opened the desk drawer. Jerry's head jerked around, startled. There was no gun in the drawer.

Jerry fumbled for a pad and pencil, darting nervous glances at Charles.

"T-810-D," he said hoarsely, and wrote. "Right?"

"Yes."

Jerry put the pad down and drew a long breath. "All right, Charley. Satisfy yourself. We'll look under the beds, in the closet and bathroom, the kitchen and pantry and hall closet and dumb-waiter."

"O. K. Let's look, just for the hell of it."

They toured the place in chilly silence, without result.

"Last night in the cafeteria," Jerry said as Charles was leaving, "you said you would fix the matter of the hock-shop guy at your place. And if Nora wasn't hurt, the person who had her wouldn't have anything to fear."

Charles tensed. He said slowly:

"It's fixed. The offer stands. All I want is Nora."

"I just wanted to know if you were making headway . . . you phone the office and I'll find who the license belongs to."

Charles let out his breath, exasperated. For a moment he'd thought Jerry was his man, ready to deal. "Thanks. I'll phone you. Are you sure you don't know where I could find Syl? She may know something."

"She'll go to work, I guess. You know her office?"

"She still at Wexler, Cree & Prather?"

"Yes, same place."

"O. K. 'By.'"

Charles went down and got into his waiting cab.

"Take me downtown to one of the burlesque shows."

"There ain't but one. The Queen. It won't be open at no seven ayem."

"That's all right. Let's go there."

Syl had said Nora met that handsome, wolfish man in the lobby of a hotel next to a burlesque for whatever her talk was worth. Fifteen minutes before Nora was to have met him. Between six-thirty when—and if—Jerry had left her at the depot, and seven-five, his train time.

Charles paid an eight-dollar cab bill in front of the Queen, and went into the small, dreary lobby of the Majestic Hotel, to the right of the show. A shabby, aimless-looking character

stood picking his teeth and looking out the plate-glass window
at the grimy depot-area street; otherwise the lobby was empty.
A gray, elderly clerk with a narrow, waxy face, looking
shrunken in a wide-shouldered serge suit, pushed a registry
card across the desk with a long, delicate hand and lisped:

"Good morning, sir." He offered Charles a pen and smiled
coquettishly.

"No." Charles pushed two dollar bills toward the old queer
and said: "I wonder if you can tell me if there's a women registered here. She's blonde, early thirties, fairly tall and slim,
dresses smartly, and she's rather good-looking in a—" he motioned deprecatingly with one hand—"in a severe way. I don't
mean tough. But haughty. Refined-looking."

"We have *very* few ladies . . . or I should say *no* ladies whatsoever . . . but very few *fe*males. And your *friend*," he said
with a delicately reproachful emphasis, "is decidedly not among
them." He folded the two dollars, pocketed them daintily. "I
thank you." He gave Charles a humorous twinkle and said
with mock grandeur, "The Majestic, sir, caters *only* to sluts."

Charles grinned and reached for Nora's picture. He hesitated. "Were you on duty between six-thirty and seven last
night?"

"No, sir. I went off at six, came on at six. Off at six, on
at six," he repeated coyly, under the impression he was making
a joke. Charles knew he shouldn't have encouraged him with
that grin. He went out, glad he hadn't let the old fool touch
Nora. He knew it was superstitious and primitive of him, as
if a look at her picture could harm her, but this tawdry, ugly
area scraped down to the jungle in him.

The hotel on the other side of the burlesque, the Supreme,
was larger, its plate glass cleaner, and far more extensive,
facing not only the street but the enclosed alley leading to the
box office of the show next door. A line of leather chairs faced
the side windows, looking out at the opposite wall which was
lined with life-sized color pictures of the strippers in the uniform of the trade. The rear of the lobby opened into a spacious
bar which, like the rest of the place, was deserted at that time
of day. The clerk was young and hard, and he listened with
an air of cynical indifference to a description of Syl.

"I dunno, buddy, have we got her or not. Stick around till we wake up; we got a little everything. Take your pick; tail's tail; she probably ain't a blonde no more anyways."

"I don't doubt it. Say, I'm trying to locate another girl, too. I heard she was in here last night around six-thirty or seven."

"You'd have to ask the four-to-midnight clerk."

"He'll be on at four this afternoon?"

"Sa-a-y, man!" The clerk gave him a derisive, lopsided grin. "Ain't you the brain! Figured it right out."

Charles looked at the clerk. He felt raw and gritty and mean as hell, and some of it conveyed itself to the clerk in that silent stare. The guy's grin straightened itself out. Charles pressed hard against the desk, his upper body leaning out across it, his hands poised tensely on the edge of the desk. "That's a goddamned insult, you cheap punk son of a bitch!" The words came out swift, clear, hard, but quiet, as if he were in icy control. "Get out from in back of there. I'm going to squash that stupid face of yours all over this lobby! Come on!"

The clerk blinked, paled, and elongated himself as if he were trying to bend over backward away from Charles without moving his feet. "All right, all right, don't get tough, buddy, don't get tough. I told you all I know and that's all I know, see?"

"Yellow punk!"

"What's the percentage me fighting you? Who puts up the purse? Beat it, willya? Wanta get me canned? Wanta get us both in the clink? Beat it, willya?"

"You ordering me out?" Charles said softly.

"Nah, you crazy jackass. I told you all I know. . . ."

"I asked if the clerk was going to be on at four, the same shift as he was yesterday, and I get a cheap insult from a cutie like you. Goddam if I take such crap."

"All right, the guy comes on at four, works the same shift as yesterday. I thought it was clear what I meant. . . ."

Charles jerked around, mashing his lips together, flipping up his coat collar, and walked out. The joint was shifty, shady, a little world of loudmouthed sports, fourflushers, thieves, thugs, sharps and grifters, hopheads, whores, strippers, queers, drunks and pimps; everybody on the make. There was an underlying breath of ruthlessness in the atmosphere and it made his flesh crawl to think of Nora caught in it.

He walked briskly for half a block, and then his pace dragged. The bottom fell out. He felt ugly. He'd lashed out and intimidated that clerk, and when he'd had him he'd kept on like some damned prison screw, or that sadistic pair of detectives, Gobi and Elton. He had let his temper get away and jeopardize everything. He hadn't had the will to hold tight, and when he'd got rolling he hadn't wanted to stop. He'd relished the prospect of a smashing, slugging fight. He'd almost been able to taste the savage joy of beating hell out of that sneering punk. His violence and hate had been bigger than anything else—pushing everything, including Nora, out of the world. He walked on, frowning down at the pavement, feeling chilled to the bone. This was it, all right: *action was character.* Syl had reminded him. In the showdown he had taken a gun to solve his and Nora's problem, and landed in prison, abandoning the woman he told himself he loved. And just now, again, that cold, tight control vital to Nora's safety had broken. He didn't know himself any more. Maybe the balance in him was shifted. He still had a capacity to love, but maybe it was diminished to the vanishing point, impotent against the hate.

He went to the depot, hoping a redcap or the taxi starter might remember Nora's arrival with Jerry and might have seen her leave. It was the wrong time of day, as in the hotels. He'd have to wait. He considered trying to contact the taxi starter at his home, abandoned the idea. It would be tricky enough trying to get the man to recall her without antagonizing him by barging in on his privacy. Syl was still his best hope. Now he'd not only have to go to her on his belly, but he'd have to sweat it out locating her before he got the *privilege.*

He walked back down the grimy block with its walkup hotels, dingy saloons, gypsy fortune joint, shooting gallery, third-run movies, oyster bars, cheap restaurants, cigar-stand bookie joints. It wasn't made for daylight. It was stirring to dull life, and there was some pedestrian traffic, cabs, and delivery trucks on the street. The dots and strips of electric light and neon lent the area a sordid accent, like flecks of bright tinsel on a scab.

Syl's other apartment might be in this area, he thought. This could be just the air she wanted to breathe.

He went into a greasy spoon across from the burlesque house, and settled down with coffee and rolls to watch the street for her. It was a vague, ridiculous hope, but he couldn't think of anything better. He couldn't think, period. He was flat. His body felt sodden. His eyes were raw, and they kept closing. He kept rousing against the insidious craving for sleep—for utter oblivion.

It was ten past nine when he entered the eighth-floor suite of offices of Wexler, Cree & Prather, where Syl worked as the senior partner's secretary. The receptionist, a plump, plain, tidy, and prematurely graying girl, gave him an overanxious smile. She sensed immediately that he was unsuitable; probably his nerve-scraped urgency clashed with the ponderous rhythm of the old firm, or maybe he just looked like a lout.

"I'm Charles Garrell. Is Mrs. Aldrich in yet?"

"No, Mr. Garrell. She doesn't arrive until nine-thirty." She wrote his name slowly, as if she doubted the propriety of it. "Will you wait?"

"Yes, thanks." He sat for two or three minutes, then went out into the corridor to watch the elevators. Some of the firm members, lofty men all, arrived. Syl hadn't volunteered to smudge herself by acknowledging any connection with him a few years back. Although her firm didn't concern itself with crime on the lower levels, it could have found counsel for him and thrown its weight around behind the scenes, he knew now. He had taken the court-appointed green lawyer rather than ask anything of her. He thought of his position now and felt like grinding his teeth.

It hadn't even been Syl's help that had got him the lawyer who worked for his parole. Jerry had arranged for the lawyer who handled things for his insurance company to take the case. Maybe Jerry had done it in spite of Syl . . . and Charles had been letting himself doubt and mistrust and even despise the guy because . . . Because why? Because he happened to be weak—kicked around, humiliated? That was it, all right! He wouldn't have despised Jerry if he'd been the one to administer the whippings, he told himself. Damn it, he had to

quit this kicking himself around, figuring himself out as some
kind of a monster. To hell with it!

He went in and sat down. At nine-thirty Syl hadn't come.
He remembered with a sudden sinking that he was due· at
the Parole Board at ten! He got to his feet, making the receptionist nervous, and looked down the corridor. Empty. He
turned back just as the phone rang. The receptionist answered,
listened a moment, then said in surprise:

"Why, how did you know? Yes, he is . . . Oh, yes, very
upset. . . ." The receptionist's glance jumped to ˙and guiltily
away from him.

He moved close to the desk, whispered loudly. "That her?"
The receptionist shook her head violently while she listened.
"Let me talk to her!"

The woman replaced the handset and said primly: "Mrs.
Aldrich won't be in today. She said to tell you that."

"Did she say where she was calling from?"

"No, sir, she didn't. She only instructed me to tell you . . ."

He snatched up the address-phone number device, ran the
indicator to A, snapped it open while the receptionist gasped
and tried to snatch it from him. The phone number beside
Syl's name was the one at the apartment she shared with Jerry.
He said intently to the receptionist:

"I *must* reach her. Please give me the number. There's another one beside this˙where you can reach her, and I know it."

"I'm not authorized . . ."

"Don't tell me, then. But call her. As a favor, a great favor!"

The girl lowered her eyes and seemed to debate, then she
looked up at him worriedly. "She *did* say I could call her back
when you'd gone. You mustn't get me in trouble for telling
you."

"May I phone you, then . . . Miss . . . ?"

"Weir. You may phone me and I'll have been in touch with
her, but you mustn't, simply mustn't ask any more of me."

"All right, Miss Weir. Ten minutes? Shall I call then?"

"It will be a half-hour before I can. She was going out for
breakfast . . ."

"Where? I'll *happen* on her . . . not involve you. I must see
her. . . ."

"Honestly I don't have the faintest idea where she'd break-fast. That's the truth. I couldn't give you a hint. I'm sorry."

"All right, all right. I'll phone in half an hour."

He took an elevator down and went into the building drug-store where he phoned the Parole Board. He was sure he could get permission to postpone his appointment.

He left the booth, looking drained. He had to keep the ap-pointment. He was a con, and the parole officer had let him know it in no uncertain terms.

An annex served as a sort of dust trap, holding those de-partments, bureaus, and sections which might sully the glorious Capitol. There were relief offices on the dingy main floor, and the sight of waiting clients depressed him as he waited for the elevator. A forlorn lot, distressed and sick and hungry and beaten and scared and ashamed. They'd lost their virtue, all right, and they knew it; they were the real criminals in the eyes of the well-fed and righteous and safe and right-thinking folk. It made him furious, and he knew he'd damned well better make a quick shift in mood. The open-cage elevator crept upward, wobbly on its cables, and by the time he stepped off at the third floor he looked insipid, and he hoped that his eyes shone with repentance and a yearning for the Right Path, and a love for the good and the true and the respectable.

The cubbyhole enclosed a desk, two chairs, a wooden tri-angle on which was the gold-lettered name: Arthur Allen Towner Pretz. A. A. T. P. himself occupied the chair behind the desk; Charles took the other.

"You made a bad start, Garrell," A.A.T.P. said. He was thick and ruddy and militant. He focused his slightly bulged green eyes on Charles and waited.

"I wanted the postponement because of personal trou—"

"We all have troubles." A.A.T.P. sat forward briskly. "How do you feel, Garrell, about things in general?"

"I have learned my lesson, Mr. Pretz," Charles said gravely. "I want to prove myself worthy of Society, which is giving me another chance. I have learned to see with new eyes." It seemed a bit thick, but then A.A.T.P. was pretty thick. "As I look back upon my crime it's as if I were another person . . . I . . . I . . . ." He permitted emotion to choke him, and he gestured helplessly, unable to express the profoundly inexpressible.

"It was a great thing that happened to you. The opportunity to learn discipline . . . the hard way, true, but, Garrell, those years in prison taught you discipline. That is what the general run of man lacks. In a sense you are better fitted for life than if you hadn't attacked Society. Charles, I'm going to talk man to man to you. Society is the father, the protector, the voice of right, the strength, and when you attack it in deed—or even in thought, yes, particularly in thought—you sin, which is far graver than crime. In this country discipline is lacking. We need a force. You are an educated man and I can speak frankly. But enough of philosophy. You're to report to Statewide Warehouse immediately. They've sponsored your parole and you are to arrange at once about the job."

"Yes, sir!" He put a salute in his voice. "You've given me a real lift . . . I feel like I can *belong* again."

The fascist bastard! he thought, leaving.

Charles left the office of Statewide Warehouse's assistant manager in high spirits. The assistant manager had been an all-right guy. The job, as a loader, wasn't going to be much. But it was sure, and enough to live on, and he'd been made to feel that he wasn't at a dead end. The company had hired lots of parolees in its various branches. If he had the ability, desire, and will to learn warehousing his record wouldn't stand in his way. It was really something! he thought. He felt focused, positive, as if for the first time he could see ahead. It put a glow in him—an old familiar surge of confidence sweeping aside all his present trouble.

He made his way down the busy, noisy dock to a loading gang working at a big over-the-road semi-trailer. Poley, the dockmaster, was supposed to be down at that end. Charles recognized a man from prison, a parolee, working in that gang at the far end. And he recognized something else that pulled some of the warmth out of his guts. Crates. Big ones. They were bringing them out on skids and putting them, via electric platform-lift truck, into the freight-car-sized interior of the semi-trailer. Nearing, he could see the labels on them—a Chicago hardware manufacturer. The crates were identical to the one he had got from Grig Proctor out at the Merry Land Club.

The crate he had used for the body had held a slot machine.

Charles reached the man in the red corduroy hunting cap and brown leather jacket. Poley.

"I'm Charles Garrell," he said as Poley turned his square-chinned, leather face inquiringly.

Poley took the cigar out of his mouth, wiped his slab hand on his pants and offered it. They shook, while Poley gave him an approving once-over, nodding all the while. "Yeah . . . Garrell . . . understand they put you to pushing a big diesel tractor up at the logging camp and you're a pretty good driver."

"I managed all right for a month or so last summer," he said. He grinned at the ex-con who waved and yelled: "Hiya, Slugger." "Of course I never drove a big outfit out on a road . . ."

Poley wasn't listening. He turned with a grin toward the ex-con. "Know him, Jim?"

"Sure. Hell, yes."

"Slugger, huh?" Poley turned back, chuckling, reappraised Charles, upgrading him. "O. K., Slugger, you're my man. I guess the boss told you you start on the loading gang."

"He said that was the job."

"Swell. When you starting?"

"How about next Mon . . ."

"Ah-ah-ah . . ." Poley shook his head, dragged his cigar. "Nah. Want a job, you start today . . . tonight. Night shift. Midnight to eight. Be here? Want a job?"

"Sure . . . yes . . . sure, but . . ."

"No buts, Slugger. I tell the parole officer you're in or you ain't. Up to you. Tonight."

"Right," Charles said. "Tonight."

Damned funny attitude, Charles thought, rushing him that way. Asking about his ability to handle a big truck when his job was to be loading. And on the night shift. He wondered, riding back to town, if Statewide Warehouse was just a great big heart, hiring ex-cons. He had a strong hunch the outfit had more practical reasons. A guy on parole was in an intimidated position; did what he was told and kept his mouth shut and stayed out of prison. Statewide wasn't known as a hot-goods depot, certainly, or it would never have got Parole Board approval as an employer. Statewide was clean. If anything dirty ever came to light, they had some ex-con fall guys—known criminals to throw to the dogs.

He knew he wasn't lined up with a job and a future, but in a trap. Those crates with the hardware manufacturer's label on them undoubtedly contained slot machines. That tied them to Proctor and to that tap on his telephone and the FBI. Maybe it was also tied in with that confidence game Proctor had told him about . . . if that spiel had been anything but talk. The con-game victim had been from Chicago—like the hardware-slot-machine crates. The con mob had resorted to the cackle-bladder—a fake killing.

Brattsford, the pawnbroker, was sure enough dead and no cacklebladder kill. But he, too, fit into this thing . . . or he very well might. His Beacon Loan was known as a hot-goods drop. He was, therefore, an expert in the moving of hot goods —just as Proctor was an authority on everything in the gambling line. What if both Proctor and Brattsford had been involved in the con game? He couldn't hope to figure it out yet . . . but the farther he went the more dangerous it looked.

# 9

HE LISTENED avidly to the eleven-thirty news on the cab radio but there was no word of either Brattsford's disappearance or the discovery of his body. He had given the driver the address of Syl's office building, but he changed it. He stopped by his apartment, hoping for mail or some sort of word on Nora, and anxious to know if the police had been around. There was no word, and no move by the police.

Leaving the cab downtown, he bought and scanned a paper on the chance that there'd been an earlier story on Brattsford, but there was nothing. He gave Jerry a ring, caught him just as he was going out to lunch. The car license clue was dead end. The car had been reported stolen last night, and it had been found and returned this morning. Anybody might have used it.

He sat in the phone booth trying to decide what he ought

to do next. He wanted to see Philip de Verre, the lawyer who'd got his parole. He had to get in touch with the receptionist in Syl's office. It was past noon, and the taxi starter and redcaps who had been on duty last night would be at the depot. He looked up De Verre's number and was surprised to see his office was in this building, on the same floor as Syl's. He took the elevator up.

The plain, plump receptionist, Miss Weir, turned pink and fluttery at the sight of him.

"Do you have good news for me? Mrs. Aldrich here? Or did she leave word for me?"

"Well, no, Mr. Garrell," she said with suppressed excitement. "And I'm not permitted to tell you any more than before, but may I suggest something?"

"Of course. By all means . . . please do!"

"We-e-e-ll." She took a breath and then fairly drooled. "This is going to sound old-fashioned, but I happen to know that deep down in her heart she's a dear, sensitive, old-fashioned girl. So, I pleaded your case. And I can tell you, confidentially." She looked down embarrassedly and squirmed. "Well, you know the saying: say it with flowers, and sweets for the sweet . . ."

"Sweets for the sweet," he said numbly.

"I happen to know," she confided, "that they wouldn't be unacceptable. Now, if you were to entrust me with buying and sending them, and if you were to contact me later in the afternoon after she had had time to receive them, I'm positive I'd have something *nice* to tell you."

"Such as her phone number and address."

She nodded brightly. His face began to redden. This was Syl turning the screws! That dear, sensitive, old-fashioned girl expected him to play lover boy, woo her with flowers and candy! He was damned if he would let her play him like that, and let her make a cheap game of this and a damned fool out of him! The smirking, nasty, sadistic bitch, hiding out somewhere and having herself a time when he was desperate. He clenched his teeth, so damned furious that tears came to his eyes. If he had his hands on that woman he'd knock the hell out of her. He turned away from the receptionist playing the delicious role of Cupid and groped for his money. He bit his lips.

"Will ten be all right?" he asked. The shakiness in his voice was authentic, no fake, but it wasn't what the receptionist imagined.

"That will be just fine," she said, and added sympathetically: "And now you just trust me . . . and don't lose hope."

"I'll try to carry on."

He left the office cursing Syl violently under his breath and found De Verre's office. But not De Verre. He was, according to his secretary, out of the city for a week.

He didn't know what good the lawyer would have done him anyhow, he thought, leaving the building and heading for the depot. He knew very little about him, except that Jerry's insurance company was among his clients. Any suspicion Charles might have confided to him about Statewide Warehouse would have fallen on deaf or hostile ears, Charles realized. The man was a corporation counsel, not a criminal lawyer. His handling of Charles's case had been a favor to Jerry. Philip de Verre had, on both visits to Charles in prison, acted quite friendly, although he had a cool, stiffly reserved personality and wasn't the buddy-buddy type by any means. The thing that had animated the lawyer, now that he recalled it, had been talk about criminals. He had solicited tidbits about notorious inmates, told episodes of criminal lore, glowing and warming as if he made a hobby of it. He'd sounded glamorstruck by crime. Lots of people were, of course, especially the horribly respectable, but Charles had dismissed the notion that a smart lawyer could imagine the underworld was romantic. He wondered seriously now if he should have dismissed it. Philip de Verre, so like Syl in surface dignity and polish, might be close to her in a lot of other ways. De Verre was a man Nora would have trusted. A message from him could have pulled her out of the railroad station . . . if she had ever arrived.

Lemonish sunlight, just strong enough to cast a shadow, lay across the lower steps at the depot entrance. The taxi starter, a ponderous figure in his uniform, stood down there absorbing the light. He listened, grave and impassive, as Charles introduced himself and his problem. He inspected Nora's snapshot and her full-face photograph, listening occasionally to a de-

scription of the coat and hat Charles thought she had worn.
The starter turned and motioned to the two redcaps who came
down. He gave each of them a picture, then asked carefully:

"Boys, isn't that the girl we speculated about? . . . came
with that fellow who hogged into that Number-1 space about
six-thirty . . . no baggage."

"Yessir! This's the one," one of the redcaps exclaimed; the
other nodded; both looked inquiringly at Charles.

"It's his wife," the starter said, retrieving the pictures. He
studied them a while longer, nodding. Charles felt a sharp
lift of excitement. He started to speak, but the other man began to deliver himself in a slightly oratorical manner. "Yes, it
was at six-thirty. A little sedan swung into the approach and
drew to a stop in this space right ahead of us. He came in at
an angle and stayed there for some seconds, in clear violation
of the rules. I started down the steps when the door opened
and the young lady got out. Well, now, sir, the anger just
went out of me, there was such a lilt to her, and whatever was
in my mind to say to the driver was wafted away, for there
was the smile of heaven on her face and she moved on up past
me as if she was singing to herself. Well, the boys—" he indicated the redcaps—"fair joshed the life out of me at the way
the miss took all the bluff out of me. Then imagine our con-
sternation when, not five minutes later, she came out again,
the smile and the song gone; the lilt hurried out of her step."

"She came back out?" Charles put in. "Alone?"

"Yes. And yes, alone. The three of us looked at each other.
Baffled. We watched her go hurrying along, down the approach,
across the street over there to the far sidewalk," he said, pointing. Charles looked in the direction he was pointing. The
Queen Burlesque and the Supreme Hotel, too far down the
block to be visible, were in that direction. "We kept her in
sight. We can see as far as that Oyster House . . . see it? . . .
about a third of the way down the block. She passed it, and
was still going the last we saw of her. All alone."

"The driver of the car that brought her," Charles said. "Was
he . . . ?" He described Jerry.

The starter nodded. "The very one."

"She got here at six-thirty? And left five minutes later?"

The others nodded. Each of them remembered her clearly.

Charles repocketed the picture, put the snapshot back in his billfold, started to take out a bill.

"No," the starter said earnestly. "We don't want that. Right, boys?"

They nodded.

"Thanks a lot," Charles said. Their whole attitude toward Nora touched him.

"It's too bad," the starter said, "but I know she'll turn up safe."

One of the redcaps chimed in. "Oh, yessir, there's just no chance that *she* won't turn up safe."

That's the way they wished it, and it was wonderfully comforting to Charles as he set out along the route Nora had taken. But it didn't mean a damned thing.

The burlesque alley outside the Supreme Hotel's side windows was lighted and the life-size color pictures of the strippers gave the noisy, crowded lobby a lush, naked background. There was a tough, nervous mood to the place, flashy, sexy, and brash, the talk loud and casually obscene, the girls, smoking, drinking, moving about, flaunting their bodies in open fur coats, their eyes restless and hot, their talk and laughter splashing out around them, their perfumes spreading a kind of voluptuous miasma. The males had the scent and there was a bawdy strut even in their voices, putting them on a high pitch, promoting everything: first-race money; the women; themselves.

Charles made his way through to the desk. The clerk who had been on last night around seven wouldn't be on till four, but this one might recognize a description of Syl. He was a kid, blue-eyed, curly-headed, like an earnest pup, and he tried, tried hard to concentrate, but a woman-in-words was just no match for the real stuff surging around the place, and his eyes just couldn't hold still. Charles gave up.

"I'll look around myself. Is it always this crowded?"

"Oh, no," the kid confided, grinning. "All the babes from next door are here . . . and that pulls! Man! We oughta charge just to come in."

He threaded his way back to the clogged, open doorway to

the bar and peered into the murkier light. A con he recognized
from stir looked at him from the bar; they exchanged imper-
ceptible nods. There'd be dicks in the place, without a doubt.
He remembered his parole, turned back out of the bar uneasily. Nora had come this way; it looked as if Syl *did* know
something. Why the devil hadn't he used a little ingenuity
with that receptionist in Syl's office? He went out of the place,
thinking he might still be able to trick her via phone.

He found a cigar store and used the public phone. Miss
Weir answered. He tried to disguise his voice.

"This is the florist you called a while ago . . . I'm so sorry,
but we're not sure we have that address . . . it's a bit illegible
. . . Mrs. Aldrich's address. . . ."

"Oh, goodness," Miss Weir said, "but that just won't work
at all. I'm ashamed of you, Mr. Garrell."

"Yeah," he sighed, "it was silly. How soon *can* I find out?"

"Not before three, surely. I'm not angry, but it *wasn't* very
clever of you."

"That it wasn't. Well, I'll call at three. 'By."

He went back into the Supreme and stood around scanning
the surging, carnal mass gloomily. Just before one o'clock the
queens, fifteen or twenty of them, began a prolonged and vol-
uble departure for their dressing rooms. The exit drew half the
crowd out, leaving a definite lull. Charles went to the desk and
gave the curly-headed clerk another try. The kid, slightly down
at the mouth, listened but he didn't recall Syl as a guest.

Charles turned, letting his gaze sweep back across the bar
entrance. His glance stopped. Sitting there alone at a table for
two and staring out into the lobby at him was Cleo the change
girl from the Circus Room at the Merry Land Club. A tan-
talizing smile spread across her pale, piquant face with its
sexy, shining black bangs. She shifted slightly on her chair
as if that exciting little body of hers, bundled in soft, dark
fur, was animated by the sight of him. Cleo brought one arm
up and let her hand lie gracefully upturned on the table, the
fingers clustered above her palm in a pattern of open curves
in a maddeningly feminine suggestion of supplication and submissiveness. Then her forefinger which had lain out flat toward
him curled upward in a slow, boneless, stroking motion—beck-

oning, pulling him. He didn't quite hold his breath, but he
was aware of breathing shallowly. She was some raggle, he
thought, his mind slipping into the tempting little grifter's
jargon, his body already moving to the crook of her little
finger. There was a sensation like feathers agitating against
bare nerve tissue on the inner wall of his gut, aggravating and
pleasant as he went into the bar, a wry smile masking his
emotions.

He wanted to say something in her language, raffish with
an edge of sharp, cynical wit. He wanted the warm sound of
appreciative laughter and a dancing in those vivid deep purple
eyes. He remembered with a surge of exultance the sight of
her body dancing as she had stood with the other change girls
watching the floor show. And before that she had scampered
ahead to open the door out of the Circus Room for him, exe-
cuting a lithe turn and twist and catching the glass door on
her hip. Then she had stood pertly, her trim, pretty legs braced
apart while she gave him an impish, challenging smile. She
gave him the same smile as he pulled out the chair across from
her. They'd clicked from the first and she sent a voltage
through him powerful enough to scramble his wits . . . or
almost powerful enough.

"Hi, Cleo," he said casually, resting his hands on the back
of the chair as if he'd pulled it out for that purpose. "You
live around here?"

"M'm h'm. Sit down, hon."

"Oh, no. Can't. Parole. Taverns are out of bounds, much
as I need a drink," he said, glancing down at the table. She
had no drink, but on his side was a half glass of beer with
a cigarette floating in it and a wet streak from the base of the
glass to the other side of the table, as if it had been slid across.

"I'm not drinking either," she said, and got up. "I was just
here talking to a girl friend from the show next door while
she had a beer. I haven't had breakfast and I never take anything on an empty stomach."

She clipped along at his side as he moved out into the lobby,
and he didn't know whether she just happened to be going
his way or considered herself with him. She veered toward the
desk and plucked at his sleeve.

"Sandy," she said to the curly-headed clerk, who split his face grinning, "this is my friend, see? Now, did you accommodate him, whatever it was he was asking you, or do I have to do what I warned you?"

"Oh, I did my best, Miss Adams."

"It's a good thing. I'll shear those curly locks one of these days if I hear you didn't do right."

"Yes, ma'am," he said gleefully. "I'm just Jesus's little lamb. See how snowy white I am, thanks to your pure guiding light."

She giggled and tucked her arm under Charles's and started with him for the street door. "He's cute."

It was ridiculous, but he was sore, *jealous* of the clerk. "He seems like a nice boy," he said, not too obviously cutting the jerk down to size. "Are *we* headed somewhere, or where are you going?" he said as they reached the door and went out. She turned her face up to him, her eyes clear and sharp; the daylight did her no harm, none whatsoever.

"Hon, I don't like to be personal, but you need a shave. I tell you what," she said, her hand giving his arm a few excited squeezes. "I've got a razor, and I could rustle you up a fresh tie . . . that thing's just not good enough for you. Why don't you come up to my place and put on the feed bag? I'll have stuff sent up and you chase down to the package store and promote a bottle."

He pulled at his tie and frowned, irritable and self-conscious. "Well, if I look so crumby . . ."

"You look good to me, don't worry! What say?"

"I could use food. Where's the package store?"

"Two doors past the Majestic, where I live. Meet me in the lobby."

He went toward the liquor store and started to turn in, then wondered what the hell he was thinking about. He stepped into the doorway, remembering the holdup that had put him in prison . . . just such a place. He didn't go in but headed back for the Supreme just in time to see Cleo come scooting out. There was a brief, quickly suppressed expression of surprise on her face. She hadn't expected him so soon. Suddenly he knew she had gone back in to talk to the curly-headed clerk. To find out what Charles had wanted?

He remembered the first time he had looked into the Supreme Bar. It had been crowded, but he'd have noticed Cleo there at a front table . . . if she'd been sitting facing the lobby, as she had been later. He remembered the streak on the table as if the beer glass had been shoved across. He had a wary hunch that somebody had sicked the hot little grifter on him and she was dangling her sex at him so she could find out something for somebody. She said she'd been with a friend from the burlesque. But all of that gang had been made up, yet neither the beer glass nor the floating cigarette had showed a trace of lipstick.

Well, if she wanted to pry, so did he. He could use all he could find out about Proctor.

"What's wrong?" she asked, coming up close to him. "No mint in the juleps, hon? Whyn'd you level with me?"

"I've got money, it's not that. It's a quirk . . . I had trouble in a liquor store once . . ."

Her eyes went soft, and she caught his hand in hers impulsively, patted it. "I'll get the jug."

He waited. She returned in a few minutes with a wrapped bottle. They went into the dreary Majestic lobby. The elderly queer's face lighted up as Cleo went to the desk.

"Hel*lo* there, sir. Delightful to have you back . . . I'm sorry," he said to Charles while he took a key down and slid it toward Cleo, "but wrack my memory as I will, I don't recall that lady you were asking about."

"Say," Cleo said scathingly, "he's with me."

"Oh." The clerk looked baffled for a moment. Then, with a disdainful smile at Cleo, he said patronizingly, "I didn't realize. I can scarcely credit my senses."

"Well, that's no surprise. Give us a menu. We want a meal. We'll take a menu up and phone down when we decide."

Cleo was moody as they walked to the elevator. She stood pressed to him as they rode up, but she just seemed to like his nearness because she was absorbed in thought and made nothing seductive of it. When they started down the hall toward her room, she said:

"You didn't pay any attention to that old queer, did you, hon?" She glanced anxiously at his face.

"I don't know what you mean."

"I mean his acting like I'm too low to stink."

"Why do you think I care what he thinks about you?" He laughed, but she was serious.

"Just so you don't let him turn you against me."

He stood aside as she keyed open the door. He looked at the earnest set of her profile, the fullness of her mouth. He realized her lips were pushed out as if she were sulking over a hurt.

"You're not really bothered about that guy's opinion, for God's sake?"

"Hell, no, but in front of you you'd think he could be decent. I never went on the make for anything he was after—and believe me I sure had to fight down the temptation to do it just for the mean hell of it—but he had to be nasty in front of you. I just don't think that's fair!"

What the hell! Charles thought. Was she conning him? Did she expect him to believe she was so damned concerned about his having a noble opinion about her? He remembered that business of hers telling him he needed a shave and a fresh tie, and her ready sympathy and eagerness to spare him from going into the liquor store. Maybe she really wanted to do things for him and she'd invited him up here for purely personal reasons.

Nuts to that sap thinking. She was on the make, always. Well, he was on the make, too.

# 10

THE HOT, airless, perfumed room made him giddy. Cleo's froufrou, ultra-feminine touch was everywhere. There was a quilted satin headboard on the bed, a rim of ruffled rose satin around her vanity mirror, blue satin skirts on dresser and stool, slick pleated yellow drapes at the window; a rich, glossy upholstery of rose and blue covered a voluptuously low, soft, semicircular chair. The place was nicely carpeted and papered and lamplit. Cleo helped him out of his coat, took their things to the closet, unwrapped the liquor and got glasses, moving

about with an air of casualness, but flicking sly glances at him
to see how he was taking the room. She poured short, straight
drinks.

"We can have a snort and order breakfast. While you're
shaving I'll promote a tie . . . And oh, hell, say—like music?
I can get a portable player and some LP's—sweet, bop, long-
hair—whatever you like."

"Don't bother."

"I *wanna* bother, hon. So, you don't like the room. Too
whorish, huh? I oughta known it'd look gruesome compared
to that high-tail blonde."

He let his drink roll down. "Blonde?"

"The one you been hide-and-seeking along the street this
morning. The one you were with at the Merry Land, I guess.
The real class."

"Your room is beautiful," he said deliberately, feeling the
slow, warm spread of the liquor. "And that blonde outclasses
you, regularly, the thirty-second day of every month. Regularly.
You know her?"

"No. I've seen her at the Merry Land is all." She was glowing. She sipped at her drink, put it on the vanity, surveyed
her room happily. "So you like it." She sighed, picked up the
menu. "It's ham-eggs-toast, double on the American fries and
coffee for me. I ain't so dainty at the trough. What's for you?"

"The same. And as for that blonde, I wasn't with her. I
want her. I need her—bad, Cleo, if you know anything about
her. But it's not a case of heartburn."

She gave him the eyes, very wide and wondrous, and sighed
blissfully. "You hate her guts, huh? Jeez, I wish I knew something that'd help you. . . . Hon, I want to call you by name."

"Charles."

"Charles. I like that name. I really like it. Charles. . . .
Well, I better get ordering!"

She phoned for the food while he went in to shave. Presently she left the room, and he went out with lather on his
face and looked out in the hall. She wasn't in sight. He shut
the door, waiting uneasily. She came clipping along and he
opened the door to see her lugging a portable player, a record
album, and a wooden rack filled with expensive silk ties. She

looked at his white-lather beard and giggled delightedly. They got the player on the bureau and she held up the ties.

"Choose."

He shrugged and pulled off a handsome blue one with a sharp kicker of color in the design, raised his brows questioningly. She nodded vigorous approval.

"Where'd you steal 'em?" he said, going back toward the bathroom. She traipsed after him, sat on the toilet seat, and watched him shave.

"I didn't steal 'em," she said. "They're Kate's . . . he's a he. There's Gloria, Mary, Nicolette, Sue-Joan," she tolled off on her fingers. "All he's, sort of. It's a pansy bed. I can sleep easy and traipse around naked in that gang without getting raped. They fixed up my room. Got me the materials at knock-down prices in the stores they work at and went to town on it. I hadda keep my yap zipped. I got execrable—ain't that a bitch word?—execrable taste. 'You're a dear creature' Sue-Joan told me, 'with an admirably rounded ass, Cleo. But in artistic spheres you got execrable taste. Go sit on your spheres.' " She giggled. She came to her feet, peering closely and frowning at him. "*Say,* that's not dirt up there across the cheekbones." She prodded the flesh lightly. He winced and pulled back irritably. She blinked concernedly. "It hurt? It's all bruised. Fight, huh?" She seemed to sense the pain in his eyes and looked away. "Finish shaving, and I think I better get my pancake make-up and touch you up. I don't want that showing, hon."

She went out into the room and he looked at the darkening bruises with a sudden sense of nausea. The raw pain of degradation and humiliation swept him. His head began to ache violently remembering Gobi and Elton, Elton's slaps! He told himself desperately that he had to shut all that out of his mind. It was past. He needed all his strength for what lay ahead.

Then he thought it wasn't in him to face the terrible uncertainty ahead. His best hope was that Syl wasn't lying and that she could lead him to Nora. There was loathsome, calculated humiliation in Syl's terms. As calculated as Elton's slaps. He felt desperate, badly shaken. And it was into that torment that Cleo moved.

Soothingly. Quietly sympathetic, sensitive, and understanding. She brought jars of creams and powder and began carefully to apply make-up, to hide his bruises, to cover his shame. She worked gently with soft fingers, standing close over him as he sat. It was bad, very bad. He had to clench his fists to keep his head up, wanting to let it fall against her. He knew she sensed his weariness, and there was something about the soberness of her expression that made him believe she felt his hurt. If he should rest his head on her breast, she would clasp him to her, immediately, instinctively, and her arms and hands would comfort and caress him. He wanted it, wanted it achingly. She would press him to that beautiful woman's warmth, and he would hold to her, close, close . . . so tightly that he would feel the beat of her heart. . . .

*The beat of thy heart is the pulse in my veins.* Nora! NORA.

He dropped his eyes, ashamed. "Cleo," he said quietly, "I'm married and in love. I'm very tired, and I like you and it's no good your doing this for me. It's too damned nice, kid; I can't take it."

"This is nothing," she whispered. She lowered herself and looked earnestly at him. "I'd do this for anybody, Charles. You more than anybody . . ."

"That's it, Cleo. I don't want you to do more." He stood up, shaking his head. She hurried away, came back with a drink. He nodded and drank it off.

"The breakfasts are coming," she said forlornly. "And you have to eat some place. . . . I won't bother you any. Please don't go."

He was hungry. It was only a quarter to two and he couldn't find out anything about Syl from Miss Weir till three. And he didn't want to go; he sure as hell didn't want to go.

Besides, he hadn't found out anything. He'd come to find out things, hadn't he—or had he? He wondered. He had wanted to go to bed with Cleo, that's why he'd come. He'd made reasons to justify it to himself.

"I'll hang around. Besides, I owe you for the food and liquor," he said.

"Forget it."

He put a ten on her vanity. It made him feel better. She

shrugged and put it in a drawer. She went across the room moodily and put on a record.

The music was soft and melodic. Cleo sat on the back of the voluptuous, low semicircular chair and looked aimlessly down at her hands and at the door and at the record player; everywhere but at him. He walked over and chucked her under the chin.

"Don't misunderstand me, kid. You treated me nice, and I appreciate it. Don't be sore."

"I'm not. I'm just waiting for the food. Take it easy. You paid for your breakfast; you got it coming. Stick around." She wouldn't look at him.

"Damn it, I didn't mean to hurt your feelings," he exploded.

"I didn't say you did mean to." She got up at a sound in the hall and opened the door. It was the waiter with their breakfast. Charles went over and had another drink.

During breakfast he decided he'd get what he'd come for. Information. But women were intuitive, and if he was going to use the love approach he'd have to try to *feel* it so that it would seem sincere. As he topped off the food with another drink, he congratulated himself on being a pretty sly son of a bitch at that. Cleo was sharp, throwing all the angles at him from tender concern to wounded feelings, but he was topping it.

The meal cart was outside, the door locked, the atmosphere soft and scented, the music sweet. Cleo had kicked off her shoes and was sitting curled in the big chair, her voluminous skirt covering her legs to the ankles. Charles stayed on his feet, a new drink in hand, feeling expansive and masculine against this feminine setting. Cleo's sulk had gradually given away to a sort of languorous content. Once in a while they exchanged glances and little smiles as he walked about, listening to the music. The thing was in need of a light touch, he sensed. The soft, cozy intimacy was dangerous to his command of the situation. He went over and ruffled her hair. Companionably. A remark, something personal but witty, should have gone with it, but it didn't seem the precise moment to intrude on the peaceful feeling.

He went over to the bottle and had another. She was behind

him, but he could see in the vanity mirror that her dark, gleam-
ing little head didn't turn. He strolled over into her range of
vision, and when their eyes met she gave him a soft, sleepy
look—somthing nearer to contented domesticity than seduc-
tion, he thought warily. Her air was smug almost, proprietary,
as if her feeding, salving, liquoring him and calling him by
name had established a sure relationship, a bond. He wondered if she were aware that the overly modest concealment
of those sexy legs was sharply piquing. She wasn't inviting;
she was just *there,* passive. He went over and stood in front of
her and grinned down, and her eyes lifted with soft expectancy,
waiting for whatever he was going to say. What the hell was
there to say? He moved nearer and ruffled her hair again.

Softly. It was fine hair. Not coarse, but like silk thread.
The touch was pleasant. He stirred it out of the smooth, flat
pattern of her coif, relishing the tickling against his hand. He
let his hand move lightly over the crown of her head, liking
its shape, its small rounding. She neither protested nor accepted
his touch by sign or gesture; she just seemed to absorb it
passively—not with displeasure. He ran his hand down onto
the softness of her cheek, lingered there, and presently she put
her hand over his and held it warmly to her face. She tilted
her head and slid her eyes up into the corners and regarded
him gravely.

His throat became dry, and he caught his breath. He felt a
slow, expanding pressure crowding in his chest, and then it burst
and seemed to flow like an actual warm fluid, as though all the
imprisoned tenderness had found release. He went down onto
the chair beside her, aching with love for her. His face was
sober, starkly sober, and his eyes were feverish, intense. He
filled himself with her loveliness, and then slowly, like a man
laying an offering, he began to make love to her. He wanted
no response from her, somehow—not yet—he simply wanted
her to exist as a thing to love, to adore, even to worship. And
she understood, knowing the fierce, the insane force of his long-
deprived need to love. It couldn't wait; it had to come out;
he had to use the best of himself.

Afterward they lay in each other's arms and slept.

Charles woke abruptly. He had a fleeting exultant sense of

well-being, an ease and a joy in his body. Then came the awful
awareness that it was not Nora beside him. He got up and
dressed in hurried silence, feeling lousy, dirty, stinking, cheap,
contemptible to have done this. At *no* time would he have felt
right about it. At *this* time, when his wife was missing, maybe
injured, maybe dead, for him to have pulled this stunt was
despicable. A betrayal. He could never forgive himself. He
couldn't have found an uglier way to violate Nora if he had deliberately calculated it. It was low, callous. Damn him to
hell, God damn him to hell! He was without honor—a man
without honor.

Cleo woke and watched him with a lazy, happy smile and
stretched a slim naked arm toward him and fluttered her
fingers. He looked at her, hating himself, hating her, wanting
to hit her. She saw his look and lifted herself on her elbows
and stared at him, stunned. Suddenly she bit her underlip and
flung herself face down and began to cry.

The sound of it and the crumpled look of her little figure
sent an instant mindless pang through him and he started for
the bed. He caught himself mid-stride, compressing his mouth.
A woman's crying—or a man's or a kid's for that matter—cut
to the raw. But what the hell were tears but a cheap relief?
She was damned lucky she *could* cry. An emotional jag.
Couldn't mean a damned thing to a slut like her; she was
loose in all directions, and shallow. Laughter or tears, what was
the difference! It was five to three by her clock. He had to
call the receptionist in Syl's office at three. He had to get out
and to a phone. He finished dressing, got into hat and overcoat, and went to the door. She was still bawling. Suddenly he
spun and shouted savagely:

"Shut up!"

The bum, the cheap cheat bum, the loose scum trash slut;
she had nothing, nothing, no standards, no quality; she could
accept thieves, killers, pansies, anything, because she was
*nothing!* He twisted at the door key, grinding his teeth. At
least she'd stopped that noisy blubbering. He yanked the door
open and went out into the hall and bumped into the meal
cart and swore and yanked the door shut, meaning to slam
it hard enough to break her eardrums. Then he thought the

stupid little tramp was so drunk on her own emotions that she might think it was dramatic as hell to slash her wrists or some such spectacular and safe clap-trap. That kind of stuff was standard with these shifty, crumby little lives. He glanced back in, and she was just lying there, face down.

It didn't matter a damn. In an hour she could have the joint flooded with new and old lovers, but she couldn't help what she was. No use to kick her around just for the sport of it. He could at least say so long. She looked so goddamned forlorn.

He went on back and lowered himself onto the edge of the bed, thinking it was just a matter of decency—a point of honor, even—not to treat her with crude contempt after she'd given him happiness. He told himself it was impersonal. He put his hand on her shoulder, stroking it a little. Then he bent down and put his face beside hers, which was buried in the pillow. Her body scooted over until it was firm against his side.

He whispered: "Don't cry, kid. I didn't mean to be a son of a bitch. It's not you . . . it's trouble on my mind . . . nerves . . . I'm sorry."

She turned over and sat up, and wrapped her arms around him tightly, pulling him forward so that their faces were mashed together, cheek to cheek. Her face was hot and wet. She started to cry again, but softly, almost comfortably, so that he could feel the small convulsions through her body, and she kept releasing the grip of her arms and tightening them, as if trying to lock them tighter and tighter.

Then he felt the heave of her breast and a noisy snuffing of her nose, and her voice came out in a sort of strangled squawk.

"Charles . . ."

"Yes?"

"Charles"—she got control of her voice—"I love you."

"No. No, you don't, Cleo. You know better; now, dammit, don't say it."

She caught his shoulders in both hands and thrust herself back from him so that she could look into his face. Her lipstick was smeared, her cheeks messy, and some of her eye-shadow was streaked, and her bangs were awry, and she looked like plain hell, and it didn't matter. Her eyes and her voice were intense.

"I love you," she said. "I love you! I love you!"

He looked away, and then back, compulsively. She was taut. Her dark eyes burned with conviction. He suddenly believed her. He remembered how he had made love to her. He had given her an intensity, a tenderness, a passion that he had given no woman in the world but Nora. It hadn't been a simple going to bed with a female. Everything about his lovemaking had said she was the only woman in the world. And she had been. At that time she had been. He'd had no right to let himself go. How the hell often had the girl ever been loved—really loved from a man's depths? Maybe never. How could she help valuing a guy who had seemed to want more than her body?

"Listen, Cleo, I believe you. I think you mean it . . . right this minute. You *always* believe it."

"Never. Not like this. I thought it was love. This I *know*. Tell me you love me, Charles. Tell me. Say it. Say it in words. You do. Admit it, in words. Say it. Please, darling, dearest sweetheart, say it. I love you. Charles, I'm yours. I'd do anything—kill, steal, whore for you, keep you. You can beat me or kick me out, and I don't care. You're my man. You hear? You know it. You knew it. The first minute. You did. Say you did. We clicked. The first minute . . ."

"Be quiet, for God's sakes; don't get so emotional."

She got on her knees, stood on them in the bed so that her face was above his. She held his shoulders and thrust her face close to him and said intensely, her voice very low:

"Stop lying. Tell me the truth. You love me."

He caught her wrists, tore her hands from his coat. She was naked. He stood up, looking away. He turned back. Her eyes had followed him. She stood there on her knees, waiting, compelling. He wouldn't say words like that. No. They had meaning. He was just damned if he would say them. He knew what she was. What? Cheap because she could accept criminals and outcasts? That was cheap? Loose because she didn't consider the act of love a crime? No quality, no standards? A lie, a stinking, protective lie, because he was trying to identify himself with the smug, virtuous, respectable, intolerant, vicious *good* people. To hell with them! He didn't belong with them . . . but with her, outcast. She had more clean instinct for justice and humanity in her little toe than all the "decent," narrow little slave-minded moralists in the world. How dared he hold himself aloof from her? He was the cheap one, a lying hypocrite. He was afraid to say it, afraid it was true.

"I've got to go. I like you. I *go* for you . . . all of that."

She sneezed, and then she swore. It was ridiculous to sneeze at such a time. He went over and got her robe from the closet and put it around her.

"See?" she said. "You care."

"Yes . . . yes . . . yes . . . yes . . . yes, dammit, I didn't deny I care . . . but . . . listen, it's after three o'clock. My life is in danger, Cleo. Think that over, and don't nag me. Don't make me worry about you. I can't, I can't do anything about it, even if I do love you. Now, you going to make it tough?"

She stood up on the floor, barefoot and tiny in the huge red satin robe, and looked up at him. "Just give me a kiss, then. Tell me what I can do to help you."

"You can tell me about the confidence game—the one that's got the Feds swarming all over Proctor, the one they had to use the cacklebladder in."

"I don't know anything but the general poop. I'm not in Proctor's pocket; I'm just the help. The score was 150 G. The Mr. Bates was roped in on the proposition that he could get his snout into the state gambling trough. So I heard."

"Who were the con babies?"

"I don't know, Charles. After the score was taken off I heard the bunch had been to the Merry Land a few times with their Mr. Bates, but they were just among hundreds, and I didn't know them from Adam. I think there's a stink in it— in the tale they're spreading about it. I can't figure how a big con man would pick a mark like the one they say was picked. On account of this mark was supposed to make slots. Now all those slot-makers are hot, real hot with the FBI watching them all the time. So what kinda deal is it to go for a sucker who's got the law on his fanny to begin with?"

"That's what I wondered. And something else, Cleo. Who the hell were you really sitting with down in the Supreme Bar? It wasn't any tail. Who was the guy?"

"I can't tell you, Charles. I . . . Please . . ."

"So that's love."

# 11

CHARLES TELEPHONED Miss Weir about Syl, and was told it was too early, to try again at four. At four, he thought, it would be five, and at five when the office closed, Miss Weir would be so-o-o regretful. In desperation he called Jerry. Syl, it seemed, had been in touch with him to tell him she'd be home that evening. Jerry was all a-gurgle with the joy of it. Well, if it came to that he'd confront Syl in front of Jerry. Later. Later. Everything was later.

He walked along the street of the burlesque house and two hotels, away from the depot toward the middle of town. The character of the street changed radically in those two long blocks, becoming a normal business and office district. Shoppers moved along the walks, in and out of stores; office workers trickled out to the cafeterias; activity surged around the entrances and lobbies of the big hotels. Once upon a time this had appeared lively enough, stimulating and pleasant. No sense of enjoyable briskness touched him now; the whole thing lacked a certain fever; it was the flush of nothing more than good health and he found its tone of wholesomeness and complacency dull. It was out of touch with the simple animal facts of existence, its senses over-larded and cut off from that edge of danger and violence and knowledge of omnipresent death which keened a man because it was the unmasked truth about life. There wasn't any security. He caught a glimpse of himself in a jeweler's side window, saw the lines of his face, set coldly and forbiddingly. It was, he realized, the same sort of expressionlessness that came over the faces of men in stir in the presence of strange civilians. Not just an isolation or estrangement—there was contempt and hostility, too. Most cons considered the average law-abider a phony, not good, just ignorant

of what they were and what life itself was all about . . . and
gutless. There was even more, Charles thought. These people
were happy in their gutless ignorance. They felt themselves
virtuous because they dared not, and clean because they had no
part in exploitations, the crime on the grand scale which was
honor. No, they had no part; they merely slaved for the masters
who did. How the hell, he wondered, was he ever going to be
able to lower himself into the torpor necessary to find satisfac-
tions in the trivialities that these good people mistook for
aliveness? Syl and Nietzsche were right about plenty—not
everything, but plenty. Slave morality. Such a morality held,
of course, that love was confined to property holders who ob-
tained a certificate from one of God's helpers, and a man
couldn't, just couldn't conceivably love more than one woman
at a time. Very bad, that, just wicked, that, it threatened the
stability of society and bitched up the economic picture . . .
*tsk tsk*. Biology had another thought on the subject. Not a very
sentimental thought. But then sentiment was an artificial aid
—kept the slaves happy and obedient. There was a going price
on sentiment—it was one of the strongest vested interests in
Society's arsenal, as a matter of fact.

So, he thought cynically, I'm spilling tears of acid all over
myself because I can't have Cleo.

What the hell kind of thinking was this? Nora was among
the good. Was he trying to abandon her? He loved her. Absolutely. Even if he didn't love her, he would never abandon
her. He was deeply indebted to Nora, no matter what else,
and if he'd retained the slightest sense of honor he must make
good on his obligation. He felt a twinge of conscience; even to
think of her as a "debt" was a mockery.

Nora wouldn't want him on that basis. It would be insult;
it would cut her heart out.

*The beat of thy heart is the pulse in my veins. . . .*

He felt so cheap he wanted to cry.

His love couldn't be so slight that a girl like Cleo could
jeopardize it. What had happened to him? To them—to the
deepest, strongest, best thing in his life. What he had done,
what he was thinking, all of it was *against* her, hurting her.
He felt lost, utterly lost. The fear of his own hardness, his

violence, his murderous thirst for revenge on people like Gobi and Elton, had worried him. But through all of that he'd felt that it left Nora intact. It hadn't. He was cut off from her. Wherever she was, he was cut off. If she were in his arms, she would be lost.

He was a stranger. Lost. A stranger.

He couldn't keep walking along the street. He turned in to a building foyer and stood against the wall, trying to hold on, to get his perspective, to find his meaning again. He had none, absolutely none, not without her. It was true. He didn't care about anything else.

Cleo had stepped into a moment of weakness, like a continuation of Nora. What Cleo had done for him was a grain of sand; his bond with her a thread compared with the bond with Nora. That was the truth. It was decked out in sentiment, but sentiment was a part of his life. It couldn't be sloughed away; there'd be nothing but animal left. He was animal and he was more, and it took more than a few minutes of sexual joy to change it. Nora had given that—a thousand times, just as she had given a thousand times as much of everything else.

And there it was! Bright, jagged, and ugly, and he had never had the guts to rip it out, and look at it. It was too painful. But there it was. He resented Nora. *Because* she had done everything, everything. Too much. She had supported herself, she had given him her whole loyalty; she had paid for even his soap and cigarettes in stir. While he had been helpless. She had had his power, his freedom. She hadn't needed him. His manhood had been stripped, trampled. His ability to give had been snatched away. His own doing, true. But nonetheless their roles had been turned around. *She* gave . . . *she* protected . . . *she* defended . . . and he had been helpless, degraded, dirt. Never had she reminded him. Not once. She was his woman, and he was the man. But he had known. It had twisted, dark and reasonless, in his unconscious until she had become identified with his keepers, his jailers, with a punishing Society, with virtue. He had hated her without knowing it. Loved and hated.

It was good. It was good to have it open and clean and in his grasp. Good to face it. Beat it. The love was strong enough to face and murder and end that unknown, underlying hate.

· Cleo? He did *not* want to identify himself with her. He was *not* going to live in her world. That was all there was to it.

He went to the Colonial Restaurant, where Nora worked. After leaving the depot she could have come on up the street to the restaurant, not stopping at the Hotel Supreme. He went in, wracking his memory for the name of the girl he'd talked to on the phone last night from the depot. Lucy? Lucy Corlon?

Lucy Corlon was the hostess. And perfect for the job, he thought. He waited, hat in hand, watching her come after the cashier signaled her. She moved with a quiet, gracious air, a slender, almost willowy figure in her basic black. She was olive-skinned and pretty with great limpid eyes, and there was an unmistakably intelligent expression about her face. It wasn't the quick, sharp, grifter-shrewd smartness of Cleo, and in fact Cleo would probably make her seem slow-witted. But only on short runs. Corlon had brains, and something else, something rare. Charm. The genuine stuff, not the insipid imitation; and her gentle air wasn't anemia but vitality muted. He had the instant conviction that Lucy Corlon was a first-rate human. This girl and Nora were of a kind. He liked her.

"You're Charles Garrell," she said in a pleasantly soft voice he recognized. She was the one he had talked to on the phone last night. She offered her hand. "I've seen your pictures so often. You found Nora all right, I suppose?"

"No, Miss Corlon, I haven't. But you said she wasn't on duty yesterday at all. I wondered if she might have come here to the restaurant last evening at any time. She might have and talked to one of the girls."

"I asked them last night after I talked to you," she said, her eyes concerned. "But I'll ask again. Will you wait?"

"Yes. She may have said something to one of them that would give me some kind of a hint. If she was expecting to meet anybody else . . . or anything like that."

"I'll find out all I can." She moved away.

He stood at the front, his gaze following Lucy Corlon's progress back and forth across the big, comfortable, and hand-some restaurant as she consulted the waitresses. She wasn't having any success that he could see. He waited. He became gradually aware of a man outside on the busy walk who stood by the restaurant window or ambled out to the curb, stopping at one or the other point to read his newspaper. He always put it in his overcoat pocket while he moved. He always took it out folded the same way and read the same small area of print each time he stopped. If he was really reading. Of course there were scores of possible explanations . . .

They all collapsed when Lucy returned. She looked past Charles toward the man outside and began to talk in a hushed, anxious voice.

"Will you look, without seeming to do so, at that man standing out at the curb and reading the folded newspaper and see if you know him?"

"I've seen him. I don't know him."

"He was here day before yesterday. He and another man. Just before Nora arrived for work. Just *after* she arrived the two men held a hasty consultation. Something about that man aroused an unpleasant sensation in me . . . I couldn't define it . . ." She caught her breath, dropped her eyes in confusion, and Charles knew she had just realized what was unpleasant about that man.

"You're too sensitive, Miss Corlon," he said amiably. "I know what you mean about him. I think you're right. He's been in prison. Lots of 'em. You feel there's a connection between his being here two days ago and Nora's disappearance?"

"I do. But there's more. Listen. That man out there didn't come into the restaurant. The man with him did—just after Nora's arrival—and the one out there now hurried away. The one who came in was another sort entirely. Young, buoyant, charming, a quite attractive fellow. I'd never seen him before, he wasn't a regular customer at all. But he asked for a table in Nora's section."

"Called for her by name?" he asked sharply. "Young, charming . . . Did—did Nora seem to—well . . ." He fumbled. Lucy caught it at once.

"Certainly not. Nothing like that. Nora didn't indicate the slightest personal interest, I assure you. I, personally . . . Well, now you have *me* embarrassed. I found him quite attractive. Quite. I managed to see him throughout his meal. He smiled and talked to Nora. But it was quite one-sided. She was civil but indifferent."

"He was making a pass, you think?"

"No. As I said, she was civil. If he had become fresh she wouldn't have been. I was quite anxious and hopeful that she would mention him to me later, and yet I didn't want to inquire and be just too obvious, you know. I put him down as some half-forgotten acquaintance or a distant relative, someone in town for the day in whom she had no slightest interest. And yet, his association with a man like the one out there . . . He's by the window reading his paper now."

"I see him. A shabby baby like that has a reason for hanging around. And he was in conference with the handsome boy just after Nora arrived? And then he went away fast while the handsome one came in and asked for Nora's table? That's the way it was?"

"Yes."

"Nora came to work at two, didn't she?"

"Yes. She's been working from two till ten, when we close."

"This happened day before yesterday—the day *before* I was due home."

"That's right. It was the last day she worked. As I said, she wasn't on duty the day of your homecoming."

"It's important. Very. I'm sure of it. Could you describe the handsome one? Tall, short, fat?"

"Not fat. Well set up. Tall. As tall as you. He dressed handsomely in matching grays. Homburg hat. It was so odd, that pompous hat on his broad, boyish, freckled face—so unsuitable, and yet . . ."

"*Je ne sais quoi?* Sex appeal."

She laughed quietly, acknowledging it. "And blue eyes . . . curly hair, blondish, not *too* blonde . . . sandy . . ."

"Sandy?" Charles frowned intently. Cleo had called the curly-headed clerk at the Supreme Hotel "Sandy." "Yeah . . . I see. I think maybe I know him. Thanks, Miss Corlon. Now, when I go, I think you'd better not pay too much attention. I've got a hunch the baby out on the walk may want to follow me. Just a hunch. I don't want to warn him in any way."

"I understand. And the best of luck, Mr. Garrell."

He went outside. He walked past the guy with the newspaper without a glance at him. He looked absorbed in something else, and he was, in fact. Sandy? It fit the hotel clerk's curly hair. He might have been off duty and swanked up. But not blue eyes. He remembered for certain. And the kid was pinkish complexioned. No freckles. Wrong guy.

Charles entered the National, the city's leading hotel, got a late paper, and went on into the lobby without a glance around. He went into an off-lobby drugstore and settled in a booth beside the plate-glass window facing the lobby. He didn't turn his head but kept his profile to the window, studying a menu. But he slid his glance to the window. The man who had been in front of the restaurant had taken a chair in the lobby and was reading that same newspaper.

To get right up and move along would tip the guy off. Charles ordered coffee and a sandwich, sat with his back to the lobby reading the paper. There was nothing in it about Brattsford.

But somebody knew all about Brattsford. Maybe his tail out there in the lobby knew. Charles gulped his food. He left by way of the lobby. His tail got up casually and sauntered after him. The guy didn't know it yet, but he wasn't tailing Charles. Charles was tailing him.

# 12

CHARLES SWUNG ALONG the broad, crowded downtown walk with a purposeful air, and when he was a hundred feet from one of the larger office buildings he began to work his way in from the curb, as though it had been his destination all the time. His tail, a tall, thin, gray-faced man in dark blue clothes, was a few paces behind as Charles turned into the lobby of the building.

Charles stood in front of the big directory, giving it a frowning scan. The gray-faced man in blue came in. Charles watched him and the elevators alternately. Charles hurried back and into an empty car. A moment later the man came in. Charles stared directly at him without a flick of interest, as if absorbed. The fellow took a position beside Charles at the rear of the elevator. The elevator filled quickly. Charles shifted as if the crowding had roused him from his private thoughts and forced him to make room. Both he and the man remained elaborately unaware of each other until Charles pressed suddenly close and gave him a swift frisk.

He located a gun in the guy's side pocket. Charles plunged his hand into that overcoat pocket, locked the guy's hand to the gun. The man was smoking a cigarette. He moved his hand casually with the cigarette cupped in his palm and he looked expressionlessly into Charles's face as he put the cigarette into his pocket and pressed the ember into the flesh of Charles's hand.

The shock wave of pain went through Charles, shuddering over his skin, bristling the very hair on the back of his neck. He flinched visibly and paled but he held on, and after the first shock he could stand it. He might have relieved it by letting go of the gun hand. Or he could have slammed his left fist up into the bastard's chin. Neither of them wanted a public commotion. He began to pry one of the fingers loose from the gun.

The elevator started up and stopped and disgorged some of the crowd, and there was a shifting of passengers. They were unaware of the silent struggle. He didn't know how long he could count on that. Somebody surely would see or sense it. He managed to get the bastard's finger in his grasp and began forcing it back. He felt the cigarette leave his own hand.

Then the guy puffed furiously, bringing the ember alive, and their eyes met through the smoke, nakedly savage. Charles was hurting that finger, worse every second, and the guy's face was drawn, his mouth pulled in a cruel line. There wouldn't be any backing down. He either had to break that finger or run, because this baby was mad enough to gun him. The cigarette mashed into his flesh again. The pain was raw, worse than the first time. Sweat popped out on Charles's forehead. His hold on the bent finger relaxed for an instant. He thought he didn't have the reserve to absorb this new punishment. He was on the verge of bursting into open violence, smashing as fast and viciously as he could with both fists, and he knew if he did it he'd either go to jail or he'd get a bullet in his gut.

This guy had a link with Nora and he was going to beat the son of a bitch! He renewed, increased the pressure on the finger with a quick force that nearly snapped bone. The cigarette fell away, the gun hand released. Charles got the gun, rammed it in his pocket. They stayed on the elevator to the top floor.

"Down," Charles said tightly.

His quarry moved out of the elevator into the hall. Charles followed. The man turned, his narrow gray face vicious, and yelled:

"Quit following me!"

Two men hurrying from offices to the elevator looked startled.

"I said stop following me," he repeated nastily.

The office men faltered, exchanged glances. The elevator operator piped up authoritatively:

"He's after him, all right. He said 'down' to me, but then when the other one left the car he followed."

It was a bad spot. He had to outbluff this baby and fast.

"I warn you, Joe!" Charles said hotly. "Explain to these people immediately! I've had enough of your moods. This time I mean it. If you force these people to call the police, I'm not only going to sue you but I guarantee—I positively guarantee, Joe, that you'll never do another nickel's worth of business with us. Explain! And damned fast with it!"

The watchers became uncertain. They frowned questioningly. Charles knew the rat didn't want cops any more than he did. He turned on the watchers with mixed indignation and bafflement. "He's sick, but he ignores his doctors. Lookit that gray sick color. He won't listen, won't rest. Nerves shot. Mind half nuts. Everybody tries to be his friend. But this is too much. Joe!" Charles spun on him, warned. "Talk! I meant what I said. I won't stand this public spectacle. I don't care if you are sick. No, sir, dammit, I'm right in the mood to call the police myself and have you put under observation." He turned to the others. "I could, couldn't I?"

The rat looked at the floor and mumbled. "I lost my temper. I'm sorry."

The others left, disgusted.

When the elevator had gone down and the curious along the corridor had returned to their offices, Charles clipped him on the jaw and simultaneously yanked him by one arm. He gave him a rush for the stairway. He got him there and through the door. In the privacy of the stairwell he rammed the gun in his mid-section, forced him down two flights.

There, he stood him backward on a step.

"Let out a peep and I'll spill you backward down those steps so goddam fast you won't know what broke your neck."

He gave him a thorough frisk.

According to a room-rent receipt from the Hotel Supreme he was Sam Keech. An identification card in a billfold showed the same name. Charles unloaded the gun, dry-fired to check its action, reloaded it.

"We're going to your hotel room, Sam. We'll walk along the street, and we'll go in the lobby, and you'll get the key and you won't give the office to anybody. You got it?"

"I got it, I got it. I got no cause to cross you."

The Supreme had no second and third floors. The fourth, where Sam Keech's room was, was on top of the burlesque show. The tinny, fast-breathing sound of an orchestra, heavy on the brass and drums, came up through the floor in a skid-around-the-turns tempo, along with the rhythmic jolt of a chorus line in a fast time-step.

"Why were you following me?" Charles said, standing against the locked door, facing into the cramped, dreary room. Sam's mattress and bedclothes had been removed from the cot and lay on the floor, Charles noted, puzzled.

"I wasn't," Sam said. He stood a pace away, facing Charles.

Charles moved toward him. "Who was it you met outside the Colonial Restaurant day before yesterday just as my wife was coming to work?"

Sam backed up into the tight aisle between the foot of the bed and the ancient, yellow-mirrored bureau.

"You got me wrong. I never met . . ."

Charles caught a bunch of Sam's overcoat at the chest and yanked him abruptly forward, off-balancing him. He held his free fist cocked and grated: "I said who was he?"

Sam's mouth twisted in a defiant sneer. Charles threw his

right into Sam's chest, jolting the breath out of him, banging
him into the bureau which slammed loudly into the wall. Sam
flailed out, going down, caught hold of the metal crossbar on
the foot of the cot. As Sam went down, the cot made a rackety
clatter and its roller screeched. Sam came up, livid and charging.
Charles caught him with a left to the head that had the moving weight of his body back of it. Sam hit the wall close to
the window and then the floor. He got up very slowly, his
hands down. Charles waited, his fists ready.

Sam brushed himself off, and held his mouth shut. Charles
could fairly see the steel-plate armor close. Sam was at home
with the rough stuff and the more he got the more he'd clam.
He could hold out for a long time, that baby. He stood watching
Charles, breathing heavily, patches of color standing out on his
cheeks against his sickly complexion, his eyes glittering, his thin
hair scraggly, his hat off. His clothes were seedy; he looked
like an animal at bay—clearly aware that he was no match
for Charles—but determined not to quit, never to quit. Yeah,
it would take a long time to break him with the rough stuff.
And, besides, Charles didn't like the bull role. Sam was, after
all, no cop or screw.

Charles began a thorough search. Socks, one clean shirt, one
change of shorts in the bureau. Suit, tacky as the one Sam wore,
in the closet, plus old shoes. There were shaving things, tooth-
brush and salt for dentifrice on the open shelf above the wash-
basin in the bathless wash and toilet room. Sam wasn't doing
so well in the world. But there *was* an extra suit, shoes, and he
should've had some kind of suitcase—maybe one good enough
to hock. But there was no pawn ticket in the billfold.

"Take off the overcoat, Sam," Charles said. "I want a better
look through your clothes."

Sam complied. As Charles began searching Sam's pockets,
a girl from the burlesque below sang a slow, sloppy ballad
in a cat-yowl voice. Charles noted a vague, relaxed look on
Sam's face as if he were listening. Sam's pockets turned up
no pawn ticket.

"Well, pal, you made a mistake," Sam said softly. The girl
below had stopped singing, but the orchestra continued to play
the same slow ballad. Sam's vague, relaxed look had turned

dreamy, as if Charles didn't really exist. Curiously, Charles looked again at the mattress and bedclothes on the floor beside the bed. He'd supposed Sam slept there in preference to sagging bedsprings. Sam's "gone" look gave him another idea.

Charles took out the gun, keeping an eye on Sam, and got down on the mattress. He moved a rug at the head of the mattress. A hole was bored through the floor. A stripper in a baby-blue spot was writhing in a slow convulsion. Charles got up, sneered.

"A peeper, for Gawd's sake!"

Surprisingly, Sam became agitated and emotional, and said belligerently: "Who wouldn't take a free show?" Sam's face flushed. "I suppose *you* wouldn't cop a free peek!"

"Sure," Charles said, grinning derisively. He wouldn't feel guilty as hell about it, the way Sam did. He'd hit a weak spot. He began to prod it. "A peeper. A grown man, fercrissakes." The tempo of the music below was faster. It swelled and broke, and there was a yell "Take it off!" applause, shrill whistling. Charles grinned at Sam. "She's peeled," he said silkily. "Can't you just see her! Grinding it. . . . Listen to that drum *wham . . . wham . . . wham* . . . every time she *bumps*." Sam gave a short, nervous, hacking cough. Just the thought of it was sending him. If he was a whole-hog peeper, and he was acting like it, the most frightening prospect in the world would be actual-flesh contact. "I know two of the girls in the show, Sam. Man, will they love to hear about you. I'm going to sic 'em on you. They'll give you a private show. And if the poop gets around that you couldn't take the stuff straight, you won't be able to show your face. And will those cats spread the word!"

Sam coughed violently. He said faintly, with an effort at bravado, "You arrange that party and be the best buddy I ever had. Bring 'em on!"

"I will!" Charles said harshly. "I'm going to give you a beating and then I'm going to sic 'em on you and make you the laughing stock of the town! Who was the good-looking freckle-faced mug you were with at the restaurant? Who set you on my tail today? Why?"

Sam became stonily uncommunicative. Charles started toward him. He changed course. He pulled the straight chair to a point under the light fixture. One of the three bulbs was dark. On a hunch he ran his finger over it. There was an opening on its upper slope, invisible from below. He unscrewed the bulb, hearing the tiny clink inside as he did. He got down, smashed the bulb. A key fell out. He picked it up, casting Sam a warning glance. The key was for a bus-station locker.

"I'll knock you out and tie you up," Charles said, "or I'll just tie you up. Take your choice. Fast."

Sam submitted. Charles used sheet and pillowcase to bind and gag him. He left him on the mattress.

He went out and to the bus station which was around the corner at the next street. The key opened a locker containing an old suitcase. Charles took it, went back to Sam's room in the Supreme. He opened it. There were telephone books.

A wrist watch! The one stolen from the pawn-broker Brattsford's dead wrist, Charles was positive.

There was more. ↝

A packet of letters.

Letters in his handwriting.

Letters he had written to Nora, from prison.

# 13

CHARLES STOOD GLARING down at Sam Keech. He clenched and unclenched his fists, unaware. His nostrils became tight, and he pulled his upper lip back flat against his teeth. His breathing became swifter. The blood seemed to have drawn from his limbs and body and compressed into his head, with his heartbeat like a ram, thrusting up with a bursting force. He was actually dizzy with the intensity of his rage. He swayed, unconsciously, just a little, from side to side. Sam Keech's eyes, stark and brilliant above the gag, watched as if Charles were a cobra about to strike.

His rage trance snapped into brittle, chopping motion. He knelt by Sam, clawed the pillowcase down past his chin, pulled the wadded handkerchief out of his mouth. Sam yelled, strained upward. Charles clipped off the yell with a teeth-snapping slug into his chin. Sam went out, unconscious. Charles got a glass of water from the basin, poured it in his face. Sam stirred, sputtered, twisting his head from side to side, and opened his eyes. He didn't yell. Charles unbound his feet.

Charles hauled him upright, forced him to walk, still bound by the hands, and sat him on the edge of the flat-spring cot facing the brick wall outside the window. He stood over him, silent, threatening.

"That wasn't my suitcase. A guy asked me to hold it. A guy with a record. Like me. Like you. I buddy any guy with a record. I'd buddy you, if you'd cut this . . . "

"How you know I've got a record?"

"The poop's every place. You been on the street all day. Guys reckanize you. What the hell, Charley, everybody knows everybody in these parts; it's all the same world. You and me, we're all in the same . . ."

"Hell with the buddy-buddy. Stop lying. Start leveling. Where's my wife? I'll kill you, man, can't you see I'll kill you? Stop the lying!"

"Yeah . . . sure . . . so this guy from Joliet, I knowed him, he had this suitcase . . ."

Charles got Brattsford's watch, dangled it under his nose. "You never saw this?"

"I never been inside that suitcase. Look . . ."

He talked loud against the upsurge of sound from below. The music was fast, the chorus line was singing, dancing. Their thin, nasal, catlike voices whined out an off-key banal melody and their feet and the drums of the orchestra trembled the decaying wood of the old building. Charles got Sam's razor, took the blade out. He got Sam's suit from the closet. Sam was spieling, lying faster and faster.

"I'll have to draw blood," Charles told him, holding the razor blade. "I'll smear your suit. Then I'll find that car you were using last night. I'll bloody it up a little. Remember I turned on the lights of the panel truck for a second? Remember? I saw the license of the car you were in. The car was hot. I know who owns it. Blood in that car and on your suit will talk if you won't, you snake-tongued bastard."

"I tellya I'm leveling. Listen, pal . . . you been in stir . . . you an me is . . ."

Charles spat out his breath exasperatedly, tossed the blade on the bureau, flung the suit down.

"Yeah, I guess you're right. We're in the same boat," Charles said, walking around to the other side of the bed. "I guess I had you wrong. Sorry I got rough. Hell, I'm just all shot to pieces. I just got out of stir last night. Got home. My wife gone. I'm beat up with it. I need a buddy." He talked steadily. Sam could see him in the bureau mirror from the corner of his eye, Charles knew. And Sam was watching without turning his head. Charles wanted him to watch, and he didn't want Sam to realize Charles knew he was watching.

"I sure need buddies. I didn't mean to rough you up. I feel crummy about it. I wish I hadn't, so you and me could help each other." While he talked, he moved. Furtively. He picked up the pillow from the mattress on the floor, silently. He took the gun out of his pocket and buried it in the pillow. He moved stealthily onto the mattress and bedclothes, holding the pillowed gun. He kept talking. Kept moving closer to the edge of the cot in back of Sam. He didn't seem to realize that Sam could see it all. Sam could see the pillow with the gun in it raising, aiming at the back of his head, and knew the shot would be muffled. He was convinced Charles was going to murder him.

"Stop!" Sam hurled himself onto his side on the bedspring, and kept yelling, "Don't shoot! Don't! Don't! I'll talk."

Charles sat on the straight chair, holding the gun, waiting for Sam to recover. He didn't say a word.

"Jeez, you'd of shot me dead. Jeez, talking to a guy easy and all the time aiming to kill him. So here's the tale. So help me God, the true tale. I ain't foolin' with you no goddam more, Charley.

"The guy I was with at your wife's restaurant was a writer. Measles Edwards. You know him."

Of course! He should have recognized Lucy Corlon's description of that boyish, freckled S. O. B. Measles Edwards. A writer . . . forger. He'd known him in stir.

"I had a bad run here lately, and when Measles put this proposition to me I copped onto it. He gimme a sawbuck deposit and half a yard to come . . . only that fifty has kept scarce from me, by God. Anywhichway, he wants me to open

your joint. So I contact him outside this restaurant your missus
works. He knows her by sight and we spot her to make sure
she ain't going to be home. He gives me the whereof of your
joint and I go out and open it up. I hang around, then Measles
himself comes out and I open for him and he gives the place
a prowl, like he's learning it to recite. Then he cops the letters.
Then he gives me orders I should get a key so's he can enter
like a gent, being he's too big to pick a lock for himself, the
way he puts it.

"So I tend to the little business, getting the key made. I give
him the key that night. I hold out my hand for the half yard,
he fills it with air. No hurry to him about putting out. So I
keep kind of burning about this stall. So, I figure to myself,
what's he? A writer. What's with the letters he copped? I
figure there's an angle in them letters that he's got all com-
passed out for some green stuff. So, I think it out. He'll put
them letters back so they won't be missed. I'll just go cop 'em
myself, then see if he screams and kicks with the half yard.
I think yes. Get me? All day yesterday I hang around that
street. Only, your missus she's in the joint. I scram outta the
area before I earn me a squeal. I come back last night . . . say
around eight-thirty, quarter nine. Lights on." That's when
Charles had been there. "I tour around. I'm in a hot crate.
Come back, oh maybe ten-thirty, eleven P.M. Lights off. I get
in. I feel around with my ears. Don't hear no breathing. I think
good. I cop the letters. I look around then, and see this stiff
in the closet. *Kee-rist!*

"When I get back to myself from the shock I give the stiff
a feel for leather, only I can't find it. So I take the ticker off
his arm so's not to draw a blank while I'm at it. I see there's
nothing fit to pick in the rest of the joint, so I scram. Then,
suddenly, it come to me . . . what's to do with the ticker? I
think, it's real hot. It just ain't a good-selling ticker except to
the right buyer. It comes to me, who should be maybe a
good buyer? The guy that give the stiff the business! You!
So I figure . . ."

"You could shake me down with it?"

"Sure. It's merchandise you'd want, I figure, and you could
take it on a layaway plan, just like business, and pay off in

installments. Y'know? I ain't out to squeeze you hard, just easy—we all gotta live! So there I am when you come in that truck and lug that crate up and the stiff down in it."

"I had books in it."

"Yeah, I know. Some books! So you gimme a real good slick and I slipped right off your tail. You got smart brains, Charley. Well, I sure wanted to contact you, so I don't know nothing but your monicker; and just by luck it turns out that when I'm asking around about you on the street around here, you walk in the lobby downstairs. A party happens to reckanize you and makes the point-out. So I'm on your tail when you and that raggle Cleo went up in the Majestic to play house. When you come out, I follow you to the Colonial Restaurant. And the rest you can figure. What Measles is doing with your letters is outta my department. I figure it's some kinda shake-down, only I don't know what. I'm leveling, Charley."

"Where's Measles now, Sam?"

"I don't know. He owes me, like I said. I been combing for him, but he ain't showed in any of the joints since last night."

"You know where he showed?"

"Sure. Here. Down'n the lobby here at the Supreme. This party says Measles met a raggle there and scrams.

"It's after the last race out at Hollywood . . . past six-thirty by us."

"You think your friend would know the girl if he saw her picture?"

"I dunno, pal, if he would or no."

"Crap! You can't stay on the level. You know where that bastard is, and by God, Sam . . ."

"Wait . . . don't get a hard . . . I take you to the guy that seen him. Take you right to him. Ask him if he seen her and Measles . . . all I know's what he said. . . ."

"We'll go, but first I'm fixing you up." Charles went around back of Sam, taking the packet of letters and Brattsford's watch. Then, cautiously, he unbound Sam's hands. He held one of them twisted up in a half-Nelson, without putting on any pressure. Then he maneuvered the watch against Sam's thumb. "Now press your first finger against it. Don't smear it or you'll keep doing it over, pal, till I get a good print. I won't use it, but I'm going to have it. You keep your trap shut about me and you got no worry." Sam gave him the prints. Charles looked at them on the crystal and smooth back of the watch. They looked clear. Then he had Sam put his prints on several of the letters. Charles put the watch in one of the envelopes, wrapped the whole bundle in a clean handkerchief of Sam's, pocketed it. Sam put on coat and hat and they went downstairs and out of the hotel to find the friend who'd seen Measles meet a "raggle."

Sam's friend was in a horse parlor in back of a cigar store diagonally across the street from the hotel. There were at least a hundred people in the big smoky room, talking and figuring their Forms at the tables and moving about. Charles stopped suddenly on the threshold and pulled down his hatbrim.

"Bring your friend," Charles said tersely. "I can't go in." He stepped to the nearest table, caught up a pink sheet and held it, concealing himself, as Sam started to search the room.

Standing in front of the big odds board along one side wall, consulting the board and their Racing Forms, were Gobi and Elton, the pawnshop detail dicks who'd slapped him around last night. Charles poised near the exit, fake-reading the pink sheet, watching the detectives warily, his heart pounding. Gobi's back and Elton's side were to him, but either of them might turn any minute. Down at the betting cage the caller began to talk over the public address in a slaty monotone.

"First quarter in the Fourth Race at Hialeah . . . it's Lacey's Lady by two lengths." The crowd's voice drone hushed out and almost everyone turned toward the caller. Charles saw Gobi, thick and red-faced, punch Elton in the ribs, and Elton's narrow, insolent face was thrown back joyously, and he laughed loudly. Then he tugged his rakish snapbrim, smacked his folded Racing Form in his palm, and swung around, his natty collegiate topcoat swirling. His glance circuited the room, touched and passed Charles. "Symphonic is second by a head, Octopus in third position, with Peevish Pretzel in fourth place, moving up fast . . ."

Elton and Gobi watched the caller, smoking, exchanging remarks, glancing around. Then Gobi's red-slab face seemed to fix, looking in Charles's direction. Charles ground his teeth, kept his face as concealed as he dared without seeming obviously to hide. His gut was tight and cold. His breath stopped. He didn't dare force attention, in case Gobi wasn't looking at him. He couldn't be conspicuous and take flight. He stood there, conscious of the gun in his pocket. They'd love catching him off base here in a gambling joint! Even if he ditched the packet containing the murdered man's watch, he was still packing a rod! His hand tightened on the gun. He knew one thing. He would never take another beating. Not from anybody. Not from that pair in particular. If they came to take him, he'd . . .

Sam was coming toward him with his friend. The second quarter call from Hialeah was coming over the public address. Gobi looked at the caller, at his Form. He hadn't seen him.

Sam, Charles, and the friend went out and settled into a booth in a restaurant a couple of doors down. The friend was an ordinary-looking guy he remembered vaguely, as "Happy" somebody from stir. He remembered exchanging brief nods with Happy when he'd first looked in on the Supreme Hotel bar. Sam Keech explained to Happy that Charles wanted to know who the girl was that Measles Edwards had met about six forty-five last night in the Supreme lobby. Charles showed Nora's picture and her snapshot.

"That's her," Happy said after considerable deliberation. Sam was visibly relieved that his pal hadn't let him down.

"Sure?" Charles said. "Positive? What was she wearing?"

"Just ordinary stuff. Coat and a hat. You know. Cloth coat, no fur. Dark, kind of. I think a belt on it. Hat was plain, just little and small like. Cute, and nothing fancy." It sounded authentic.

"I guess you did see her. How'd she act? And where'd they go? You pay any attention to that? Which way? They walk or take a cab or . . . ?"

"They light out toward town. Walking. They never spent half a minute there in the Supreme. She just breezes in, see, and Measles makes contact, and he don't ease her off with no drink nor nothing, just walks up to her, gives her the fast patter, and hustles her out. She sure acts gone on him the way she got no eyes for nothing in the joint, only him. She gives him the face . . . you know, all turned up and blanked out. Man, she's his zombie. . . ."

Charles felt his face color, and Sam broke in on Happy. "Don't rub him, Happy."

"Oh . . . oh . . . that's your heart, huh?"

"Yes," Charles said. "Well, thanks for the dope."

"Listen, Slugger," Happy said, anxious to please, "when you catch up with that son of a bitch, give him a little for me. Cut 'em out for him. That's what I'd do for a laddie boy that went around making time on my woman while I was cooped, believe you me, Slugger. That Measles Edwards!"

"That rat didn't make time with her. It was something else."

"I bet that's true. But if it was me, I'd mark her puss up so she'd never be no good for nobody else to look at. Like Jack Pake fix up that pig used to hang out down by Raimey's joint trying to pay guys to lay her she was so goddam ugly. And that pig was a zizz kitty of a looker oncet. Man, he done her up slow with acid. Took him a good full week before he finished her puss."

Sam said, "Whatever became of her?"

"Booby hatch. Jack Pake sure fix her wagon. It never spoiled her from wanting it, but Christ, a guy vomit just to look at her. Jack, he don't like nothing good-looking to begin with. I see him just a couple hours back taking a beer with that good-looking black-head raggle Cleo Adams. First time I see him since I dunno when."

"Is that the Jack Pake that works for Proctor?" Charles said, trying to make it casual.

"Same guy. Proctor's knife hand. Real hard man. I dunno what come over him. He's in there in the Supreme bar right when that burleycue gang is strutting the place. Way he hates a good-looking broad it's pitiful, but there he sits with one right in the middle of all them others. It's a wonder he don't start kicking their tails in."

So it had been Jack, that stone-faced hood of Proctor's who had got the truck and crate for him, sitting with Cleo. A guy that hated lookers, sitting with her. Proctor's knife? Maybe Cleo had been scared to admit who she'd been with, who had sicked her on him. Well, Cleo could take care of herself . . .

he was sure of that. He got up, leaving a dollar for the coffees on the table.

"I'll shove off. Thanks, Happy. And thanks, Sam, for the loan of the hardware—temporarily. I'll try and collect that half yard from Measles."

"Give him something for me, Slugger," Happy said. Sam nodded.

Charles left, crossed the street, glancing back at the restaurant to see if Sam followed. He didn't. Charles looked at the cigar store fronting the horse parlor, afraid he might see Gobi and Elton. It was clear. He walked past the Supreme, the Queen Burlesque, the Majestic, toward midtown, away from the depot. Measles and Nora had walked this way.

To a waiting car? Cab?

It was clear that Measles had used Charles's letters so he could forge a message to Nora in Charles's writing. The sudden thought that the scum had probably used the line *the beat of thy heart is the pulse in my veins* made him suck cold air through his teeth.

Measles had probably had the fake note delivered to the depot. Careful. Not showing himself for the station dicks to remember. Waiting at the Supreme, ready to lam if she smelled a rat and didn't come alone.

The message in Charles's writing would have been urgent. Charles in trouble. An old prison buddy was waiting at the Supreme to help. The buddy would know her. Measles would have been too cagey to name or describe himself. When Nora had come, he'd got her immediately out of sight.

Charles paused at the corner of the next street. To the left was the inter-city bus station from which he'd got Sam Keech's suitcase. What if Measles had hustled Nora out of town via bus?

He went into the station, got in the shorter of two ticket lines, lit a smoke nervously, glancing around. If Sam Keech had tipped Gobi and Elton . . . But he wouldn't dare. Proctor's vicious hood Jack Pake had been with Cleo, watching him. There might be another Proctor man tailing him for some damned reason.

He couldn't stand around chasing will-o'-the-wisps. It was

past four. Time to call Syl's office. Syl hadn't lied about seeing Nora with a wolf in a burlesque-side hotel. *She* knew something specific. Where to find Measles, maybe, and Nora.

Whatever Syl's terms, damn her to hell!

# 14

HE WAS PREPARED for a stall when he phoned Syl's office. But Syl had left her phone number. He called the number. Syl answered almost at once.

"This is Charles, Syl. Are you through playing? I want to know where that freckled-faced son of a—"

"Not so fast, darling," she drawled. She laughed softly. "All hot and bothered, aren't you?"

"It's not funny, Syl, not by a damned sight. I think you've been just about as nasty as even you can stomach. Enough's enough."

"I've had such a bad hangover today . . . and the candy and flowers were so lovely. They brought my spirits up so beautifully."

"O. K., then. Now you feel better, so tell me whatever you can that'll help."

"Charles, I don't get you, not at all, really I don't. You worry the girl in the office to death over me, you send me gifts. Now you phone me and begin acting out of character. You certainly do not even use the tone of voice of a suitor. . . ."

"A suitor! Why, damn you to . . ."

The receiver banged in his ear. He rattled the hook. "Hello . . . hello." The line was dead. He swore, put in another coin, dialed, ripping the spinner around, poising for the next spin before it settled. The number began to ring. He sat tensed forward, ready to blast into the mouthpiece. The number rang and rang and rang, and she didn't answer. A slow, sick look spread over his face, and he began to gnaw his lip. He'd ruined it! Oh, damn her! damn her! But why hadn't he had the guts to swallow his medicine? She wouldn't answer. He edged the booth door open, feeling stuffy. His face became feverish. Maybe he could find a cross-reference book and get the address from the phone number. But she could leave or refuse to admit him.

"Yes!" At last her voice. Harsh, like the crack of a whip. He thought of Jerry saying Syl used a whip on him.

"Why did you hang up?" he said weakly. "I'm desperate, Syl. Fercrissakes"—he hated the wheedling note in his voice—"for the sake of friendship . . . old times . . . my whole marriage is shot."

"Hell!" she said coarsely. "Friendship. You professed to despise me—maybe not in words, but it was there. What a chump you thought poor Jerry was to put up with a bitch like me! Admit it!"

"It wasn't like that."

"Cheap, whining liar! Admit it, or sign off."

"All right. Maybe it was my attitude. A lot of water has gone under the bridge since then."

"A lot of things have changed, you're damned right, Charles Garrell. I should help you salvage your marriage with that little . . . Well, whatever she is. What about *my* marriage? I should be worrying about yours! Now, listen, I get tight, but never too tight to forget. I remember that I told you my terms. I know something and you don't, and you want to know. Well, before you know, you will have given irrefutable proof to me that you acknowledge my superiority in every way to that trivial creature you used to prize. She's not top consideration now, though, *is* she? I come first, don't I?"

"Well, hell, you know the situation, Syl. We know the situation."

"What is it, Charles, in so many words?"

"You want me to make love to you, and if I don't . . ."

She laughed acidly. "*I* want you to? Did I send *you* flowers?"

"No. I sent them. I want to see you, be with you. I . . ."

"Not so articulate, huh? Well, darling, action speaks louder than words. Perhaps you shall have a chance to see me. Tell you what I'll do. I'll call the caterer and have three dinners sent home. Come dine with Jerry and me."

"Not that. Damn it!"

"What, then?"

"I want to be with you alone . . . all alone . . . please . . ."

He took a deep breath. He stared at the mouthpiece and moved his lips, forming silent words of the most scurrilous obscenity he could dredge up.

"You want me to deceive my husband in your behalf, darling?"

"If you will. And listen, Syl." His voice sharpened. He was ready to threaten her if she double-crossed him. He stopped himself.

"What were you going to say?"

"Nothing . . . just to make it stronger how much I want . . ."

"Hate me?" She whispered it.

"Do I have to answer?"

"Hate me hard. Chew nails, darling!" she whispered. "Remember what I told you. The extra dimension. Intensity, darling. It will mark us . . . bind us with fire . . . and you're going to hate me even more, sweetheart. You're so proud, so proud . . . it will be unendurable to submit unconditionally to me."

"Yes, bitch! Unendurable."

"I know how to slash down to the quick. . . ."

"That you do! Admitted. Now, what's the address?"

"The Kessler Apartment Hotel at 73rd and Dane Boulevard. And, Charles, I do hope your skin isn't tender." She hung up.

He knew what she meant by that. No, by God, he wouldn't submit to a whip in her hands. Submit unconditionally, she said. And along with it she would demand acknowledgment that he preferred her to Nora.

Words would be easy. Meaningless. But a man couldn't fake completely. His was the active role. If ever he met her conditions, his body must give evidence, prove in action that he accepted her as a love object . . . no matter how his mind denied.

He took a cab to the apartment hotel. It was dusk, early winter night. The place was swanky and hushed. The desk was expecting him. She had sent down word. He was to wait.

He cooled his heels. She took her time. It would be futile to try sneaking up. She'd just let him bang the door and get a bigger kick out of the whole thing.

Furtively, he unloaded the gun. He didn't dare trust himself to have it loaded and handy when he and Syl were alone.

Never, he thought, never had he so completely hated another human being. He stopped himself from thinking about her. To hate her was playing it her way, giving it a depth and intensity and raw nightmare quality of unforgettableness. He had to lift himself, see it in perspective, remember the vital reason behind it, reduce her to her actual position as a simple obstacle in his path to Nora. On that level, coldly, he could take it.

But it couldn't be cold. Love, with or without hate, with or without the consent of the mind, was physical, and it couldn't be cold. Damn her! damn her!

The functionary came to the lounge where he waited and gave the glad tidings that Syl was "at home."

He took the elevator up and stepped out into the empty, soft-lighted, carpeted corridor, and walked down it toward her apartment. He felt out of breath. He stopped at her door and tapped. He kept one hand clamped around the unloaded gun, his forefinger curled on the trigger, easing out the slack with a slow, steady pressure, then letting up, before activating the hammer. Then she opened the door. He heard the gun dry-fire in his pocket. He pulled the gun out, and pushed into the apartment, silent. She stepped aside, smiled down at the gun.

"My, my, is this my rendezvous with death? The dead don't talk, Charles. I thought you wanted me to tell you things."

His eyes were glittering. He cast them nervously about. He strode into the other rooms, opening doors, searching.

"We're alone, lover," Syl called. "Don't worry. Now, come on back and relax. The shades are drawn, the door locked . . . this is our world . . . shut off, darling . . . just yours and mine. Special . . . very special."

Charles went back to the front room.

She had prepared herself. Her blonde hair was down loose about her shoulders. She wore a diaphanous silk or nylon negligee which gave her skin a softened, shadowy tone, and it flowed out about her as she crossed the room to a settee. The negligee was girdled with a silver rope that matched a ribbon in her hair and the sandals on her bare feet. He could see clearly the outline of a black lace bra and panties through the smoky veiling of the negligee, and there was an odd, spicy scent of perfume about her. She moved supplely, the pliant soles of her sandals making no sound. She sat on the little sofa and nodded toward a chair facing it from across a glass cocktail table on which was a shaker and glasses, a box of cigarettes and a lighter.

She poured martinis. He sat. He watched her sip her drink and replace it. He didn't touch his. He said nothing. She said nothing. It was up to him. He got a smoke, snapped the silver lighter aflame, lighting, his eyes dark and hard. He replaced the lighter, inhaled deeply. She draped herself with her arms outspread along the continuous curve line forming sides and back of the settee. Her negligee opened on bare white skin in a long V between her breasts to the silver-rope belt. He looked away. The couch was severe, its upholstery gray silk. The wood was fine and delicately carved. The legs formed exquisitely fragile bows. He had to get to it, instead of kidding himself with furniture appraisal. Her body, there for him to see . . . she had gone to considerable trouble to make it enticing. The bitch! She extended one leg, a casual gesture, breaking the silence, drawing attention to herself. The silver T-strap sandal set off the long white line of her foot; the toenails were bright red . . . even the heel looked as if she had rouged it. She crossed her ankles, giving him an arch-line view which she evidently considered charming. He looked at her face with an expression that made her flush. He didn't have to say she *still* left him cold.

"You're a good-looking woman," he said coolly. "Any man would admit it."

"Thanks," she said.

"Now, will you tell me where Measles is? Edwards, the boyish darling who met Nora at the Supreme Hotel."

She leaned forward, tossed off her drink, remained in the forward bend, and said nastily: "You know that much . . . well, find out the rest. Get out. You're not going to make me prompt you again. So get out. I'm bored with you. You can't sit there and think you'll wear me down. Get to it, or get out. Or maybe you want me to start it. . . ."

"Well, I . . . Listen, Syl . . ."

"Well, you're not leaving, and you're not starting things."
She got up and swept across the room. "I'll put you in the
spirit!"

He got to his feet, twisted about, watched her streak into
the bedroom. "What are you up to?" he demanded. She didn't
answer. He stood staring at the door, gnawing at his lip. His
throat dried. He took a drag from his cigarette.

She came back, stood there in the bedroom doorway, her
face upraised, flushed and radiant, her eyes snapping, a tight,
challenging smile on her mouth. She held a whip.

"Come here."

"You're crazy."

"Come here."

"Don't push me, Syl. You hear me? Don't push me . . .
don't monkey with me like this." He was deathly pale. He
twisted around, dropped his cigarette. He rubbed his palms on
his pants. His breath came very slowly in long inhales through
his open lips. He didn't move. He looked at the door to the
outside hall; his gaze snapped back to her, compelled. Their
eyes met, held. She looked at him steadily, command, amusement, assurance mingled in her expression. Her wrist snapped.
The whiplash made a faint whooshing sound, fell in a muted
thump to the carpet.

"Come here . . . or get out."

"I won't do either." His voice was harsh. He moved his
head jerkily, scanning the room as if there might be a miracle
solution somewhere. He started toward her. "Give me that!"
he ordered. She took a step back into the bedroom.

"I'll give it to you. Strip down, baby . . . I'll give it to you."
She backed farther into the room. "I'm going to beat you till
you cry. Hear me? You'll kiss my feet, you hear me? You'll
beg for it. . . . That'll tap down to the fire in you if you can't
bring it up of your own accord. . . ."

He kept going toward her. He crossed the threshold. She
lifted the whip stock to shoulder height, started to draw her
arm back. "Don't throw that lash at me," he said quietly. "I
won't take a whipping from anybody, not for anybody . . .
not for any reason."

Her shoulders lifted faintly. She lowered the whip. "You

mean it, all right." She tossed the whip aside. "And I mean it. I'm going to have you, Charles, or else get out. Do it your way, but do it or get out."

He stepped to her, encircled her waist, yanked her to him roughly and kissed her mouth hard. Then he jerked his head toward the bed. "Get set, kid."

She sneered. "What am I, a cheap whore? You think I'd go to bed with anybody who didn't make me want to? I'm a bit human, not quite yet a mechanical woman. You've done nothing but repel not *rouse* desire. I know you didn't mean that kiss."

He had to *mean* it, in spite of the loathing, did he?

"All right. Softer." He drew her to him gently. He stroked her cheek. He kissed her forehad. He pressed her body closer to his and caressed his hand along the curves of her back. There was an automaton's stiffness; the hand didn't fit itself relishingly to her contours.

"What're you measuring me for?"

"A shroud." He kissed her mouth again, less roughly.

She pulled her face away. "Is my mouth gall?"

"No. Don't be insulting. I don't happen to be a Romeo . . . it's the best I can do."

"Well, then, it's just too bad. It ain't good enough . . . you don't *mean* it. . . ."

What the hell! What the hell! Did he have to convince himself before he could put it across? No, dammit, he could fake, and he would fake—up to a point. After that, who knew? He couldn't permit himself to find her desirable when he *hated* her guts. He wasn't *capable* of finding this detestable creature desirable. He was cold, stone cold. And if he let himself warm up, it would be an admission. And never could he face her and deny it afterward, nor face himself.

A woman's throat was impersonal . . . and beautiful . . . almost any woman's. He put his lips to the softness of her throat, and his lips softened and warmed. The scent of her body rose in a delicate, faintly spicy warmth. He kissed her throat easily, several times. Any throat in the world. He kissed her shoulders, pushing the negligee away. She put her hands in his hair, responding to him. She played with his hair, then ran her palm in an artfully silky caress along his neck, and a certain not unpleasurable sensation ran over his skin. *He* was responding to her. No . . . he wouldn't permit . . .

He slipped his hands under the negligee and moved them on her bare flesh, and it was not repulsive to him. He looked into her face, and her eyes were muzzed a little, and there was a beginning slackness to her mouth, and he thought that there *was* rather a delicacy to some of her features when the harshness was warmed out . . . warmed out in this case by him. Her mouth clamped suddenly to his, and she surged up, molding herself to his body, arching herself in a taut, vibrant pressure against him, drawing his head forward over her. She opened her lips under his and rolled her head just a little and moved her lips as if she were talking rapidly to him, and she darted her tongue fierily into his mouth, and he could taste the sweetish flavor of her lipstick. Then she broke, gasping, and he found himself crushing her to him, seeking her mouth again, his senses giddied, and suddenly there was a wild surge of the most intense desire imaginable, and he thought there's everything in what she said . . . they belong together, the love and the hate . . . she *knew* all along . . . about us . . . our minds are the same . . . and our bodies . . . She was writhing against him, an animal, blind and lost, and he thought again of her personally, in her cold and ugly phases, and the very thought of it had a pique, a whiplike stimulus. She was everything he loathed, and yet this was beyond him, the power of their bodies obliterated it, and to lose oneself was glorious. . . . The mind, with its comfortless discriminations, its guilty pain, was washed away. . . .

Her perfume made him drunk . . . powerless. . . .

Submission!

His senses bleared out.

And when they cleared, she was on the floor, limp, and he was beside her, crouched, and his hands were locked to her throat. Her face was horrible. There was a tortured, feeble convulsion in her body, then she lay still.

He loosened his fingers, and stared down at her with glazed eyes, his mouth open. His tongue lolled inertly in his mouth. He felt like an animal, a stupefied animal, a killer animal.

# 15

He came upright out of his crouch, turning to the open door into the front room. He couldn't look at her.

He couldn't keep from looking.

His glance snapped back and down. The quick motion dizzied him. He stood on the balls of his feet, regaining his balance. He started out of the room. He stopped in the open doorway and looked back at her. He shook his head, turned, and went into the front room.

Empty. Silent.

He went over to the cocktail table and picked up his untouched drink. It splashed all over. He set it down, hastily, noisily. He stood there trembling. He looked back at the open doorway, then shuddered a little and looked away.

He had to get out.

Where?

It was broken. The continuity of his life. Shot.

It hadn't been his fault! He'd been out of his head; he hadn't known what he was doing.

No reason.

Caught. He lit a smoke. He looked at the ugly burn on the back of his hand, frowning, not remembering it. His wrists itched.

Then he saw the raw, pink claw lines across his wrists from her nails. He lifted his arms, saw the frayed areas in the cloth of his sleeves. She'd fought. Maybe his face was clawed, too. He scanned the room for a mirror, saw one, started toward it. He stopped. He went to the wall switch beside the entrance door, snapped off the lights. He wanted dark. Quiet. Time for thought. A long, narrow fan of light stretched across the end of the room from the bedroom door. He looked away. Think . . . think . . .

Now he was hunted. Alone. He didn't dare find Nora. She'd be the trap, the obvious trap. They'd be watching her night and day, waiting for a word, a move from him. Wherever she was, she was gone from him. She was death.

He would have time. A few hours. Maybe till morning. He would be on the lam, far away. From now on, running. Hunted.

He couldn't stand the silence, the dark. He snapped the light on.

He snapped it off. He dragged at his cigarette, trying to think. He mustn't rush, planless.

He had really killed.

No.

He hadn't known what he was do . . .

He had.

There it was. Compressed and concealed. But there it was.

He'd known. He remembered. The whole swift, incredible sequence.

He had hurled her away from him with such violence that her upper back had hit the floor first and her legs had shot up, naked, kicking, and he had leaped at her, his hands going directly to her throat and clamping mercilessly into the flesh, and she had gagged and coughed, and her eyes had bulged out at him in blue terror, and she had kept chewing at the air, trying to talk, shout, beg, and all the while he could feel the thrashing death struggle of her body and the tearing at him of her clawed hands, and several times he had felt the impact of her knees against his back, but he'd held balance, and her face had become scarlet and then purple, and unrecognizable as human in its death contortions, and he had been aware of the feeling of her struggle, and he had sensed the dreadful approach of death, and her hands had fallen slack to the carpet, the power drained from her arms, her fingers scratching aimlessly and futilely into the nap of the carpet, and he had known something, something terrible, an exultance, brief but powerful, and there had been a raw flash of insight, and he remembered the good feeling he had had in the police station when he had seen Gobi and Elton, the good sense that everything was all right, and he knew why, without the slightest obscurity . . . he had decided that Elton was dead, already dead, living only until Charles had found the moment to kill him . . . and he sensed that it had been inevitable for him to murder, that he had known there was no other way to ob-

literate his humiliations . . . and Syl was an even more logical
victim, for her cruelty was the same, but her torturings reached
far deeper . . . and she was the enemy, the dead enemy . . .
the struggle had dwindled to spasms in her thighs and in pel-
vic muscles, and it had come to him as curious and fitting that
the womb area should be last to go . . . and he had looked at the
area, regretful somehow, and his intensity had vanished, the conscious control had returned, and he had been aware of himself,
a crouched killer animal. . . .

And it came. Remorse. Tears.

He gave way as much as he could. It wasn't much. He remained conscious of himself, relentlessly conscious of himself.
Blubbering. It made his flesh crawl. Fake. He wasn't remorse-
ful; he wasn't crying about Syl. Maybe he was a little, very
little. He was crying about himself. Pitying himself, he thought
with contempt. And he wouldn't even be sorry about himself
except that he was scared. He wouldn't be slobbering over himself for an instant if he thought he was going to get by with
the killing.

He wiped his face, muttering at himself. What a big hero!
Well, what next? Money, naturally. The first corpse loot was
running low. Brattsford's money. He'd take Syl's now, if he
could find any, plus whatever else he could get by with. He
could stall around a while and wage mock war with himself
and finally pretend that he'd just had to twist his conscience's
arm, and in the end it would be the same. He'd rob the victim. It was no longer good taste to eat the kill . . . logical, but
not the thing, so he'd take her money and whatever jewelry
there was. No, he'd have to bypass that. It would leave his
tracks in pawnshops behind him. . . .

He went across the dark room toward the fanspread of light
from the bedroom. And suddenly a shadow slid over the carpet.

His breath caught; he went motionless. He stared toward
the bedroom doorway. She was looking at him.

Holding her hands at her throat and staring with enormous,
accusing blue eyes. Her blonde hair was awry about her naked
shoulders. Standing there, almost nude, her hands holding her
throat, her eyes on him. He moved from shadow to the lighted
strip, and one of her hands shot out, arm's length, outspread,

fending him off, and her right foot slid back, and she caught her weight in balance awkwardly as she moved the other foot back. She didn't speak, nor move fast, just backed up. He didn't know if she were real in herself or his terror projected. He caught up the distance between them and reached out with both hands to span her. He brought his hands in toward each other in a pincer movement, certain that they would pass through the apparition and meet. Her mouth opened wide and her eyes shut but there was no scream. Her skeletal structure seemed to turn liquid and she sank down. She was flesh, all right. He tried to clamp her to him and keep her from falling, but she slid heavily away from him.

And there she was on the floor again. Where she had been. And maybe she hadn't walked at all, and the hallucination had been complete . . . visual, tactile, everything but auditory.

No. It had been real. She wasn't in just the same position she had been. This was a faint. A fright-faint. She'd thought he intended to finish her off.

He got a wet towel and sponged it over her face, and after a while she came to and whispered: "Please don't kill me."

"I won't," he said. His voice was husky, shaky. He cleared his throat. "That's done with. But don't ever do that. Don't ever push me like that, Syl. Now, get up. Tell me where Measles Edwards is. Has he got Nora?"

"I don't know. Really. But he had a house at 5410 Anderson Lane. He hasn't been there, but he may be there."

"Anybody with him? Anybody who'd be dangerous? Is he armed?"

"I don't know . . . I don't know . . . Oh, Charles, I didn't realize what I was doing to you. Oh, God, it was the end. I felt it. Death. I knew I was dying. Thank God you quit."

"We can both thank God. Syl, I don't know what stopped me. I got my senses back and I thought you were dead. But I remember dimly, very dimly, that you hadn't quite stopped moving. There was a little tremor of fight left in you. Not much . . . not much. Sober up now, you hear, and get all that hate-thrill and death-thrill out of your mind."

"Yes!"

"Get up and dress. I want you to go with me and front for

me so I won't have trouble getting in. I don't want to get him jumpy, understand. I have to get the jump on him. He might kill Nora . . ." He paused as she lifted her hands. He helped her up. "Does he trust you? Do you think he'll let you in?"

She nodded steadily, her blue eyes wide open and staring hypnotically at him. He snapped his fingers angrily under her nose.

She said breathlessly: "I'm fine. Fine. And done with all that nastiness. I'll dress. We'll go to his place. At once! I want you to get that Edwards rat . . . Measles, you call him. A good name! I want you to get him. And beat him! I'll never talk if you kill him. And you can do it. You can do anything, *anything!* My *God,* I underestimated you. . . ."

He snapped: "Get dressed!" Sobered? She was drunker than ever. Thrill drunk. "And snap into it!"

She moved with alacrity, getting a dress and shoes from the closet, a slip from the bureau. She began at once to dress, casting shy and docile glances at him. "You see I'm hurrying," she said, her tone submissive.

"Cut the coy!"

"A woman knows her man."

"Damn it, I'm not your man! Snap it up. And shut up!"

She was mute from then on. Spectacularly silent, as if to say: you have spoken, I obey. That's how she played it. A game. The damned fool still thought it was a game. He went in and switched on her radio, and kept searching the dial. There was music, a horse opera, sportscast, a network commentator with world news. No local news. He returned to watch Syl briefly, then got into his hat and overcoat. He opened the cylinder of the revolver, inserted the bullets, .38's, in the chambers, snapped the cylinder shut. He went back to the bedroom door, holding the gun for her to see as she got into her coat. Then he pocketed it, saying nothing. His eyes watched her, bleakly at first, then thoughtful. He really had scared her witless and she might be in a state of shock, which would account for her almost sensual air of submission. On the other hand, she'd been looking for a beating all her life and maybe she relished what he'd done to her. Maybe she'd done her damnedest to goad her husband into some male assertiveness

which would have permitted her to feel like a woman instead
of a governess, but Jerry hadn't been up to it. Now she was
trying to show him, Charles, that he was the master. And by
damn he was! She fluffed a silk scarf high up under her chin
and came to him, holding out a set of keys with a miniature
auto-license tag. He took them, then snatched her purse. He
looked into it, saw no gun, and handed it back. She stood
passively before him, her eyes uplifted as he patted her coat
pockets, then opened the coat to see if there was a pocket in
the lining.

"All right," he said, "button up." He touched his overcoat
pocket where the gun bulged. "Remember, Mrs. Aldrich, I'm
looking for a double-cross out of you. Every minute."

Her fingers were trembly on her coat buttons. She shook her
head emphatically, opening her lips.

"May I speak?" she whispered.

"Talk!" he said exasperatedly. "Cut the coy stuff."

"Kill him for me!"

"Not for *you*. Get that! What's your score? Hell hath no
fury like a woman spurned?"

"That *was* it. Not now. There's no feeling to it now," she
said softly. She cast her eyes down. "There's none left over
for him."

"Let's go," he said stonily. On the way out she took up the
martini shaker, removed the top. She offered the shaker to
him. He shook his head. She drank. He let her. She was jittery
as hell.

As they settled in her coupé with Charles at the wheel she
said: "5410 Anderson Lane. You know the way?"

"I do."

It was within two miles. He pulled out, switched on the
radio, searched the dial for local news. It was six twenty-five.
No news at the moment. Syl lit two cigarettes with the dash
lighter, gave him one. To throw it out would have been playing her game, giving the intimate touch significance. She sat
very close to him. He caught a lazy-soft smile on her face, felt
her hand messing around his coat pocket where the gun was.
He rammed her with his elbow.

"Sit over there away from me!" he snapped, transferring the

gun to the opposite pocket. "You haven't got a chance of getting it."

"I wasn't trying," she said dreamily. "I like the feel of it."

He looked sidewise at her, and her eyes slid to the corners toward him, and she ran her gloved hand over his sleeve. He pulled away from the touch.

"Move anyway."

She slid across the seat. Maybe she *was* subdued. "The way you're laying it on," he said, "gives my ego a big boost. I just can't resist you." He laughed derisively.

"It was even better than I'd hoped," she said. "And you can't deny I was right. Our experience was unique, yours and mine, and the bond is deep and dark and strong. Something neither of us could have created with any other partner. The roles could only have been played by you and by me, together. The thing could *never* exist between either of us and anyone else. It was *rare*. A jewel, Charles, a jewel . . . terrible, but utterly without similarity to anything else in the world. Don't you *see*? We, we alone went together to the brink of death . . ."

He snorted. "You thought it was wonderful. You were having a high old time, I suppose! Crap!"

"It wasn't wonderful then. Not at the moment, no. If it had been, it wouldn't have been valid experience. Don't you see? If we had felt ourselves to be simply experimenting, acting, it wouldn't have been valid. It was real, beyond us, and it banished the world. What we had was a matchless combination of love and hate. And what we had wasn't imposed—it was our own making, each of us indispensable. It was our world, private, shut off, dependent on nothing but each other. It was macabre, Charles, a death dance. Think of it, its intensity, Charles. It was with me, Charles, with me, that you created the most powerful experience of your life!"

She was right, damn her! It had been the most powerful experience of his life. Hateful or not, it was stamped irrevocably into his very fabric, and he'd never be able to forget. He resented her for it; he wanted to smash her face. He held himself. His head began to ache, and the muscles in his shoulders and the back of his neck became rigid with restraint. He was shocked to realize the effort it took to keep from hitting her. It was ugly, ugly as hell to know her power to tempt him —like a negative pole inviting the discharge of the pent-up violence in him. She offered herself as a vessel for his hate, a release for his acid frustration. She could give him relief, gratification, and she knew it! If anything happened to Nora, Syl would like it; she'd have a morbid and maybe indispensable place in his life. He mistrusted her doubly now. She might deliberately pull some trick in order to recapture that experience; she might try to draw that lightning again, tempt him to rage, and the more deadly the situation the keener the thrill. He watched her in the rear-vision mirror. Her features were indistinct in the dull glow of the dashlight except for the surfaces of her eyes which caught the light like polish. She was looking forward to trouble with unconcealed relish.

There was no mention of Brattsford on the six-thirty local newscast. Evidently his body hadn't been found.

At Forty-fifth he turned onto Anderson Lane, headed for 5410. It was an opulent neighborhood. The houses were expensive and the grounds, while not in the estate class, were spacious. At Fifty-fourth he could see that the second house on the even-numbered side, a high, square, solid old house with roofed porches across the front and along the side, was dark.

"Isn't that 5410?" he said tightly. "The number you told me? The dark one?" He slowed without stopping.

"Yes." She nodded, watching it. "That's it."

He drove to the next corner, turned, then turned again into the alley. He drove past the back. No light showed anywhere. Leaving the alley, slowing into the curb, he felt inside the glove compartment.

"I need a flashlight."

"Sorry," she began.

"I'll get one," he cut her off, accelerating again.

At the drugstore a few blocks back he made her go in with him while he bought a flashlight and some adhesive tape. Returning to Fifty-fourth, he parked near the alley, cutting engine and light except for the dash. Then he sat and taped the head and lens of the flashlight. He tested to see that no light showed. Then he punctured the tape with a pin at one point, tried the almost invisible beam. He took out the gun, reached across Syl, and opened her door.

"Get out. We're going back there."

"We? But obviously he's gone, Charles."

"Never mind that!"

He forced her out of the car, hurried her to the mouth of the alley, where she balked. His grip tightened warningly on her arm. They moved into the alley and down to the closed triple garage behind 5410. He stopped at the rear gate.

"Did he have rooms," he said in a gritty undertone, "or lease the whole house?"

"Whole house." Her whole body was shaking from cold or fright. She whispered agitatedly: "I don't want to go in there!"

"You're going, and you're going to be all right, Syl. If nothing's happened to Nora, you're going to be all right!"

"But you can't hold *me* respons——"

"Damn you! For almost twenty-four hours, when her life was in danger, you held out on me. And God help you, Syl, if we go in there and find Nora . . ." He wouldn't say it. Dead. He had to keep himself in cold control. "Let's get going!"

# 16

HE OPENED THE gate beside the triple garage and went in along the walk, Syl following closely. At the side window of the garage he stopped. He gave Syl's arm a warning pressure and she stood motionless as he snicked on the flashlight. He probed the garage interior with the pinpoint beam. The light emerged, a tiny dot on the opposite end wall, then zigzagged back toward him along the oil-splotched bare concrete floor. No cars within. He put a finger on the pinhole in the adhesive across the flashlight lens and walked silently to the corner of the garage. The wall of the garage and the overhang of its roof provided a deep gray cover, but the walk from the garage to the back porch of the house was flanked by patches of dully luminous snow which would silhouette him clearly. He stood adjusting his eyes to the details of the square dark mass of the big old house, conscious of the faint pressure of Syl's coat against the back of his. He could hear her quick breathing. His hand shifted on the gun. If she grabbed it or shouted he was prepared to spin and club her.

The muscles in his gut were clamping in a slow, tight rhythm like hunger pangs without hunger. This locked feeling of caution made him feel demeaned . . . and maybe hysterical. He wanted to charge the house, smashing and blasting, and forget the possibility that someone might be alerted and watching from one of those windows. They were black . . . and probably deserted. Nonetheless, he aimed the tiny beam at them, one after another. From the four on the third floor down to the pair of small basement windows he darted the spot of light across each of the lower panes. None of the windows were open, none of the blinds were lowered. No one was at any of the windows.

He hurried Syl up the walk to the short flight of steps to the porch. They entered the porch, where he inspected the window and the door there. Both were locked. Without further ado he smashed a small pane in the door, reached in and opened it. He stepped back onto the porch, concealing most of his body against the outer wall of the house, his gun aimed and ready. Nobody came.

He pulled Syl inside and shut the door and stood fighting off the sudden unreasoning surge of panic in him. The house was chilly, as if the furnace had been untended for some time. He opened the pinpoint flashbeam and shuttled it through the large kitchen, located and crossed to the light switch. He clicked it on-off without result. He jerked around, felt the darkness with the thread of light until he found Syl. The light skimmed like a disembodied coin over her coat and settled on her cheek. He darted it over her face, his mind piercing the fragments of light into a pattern. Her face looked drained, stark. He ripped the adhesive off the light, crossed to her.

"We're going through this place," he said in an undertone. "From attic to cellar. I hope we don't find anything. . . ."

She clutched his sleeve. "We won't! We mustn't. . . . God, don't hate me, Charles, I . . ."

"Come on."

The furnishings were all there, since, as Syl explained, Measles had rented it that way, but it had the cold, empty feel of death. The sound of their steps, the pervading darkness, and the impending sense of dreadful discovery held him taut. Each new room, each closet and nook was a threat, and he moved warily, shooting the wide white beam ahead and occasionally behind them.

They went through bureaus and desk drawers, but there were no clothes or papers or anything to indicate Measles had been there.

Finally they were through except for the basement. He opened the door, motioned to her. She stared at him, shook her head.

"You don't believe he ever was here."

"I haven't seen proof!" He blinded her with the light.

"I don't want to go down," she pleaded, turning her head, her eyes squinting and turning to the corners toward him. "Look at you. You want to kill me. . . ."

The glow of light spread up to his face, giving him a shadowed harshness. He clenched his teeth, shot out an arm and yanked her so hard her head snapped back. He thrust her at the cellar steps, pushed close behind her. She gripped the rail going down, and at the foot of the stairs she spun and stared at him, her underlip and chin quivering helplessly.

"He had servants. A housekeeper. A cook. A maid. I could take you to them, and prove . . ."

He shook his head abruptly. His chest felt banded, his breath constricted. He scouted the laundry room, the "rumpus room" hastily. He returned to the furnace-room door, there near the foot of the stairs. He thrust her in. He felt the furnace, which was cold. He opened the grate door and the feed door and squatted, beaming light into the black interior. He hadn't expected to find anything, he told himself, rising slowly. No. He hadn't. He felt giddy. He went into the coal bin, ordered Syl to hold the light. He shoveled into the pile for several minutes, then hurled the shovel, clanging into the back wall. Measles wouldn't kill her and leave her where he'd lived. He got the light from Syl and went up the stairs.

"Come on, come on," he said, shining the beam back down the steps for her. "Let's get the hell out of here!"

They returned to her car. He started off in the direction of mid-town with the idea of going to the bus station on the cross-street a block from the burlesque-side hotel. He should have shown Nora's picture there on the chance Measles had simply put her on a bus to get her out of town. But Syl had seemed the best bet.

"Where are you going now?" she ventured after a while.

"The cops!" he snapped.

"But, Charles, you can't . . . you're on parole and carrying a gun."

"You sweet, tender thing. Don't you break your little heart about me. Worry about yourself. You won't level with me. O. K. Maybe you will with the cops. You'll explain your connection with Measles Edwards and the con game and Brattsford's murder—and I'm sure you can clear everything up—and they'll tell you to dry your tears and go home like the good little girl you are."

She was silent for several seconds. "All right," she said. "There was more to my relationship with Edwards than passion. But there hasn't been a murder, and Measles got her out of town to protect the money involved in the con game. It was wrong of him, yes. But she's suffered nothing but worry and inconvenience, Charles. You're quite mistaken about Brattsford being murdered. He pretended to be shot in order to scare the victim of the swindle into thinking he was an accomplice in a murder. . . ."

"Where's Nora?"

"I don't know."

"Brattsford's dead. Not a cacklebladder dead, but real. Stabbed to death. I found him in the bedroom closet in my apartment when I got home last night!"

"You mean," she cried, genuinely alarmed, "he's *really* dead . . . and in your *home?*"

"Not now, he's not in my home. I moved him. Now, are you going to tell me where he sent Nora?"

"Line City. It's just across the state line. She went on the seven-o'clock bus. He forged some notes from you, and made

her believe she had to leave at once and tell no one because
you were in serious trouble."

"What name is she using? Where's she registered?"

"Joan Arrell, Line City Hotel."

In five minutes he was in a phone booth in a drugstore with
a handful of silver. Syl stood just outside where he could watch
her, although he didn't think she would try double-crossing
him again.

"Line City Hotel," a man said over the phone.

"Do you have a Joan Arrell registered? She got in last
night"—he calculated time and distance to the city rapidly—
"about eleven or so."

"Just a moment, please. I'll check."

Syl edged the door open, whispered: "She there?"

He shook his head impatiently, listening, waiting tautly. The
clerk's voice came through the receiver. Charles edged forward, holding his breath.

"I'm sorry, sir, but Miss Arrell has checked out."

"When? Where'd she go?" His words were challengingly
abrupt. He changed tone hastily. "This is most urgent. I'm very
worried about her, and I'd appreciate anything you could tell
me. I . . ." He hesitated. "I'm her doctor—Dr. Galen. She's
been in a state of hysterical shock. Would you say she appeared hysterical?"

"No, Doctor, she didn't give me that idea. She was quiet
and calm and kept to herself. She got a telegram a little past
four this afternoon. Just afterward she checked out. She didn't
offer to give a forwarding address and we didn't inquire."

"She was alone, wasn't she?"

"Yes."

"You have any idea if she went to a bus station, or train
depot, or the airport? Perhaps she took a cab from the hotel?"

"I know she didn't use any of the cabs stationed here, Doctor, because one of the drivers stationed here mentioned it to
the bellboy. She walked away with her suitcase and turned the
next corner. There's a bus station up that way, but . . . We
can't say. Maybe that's where she went, but . . ."

"I understand. She had a suitcase, then? She left here without one."

"Well, it was quite inexpensive—something you can get in drugstores."

"Tell me, are you a clerk? What's your name?"

"I'm a clerk. John Latham."

"If you'd give me your home address . . . Is anyone listening?"

"No, sir, Doctor."

"If you can tell me what was in that telegram, who sent it, where it was from, I'll send you fifty dollars."

"I'm awfully sorry, Doctor. It came here to the desk, closed, and it was sent up."

"A hundred dollars. Cash. To your home address. Her family is terribly worried about her. I'll send it registered tonight."

"Believe me I could use that. I'm sorry, but I didn't see it. I couldn't even look in her wastebasket because she carried the telegram away with her. I really can't give you any more information."

Charles opened the door, beckoned to Syl. "How was she dressed?"

Syl told him. He repeated to the hotel clerk, who confirmed it.

He came out of the phone booth frowning and left the store with Syl. "Well, you weren't lying on that," he granted when they got in the car.

"Not with murder involved I wouldn't."

"Let me think . . . let me think," he said, half to himself, his fists unconsciously clenching and unclenching on the wheel as he stared out the window at nothing. Abruptly he nodded his head, started the car. "That must be his next move!"

"What?"

"Never mind. On the way you can get right with me . . . and with yourself, Syl."

"I want to, believe me I do," she said earnestly.

"Tell me from the first. How you got in with Measles, the details of the con game, as many as you know."

"I met him three months ago at the Merry Land Club while I was on a date with Phil de Verre . . ."

"Philip de Verre?" he asked sharply, shifting his attention

from the street traffic. "The lawyer who arranged for my parole?"

She nodded emphatically. "Phil was tight and boasting. He had a lot of cash he'd never reported as income. This Measles Edwards was standing near, playing roulette, and he started giving me a play. I went for him. We dated, and he began to feel around about De Verre. I told Edwards to come out with it, that I smelled a rat. He admitted it was less my charms than Phil's cash money he was interested in, and that he was a con man. Which gave me a big kick."

"It gave him a big kick," Charles said sourly, "to think of himself as a con man. He was a forger!"

"Maybe he *was*. But anyway, he played a con game on De Verre. I introduced him to Phil as a scion of an old, aristocratic Southern family who was now connected with the gambling syndicate, supposedly a big man in New Orleans, Miami, Chicago. This was perfect for Phil de Verre—not only socially proper but exciting and sinister. Measles Edwards really took Phil in. Good manners, good tailors, a smooth, lavish host —lots of cornpone dialogue about the old plantation days of grandpappy, plus name-dropping of underworld gangsters. Phil even thought he met some of the real big shots. Edwards took him to New Orleans and showed him the old plantation and oh, scores of convincers. You know."

"You mean De Verre was the sucker in the con swindle?"

"Yes. He had $150,000 cash."

"I heard it that the victim was a slot-machine manufacturer. Grig Proctor at the Merry Land Club gave me that impression," he said uneasily. He didn't like the implications of Proctor's deceiving him.

"Well," Syl said, "the play did involve slot machines and a manufacturer. Except the manufacturer wasn't authentic; just a shill. A convincer for Philip de Verre." She mouthed the jargon words as if they were succulent. "The pitch was this: Measles Edwards had a chance to invest some of his own cash capital in a manufacturing and distributing corporation handling the slot machines which were used by the syndicate all over the country. But he didn't have enough to swing it alone. The profits would be enormous because they would have a monopoly and because it was so dangerous, shipping across state lines in violation of Federal laws. Measles introduced him to Grig Proctor who showed them the system for getting the illegal machines through to the different outlets, such as the Merry Land Club. Supposedly they came in hardware crates, and came through this Statewide Warehouse. He was allowed to see the crates at the warehouse, and in the basement of the Merry Land Club, and a foreman out there . . ."

"Poley? A big, tough guy?"

"Yes. Well, Poley acted like he was in the 'know' and part of the underground system. Phil de Verre thought he saw the workings with his own eyes. Actually, it was a laugh, because Statewide hasn't a thing to do with shipping slot machines."

"You mean De Verre was given the story and shown crates, etc., and told about the parolees and ex-cons who worked there?"

"Yes. Everything was worked out with a lot of careful, convincing detail. You know."

"I know," Charles said.

"Even you were supposed to be in on it."

"Me?"

"That job at Statewide. De Verre got it for you because he was made to believe you'd do what you were told."

"Or get slapped back into prison! No wonder he was so willing to step down out of the castle and get me a parole. I thought he did it as a favor to Jerry."

"So did Jerry. Phil de Verre does his favors for De Verre. Statewide sponsored your parole by the job offer because Phil de Verre pulled strings with some people who know one of the big stockholders."

"I see . . . Well, when did the playoff on the con game come? And where? And how'd Brattsford come into it?"

"The playoff was three days ago in a suite in the National Hotel. In the afternoon. Brattsford had been in it all along. He helped build up De Verre's confidence in Measles Edwards by going behind Measles's back to De Verre and trying to double-cross Measles—squeeze him out. De Verre and Measles were gentlemen and men of honor and they were mistrustful of Brattsford. Two fake FBI agents walked in on them to arrest Measles and De Verre and some others. Measles knocked the

FBI men out, tied them up in a closet, then got into a fight with Brattsford, saying he'd double-crossed them and squealed. Then Measles shot Brattsford . . . or pretended to."

"So De Verre was really scared. In the shuffle the money vanished, eh?"'

"Yes. So did Brattsford. Proctor thinks he lammed with the money. Proctor's money, too. He financed Measles . . . all his living and entertainment and travel expenses. Plus $50,000 cash, which Measles had to put into the deal in order to look like an authentic co-investor with De Verre."

"So there was $200,000 cash, including De Verre's. Brattsford vanished right after the blowoff . . . so did the money. Then it's worth plenty to Measles . . . that murder. . . . What a tear-off rat he is!"

They had reached his street. His attention focused on the dreary old building housing his apartment as he cruised past. The lower apartments and the upper one across the hall were lit. His own was dark. He scanned all the cars parked along the street and saw none occupied. He parked on down the street. Whether or not there was a trap waiting he had to go.

"We'll both go," he said quietly, getting out.

They crossed the street and headed back. He glanced warily around as they turned in along the cracked and tilted walk toward the building. No one followed. They made the porch. He could see that the lower hall and stairs to the landing were empty. He went inside, peering toward the mailboxes. There was something in his. His heart quickened as he opened the box. As he had expected, there was a letter in Nora's writing. It was on a Line City Hotel envelope. He took it and went back outside, cautioning Syl:

"Quiet. We're going up the back way."

They went down from the porch, crossed to the side of the building, and went to the back. They went up the steps to the upper rear porch. He let himself into his apartment. Syl followed. He took out the gun and flashlight, shot the beam into bathroom, kitchen, dining room, and moved through to the hall, the light feeling ahead. There was no one in the front room or bedroom. The bedroom blinds were closed and he urged Syl in, shut the door, and turned on the overhead light.

The straight-mail letter from Line City had been postmarked at 11:45 P.M. last night. Her bus should have arrived there by eleven or so. He tore the envelope carefully, removed the contents. There was a hundred-dollar bill folded in the letter! He frowned; then aware of Syl's watching him, glanced sharply, almost defensively at her.

The letter on Line City Hotel stationery was Nora's hand-writing, or a good copy. He had to put it down on the bureau top for a moment because his hands were suddenly too shaky to hold it. He picked it up again and read:

Charles dearest:

I will be waiting for you in Chicago. Darling, I'm forwarding some cash. Fly here and use the name Carl Gare when you register at the State Street Hotel. Hurry. Trust me, sweetheart, as I trust you. It will be all right about the money and everything. I will get in touch with you when you arrive. All our troubles will be over and we will have a new life. The beat of thy heart is the pulse in my veins.

Always love, always your

Nora.

Her writing, her phrasings. An intimate, compelling letter capable of pulling him blindly to her. A letter calculated to make him suspect she had taken guilty flight because she had killed Brattsford . . . and perhaps robbed him. A letter he couldn't ignore, didn't dare ignore (*The beat of thy heart is the pulse in my veins*), a letter cunningly manipulating all the softness and love and tender concern and fears in him. His mouth tightened. He strode to the closet, yanked it open.

He pointed in, said to Syl across his shoulder: "Right here he was. Brattsford," he said huskily. "Stabbed to death." He got his suitcase from the closet, lay it on the bed. He gave Syl the letter. "Read it!" he said bleakly. He opened the suitcase, got out the thick packet of letters he had received in prison from Nora. He shuffled hastily through. They were out of sequence.

"Are you going to her?" Syl whispered.

"Hell, no! He's trying to get me to lam out of town as if

I'm running. Guilty and running! No, by God! No! Never!"

He began to open Nora's old letters. Clearly, Measles had been here, using these letters, since last night. And the chances were Measles was in town. Innocently on the scene. Trying to prove that Charles was the killer and thief. Trying to sign his and probably Nora's death warrants.

"Here!" he said grimly. "Here's *one* sentence in that letter, you just read. 'Trust me, sweetheart, as I trust you.' A literal copy." He opened another and another letter in rapid succession, scanning swiftly. "Another! 'Darling I'm forwarding some cash.' Not, I'm *enclosing* some. Because she didn't enclose it. She forwarded it to the prison to be put to my account, see? Here's another. 'It will be all right about the money and everything.' She was talking about things as they'd be when I came home. And here: 'All our troubles will be over and we will have a new life.' This wasn't a forgery job. But a copy. He simply composed the letter out of exact copies of parts of her actual letters. And I'll stick him with it, believe me, I can stick him!"

"How? I want you to. I'm all on your side. All the way!"

"He'll be with the sucker, keeping him calm, keeping him from getting hysterical and confessing to the cops. Most of all he'll be right in evidence to prove to Grig Proctor that he's no thieving tear-off rat."

"But he's not at De Verre's. I've tried and tried to reach De Verre. I'm sure De Verre's out of town."

"We'll see about that!"

# 17

CHARLES STOOD ACROSS the ornate foyer from Syl in the big apartment building as she rang the lawyer De Verre's bell repeatedly. There was no response. She peered into the lobby toward the elevator, gnawing at her inner cheek. Then she rang again. Charles remained within the angle of inner and side wall, concealed from the inner lobby, his hand around the gun in his pocket. Syl looked questioningly at him, turned up her palm briefly.

"Go out to the main sidewalk," he decided. "Look up toward his windows. You'll be visible in the street light out there. They'll see who it is, and if you give an urgent, nervous impression they may think you've got something to tell them that's important to them."

She nodded and went out. He watched her pace and crane upward, fairly wringing her hands. The chance of finding De Verre and Measles here hadn't been bright in the first place. Still, if De Verre believed not only that he was involved in killing Brattsford but also in an attack on FBI agents, he would keep out of sight, and he could be convinced that leaving town would expose him. Playing a con game in the victim's own home town was against the basic principle of the racket, and a dangerous blunder. So it wasn't hopeless to think this part of the play was illogical, particularly since Charles was positive that Measles Edwards wanted to stay where Proctor could find him and divert suspicion from himself. Syl came back into the building and began to ring the bell insistently, rapidly.

There was a buzz. She unhooked the house phone. Charles stayed where he was, keeping out of view of the inner lobby.

"This is Syl. I must see you at once!" She listened for several seconds, then broke in: "It's *not* personal. That's done. I accepted it; I chase nobody. . . . No, I cannot tell you over this phone. This is damned important. . . ."

"Measles?" Charles whispered. Syl nodded.

"Of course I'm alone! Release the door catch and let me in, or you come down. . . ."

Charles motioned to her, said hurriedly, "Tell him another tenant's coming in and you can get in anyhow."

Her voice hushed into the phone: "Somebody came in. No . . . no . . . just someone who lives here and they're opening the inner door. . . ." She listened, then snapped, "No. I promise. I won't tip De Verre." She listened again.

"He's stalling," Charles said. "Turn the screws!"

"Damn you! You stalled till those tenants got through and locked the door again. All right! If you don't release that door catch instantly, I'm going to the police whether I land in jail, too, or not!"

There was a raucous buzz. Charles seized the knob of the

inner door, motioning violently to her. He ran across the empty lobby and entered the elevator. She caught up. He yanked her inside, pressed the "8" button. The doors rolled shut and the car started up.

"He's on ten," Syl said, panting a little. "Not eight."

"I know. I wanted to get on here fast, so he'll think—I hope—the elevator's being used by the tenants you said just went in. We're going to eight first. You'll show me the floor plan. Then you'll go down to the lobby and I'll go up by the stairs. Then you'll take the elevator up from the lobby to ten."

He took out the gun, released the safety. "When we get to eight, you'll show me the location of the apartment corresponding to De Verre's on ten. As fast as possible, because you're supposed to be in the lobby, impatient and ringing for the elevator. It should start down again within *seconds* after it stops. Don't mention that it went to eight. There's no indicator. You couldn't know. Now, when you get off at ten Measles will probably be watching the corridor from the apartment. He'll see you're alone. That'll help. But when you get to the apartment, stall. You're nervous, fumbly. Get it? You'll be fooling with the clasp of your purse. In the doorway drop it, open, so it spills. If possible, he should be inside the apartment, not looking in the corridor. That's to give me a chance to get from the stairway door to the apartment. But better take off your scarf and be carrying it. If he's got a gun, drop the scarf instead of the purse. Got it?"

She nodded. "I'm nervous. I stall. I drop my purse there in the apartment doorway, and things spill out. Keep him from looking out into the corridor . . ."

"If possible. But if he's got a gun . . . ?"

"I drop my scarf."

"Right!"

"He threw it in my face," Syl said viciously. "That tramp he dropped me for! He thinks I'm panting for him, chasing him! I'll chase him to death, that's what I'll chase him!"

"Calm down!" Charles snapped. "You'll blow everything!"

"Calm," she said tightly. "Calm. I am. You *get* him!"

The elevator slowed, settled to a cushioned stop. Charles loosened then resettled his grip on the gun as the doors rolled open. He expected nothing, but he was alert as he stepped out, his gaze jumping right-left in lightning flicks. The corridor was empty. Syl pointed toward the front at the apartment corresponding to De Verre's, then pushed the "1" button. The door rolled shut, and Charles went at a cat tread to the stairway door. He didn't open it but stood, gun ready, at the opening edge, watching, waiting. Measles might have anticipated this play and listened from the stairwell above. He might come down to see who had got off the elevator. Charles listened and watched. The door didn't move. Measles could be waiting him out on the other side of that door.

Charles pulled the door open very slowly.

No one on this floor. He moved cautiously into the stairwell, his gun angled upward toward the midpoint landing where the steps turned between floors. There was no one up there. He ascended stealthily, paused at the landing, searched upward. He went on up to the ninth-floor landing. For several seconds he stood, motionless and silent, breathing through his open lips, listening to the descent of the elevator. The gray concrete steps, the iron handrails and newel posts smacked unpleasantly of prison. The light was flat, dull. He moved across to the ninth-floor exit door, peering upward. The midpoint landing was clear, and no one was on the steps of the half-flight leading up to ten. He risked moving to the newel post from which he could see, in the gap between stair railings, from basement to roof. He looked up, prepared to see someone looking down. No one.

He waited. He heard the elevator's machinery stop. In a moment it started again and Syl was coming up. There was an emptiness to the stairwell, an oppressive, tomblike air. Its utter silence began to work on his nerves. His finger curled and relaxed on the gun trigger. His palm was sweaty. Maybe he should get up there to the tenth floor. He forced himself to stay where he was and to remain utterly soundless, not even daring to shift his weight for fear of a gritty noise under his shoe. He was positive, absolutely positive, that Measles would be wary enough to check this stairway, particularly in the face of Syl's delay.

Then it came. Almost thunderous in the wake of the long-strained silence. The snick and hiss of a lighted match. From overhead! Charles heard the door on the floor above open and thump shut. He stepped noiselessly across the landing, pressed himself into the corner, the point which was as far as possible from the door and out of view to anyone peering down from the newel on the floor above. It was possible that Measles, or someone, had lighted a smoke and then actually left the stairwell. It wasn't likely!

Then he heard it. A cautious descent. Only a few steps. Charles could visualize it. Slow, crouched, peering down through the widening angle from between the iron uprights of the handrails. Seeing the door and the area just before it. He would have to come clear to the midpoint landing before he could see Charles. Charles aimed his gun, waited for a glimpse of his legs. Charles would see him first!

But Measles, or whoever it was, satisfied himself without coming clear down to the landing. Charles heard him go back up and leave, really leave the stairwell he was sure.

Charles went hurriedly up to the next floor. He heard the elevator stop. Then he could hear Syl's step passing the stairway door. He pushed the door open a slit. Measles stood in the open doorway of De Verre's apartment holding a gun. As Syl neared the apartment, Measles kept watching the elevator. At last, satisfied no one else had come with her, he lowered the gun. Syl reached the threshold of the apartment, gave a short, exasperated cry, and dropped her scarf *and* her purse, spilling its contents. Measles had retreated into the apartment, and Charles heard him swear at her. She pawed out, trying to retrieve scarf and purse, and then she crouched in the doorway, feeling out clumsily for her things, babbling out a string of nervous apologies. Charles slipped out of the stairwell and was down the corridor at the edge of De Verre's door by the time she regained her feet. Charles pushed in ahead of her, bringing the gun forward at hip level and imbedding the barrel in Measles's gut.

Measles brought his gun up, tried to back away. Charles pressed forward, keeping the advantage of bodily contact. Measles would have to aim and fire. Charles would only have to fire.

"Drop it!" Charles ordered.

"Stop this!" a hysterical male voice shouted. "Garrell, how dare you?" It was Philip de Verre, unshaven, disheveled, almost unrecognizable as the smooth, grand-mannered, silver-maned corporation counsel glamour-struck by crime. He just looked struck now—shaky, terrified, completely demoralized. And a little drunk.

"Don't *you* monkey with me any more, De Verre," Charles said levelly, his eyes turning to him briefly. De Verre's glance skittered away, seeking shelter. Charles rammed forward with the gun in Measles's gut. He said in a barely audible voice:

"It's private. Between you and me. I won't rumble De Verre and knock your racket, but drop the gun. If the gun's in your hand when I count three, I'll kill you. ONE!" Measles's eyes met his defiantly. He held onto the gun. Charles raised his voice. "Syl, shut the door. TWO. . . ." He heard the door close behind him. The blood had pulled from Measles's face, leaving it blotchy with ugly brown freckles. The boyish charm was nowhere in evidence. He was going to drop the gun. It was clear in his eyes and in the sickening around the edges of his mouth. "THREE!"

The gun dropped. Charles picked it up, pocketed it. "Turn around and walk through the apartment. We'll see who's here."

"There's no one else," Measles announced with an air of condescension.

It was pure reflex. Charles's free fist smashed into Measles's chin. The impact was solid and gratifying. Measles's teeth clicked, his head snapped back, and he staggered backward. Charles followed, ready to drop him if he asked for it.

"Infamous," De Verre croaked. "Striking a man . . ."

Charles gave him a brief scathing look of contempt, turned back to Measles. "Get going!"

They went through the place. Charles was satisfied that no one else was there. He stopped Measles in a little hall off the front room.

"Where's my wife?"

"I don't know what you're talk . . ."

Charles smashed his face, banging the back of his head resoundingly into the wall. Measles's eyes rolled and he began to wobble and sag, semi-conscious. "If you give me one more

stall, Edwards," he said dispassionately, "I'll let you live and
wish you were dead. I'll slice your face to ribbons and leave
you looking like . . . I don't know. You figure it. But that's
only the half of it. I'll fix you downstairs so you can't go near
a woman. Is that clear?"

"Don't lose your head, Charley! I never touched your woman!
She's O.K. in Chi."

"Where? Phone her!"

"Alvin Hotel. She's maybe not got there yet, but . . ."

"What name? Joan Arrell . . . like you had her use in Line
City?"

"Sure. Joan Arrell. And look, Charley, it ain't near as bad
as you think. I can explain the whole . . ."

"I know you can, and will. First." He pushed Measles into
the front room, toward the phone. "No," he decided. He nodded
at Syl. "You make the call. Joan Arrell. Alvin Hotel, Chicago.
That's it, Edwards?"

"So help me God!"

"I demand to know," De Verre began as Syl started the
call, "the meaning of . . ."

"Shut up!" Charles snapped at him. "I can blast you to
hell. I know all about a certain dead man, and a big deal of
yours concerning slot machines, and a pair of FBI agents. If
you think everything's being cooled off and fixed for you, by
God, just monkey with me and I'll surprise you."

De Verre looked desperately at Measles, who nodded gravely.
Charles stood over Syl who was speaking in a low, rapid voice
over the phone. She nodded up at him. He kept his eye on De
Verre and Measles, but they had become unimportant. Everything seemed to disintegrate and to reintegrate within him. He
felt a slow, seething rise of excitement. It was warm, expanding. Her nearness . . . minutes, maybe only seconds away
from the sound of her voice! He hadn't realized the meaning of
this . . . this was *it*. What the hell else mattered? There was a
gun in his hand; there was De Verre and Syl and Measles,
enemies, and there wasn't room in him to hate their guts.

"She's registered," Syl said. "They're ringing her room."

"I'll take it," he told Syl, "the phone. I'll hold it." His voice
was vibrant; he wanted to let his face break loose into a silly

grin; he wanted to clear the rest of them out. He sat down. He got up. It was surging in him. Joy. His eyes misted.

There was a faint, unrecognizable "Hello" from the phone and the operator's. "I have a person-to-person call for Joan Arrell. Is this Joan Arrell?"

"Yes." It was Nora's sweet-soft voice, uncertain and afraid.

"Darling, it's me!" Charles burst in. "Baby, you all right?"

"Here's your party, sir. Go ahead."

"Charles! Is that you, is that you? Where are you? What's wrong? I want to *see* you! I can't stand this . . . I . . ." She started to cry.

"Be calm. Don't cry. It's all right now. All right. Are you safe? Alone?"

"I'm alone . . . safe."

"Got money?"

"About sixty left from the hundred you sent by that man."

"A freckled-faced, good-looking man? Did you go from the depot last night and meet him in the Supreme Hotel? He the one who put you on the bus to Line City?"

"Yes . . . yes. Your note came to the depot that you wouldn't be on the train; then this man—Jimmy Cain, he said his name was, he'd come to the restaurant the day before and asked when your train got in, saying he was your friend from there" —she meant prison—"and he had another note from you and money. The note said you'd have to leave the state and break parole, and I must tell no one where I was going, and I must use this name . . ."

He cut in: "He's a forger. It was all a part of a scheme of his. Did you send me a letter from Line City last night?"

"No. I didn't. I wasn't to write, and I tore up your notes. I got the telegram from you—Carl Gare was the name—this afternoon telling me to leave Line City for here, and to wait here for further word. You didn't send that telegram either, is that it?"

"That's it. Did it come from this city?"

"Yes. Sent at two fifty-five. I got it just past four. Darling, I'm out of my head. What shall I do? I *want* you, dearest, I . . ." Her voice broke again.

"Come home. It's all being cleared up. Get out of that hotel at once, baby. Go direct to the airport and wait there for the next plane home. I'll meet you here and explain everything, and it's going to be all right."

"I'll come. First plane. I love you."

After he had hung up he became aware of Measles cracking his knuckles, Syl frowning at the floor, De Verre looking uncomfortably away. Charles felt the coldness on his face. Unaware, he had cried with her. He wiped his face. He realized, with shamed anger, that they had seen him naked, his most private emotions exposed. He got up, his head thrusting forward a little, and he started for Measles slowly.

"Now," he whispered. "Now. No gun. Just you and me. Nobody's going to interfere."

Measles moved agilely back across the room toward the little hall. "Wait," he said, shaking his head, holding out one hand, palm open. "We could deal."

Charles laughed coarsely; quickened his pace. He caught up and spat in his face. Measles wiped at it numbly, without lifting a hand in defense. Charles drove his fist into the hand on his face. Measles retreated, turning into the hallway. Charles pressed him, threatening to strike, not striking; backing him until there would be no further retreat. He kept looking at Measles's face, liking the cowering, intimidated expression he saw. He lashed out suddenly, knocking Measles down. He stood over him, hands cocked, a gloating feeling of power in him. Measles tried to stay down. Charles drew back his foot. Measles scrambled up and Charles got set to hammer his face into a bloody pulp. He was aware of the grimace on his own face. There was a high flush on his cheeks and a brilliance to his eyes. Abruptly he felt self-conscious and guilty because his grimace was phony, a mask for a grin! A sense of revulsion swept him as he realized he was looking, acting, thinking, and feeling like a prison screw! Measles had a beating coming, and it would be simple to rationalize himself, except that he knew, he couldn't blind himself to the knowledge. . . . He wanted to administer a beating for its own sake, indulge himself in a kind of pleasure that degraded him. If he let himself yield to an orgy of hate, he'd be admitting they had broken him. Proving what they said back in stir, that the man who went into prison never came out—a stranger came out. Nora had something better coming to her than a stranger turned vicious.

"What's the deal?" he asked Measles.

"Money." Measles composed himself, repeated, "Money." Charles waited, watching him coldly.

"Ten grand," Measles offered.

"Don't make me laugh. A hundred and fifty thousand from De Verre plus fifty from Proctor. Out of two hundred grand you can do much better."

"So Syl told you about the con game. And you think I was a tear-off rat and hijacked the game?"

"What's your story?"

"Proctor got it. Brattsford was responsible for the money when the blowup came. After we blew De Verre, Brattsford was supposed to handle the suitcase with the cash. But he vanished. I think he was held, drugged probably, somewhere. By now he's probably actually dead."

There was nothing to be read in Measles's face. Charles wavered. "Wait a minute, wait a minute. How could you offer me even ten Gs? Where would you get such money?" Even as he said it he could think of several explanations.

"There was a boat ride down at the Fairgrounds track in New Orleans. Proctor was financing me while I was building De Verre up, so I had some cash to play with."

"Well, I know you put my wife on the send! She told me, so did Syl. I also talked to Sam Keech. You hired him to help you get in my place and forge those notes to Nora."

"Orders. From Proctor."

"Why? Just what did he order?"

"Well, two days ago, the day before you got home from stir, Grig Proctor came here—to this apartment. He and one of his hoods, Jack Pake, took me in the bedroom, private, and said everything was fouled, and I'd have to do something if I wanted my cut from the con game. I was to go see your wife at her restaurant, find out when you were due in. Then I was to hire a *gonif*, get in your place, and write notes to her—get her out of the way."

"I'm going to phone Proctor."

"That's up to you. But be careful. Like I said, I think Brattsford's really dead. Grig Proctor has to have a fall guy. I've been scared crazy thinking I'm it. Maybe you're it."

"Why?" Charles demanded. "I mean, why would *he* hijack the game? He's got plenty, And why would he risk murder?"

"Why did Rockefeller want another million? And what's risky about murder to a guy that owns as much law as Grig Proctor does?" Measles said reasonably. "Especially when he can provide a fall guy."

"Why should he want to put my wife on the send?" Charles said. He felt inane. Measles could answer that one and make it sound good . . . and it might even be so, that was the hell of it.

"He told *me* that it was because she'd tip off De Verre. Or when you got home she'd tell you she hadn't been able to contact him and you'd cause trouble. Because you've heard about the con game over the prison vine. You'd try to cut in and make trouble. If I had doubts, Charley, I also kept it in mind that Grig Proctor could fix me for keeps. I'll admit this. I smelled something. But I thought: it's me or Charley."

"God damn you, I could take that part. If it was me or you and I had to choose, I'd throw you to the wolves every time. But what my wife's been put through . . ." He broke off, shaking his head, as if trying to clear it. It wasn't what *had* happened to Nora, but what *might*. He kept telling himself Measles was a smooth fake, a professional liar, cheat, forger, but beneath that certainty was another knowledge. He wanted to believe Measles had hijacked that game and murdered Brattsford, because he was an easier enemy than Proctor.

"I feel guilty about your wife, I sincerely do, Charley. I could make that fifteen grand. The two of you could be in the peso country in twenty-four hours. I'd like to help you lam. She's a nice girl. She loves you to hell, and that's something damned precious in this crappy world. I've been a wrongo too long to be anything else, but you know nobody's all rat. If I've helped bitch you up, I can square it a little."

Charles just looked at him earnestly. On the surface Measles was convincing, but that blend of boyish innocence and the broad, wholesome-looking features were part of his stock in trade. His gaze was straight, his voice serious, his admissions disarming, and of course the tribute to Nora and the contrition were powerful appeals. Certainly it was true that nobody was all rat, and there wasn't a human alive who didn't want to square himself sometimes. Charles thought he himself would be in a bad way it he'd lost the capacity to trust anything. He fumbled in his pockets, one after another, doubting Measles, doubting himself, his power of decision paralyzed. He felt the towel-wrapped packet of letters and Brattsford's wrist watch which he'd taken from Sam Keech. He felt the letters he had taken from his suitcase an hour ago, the ones from which the letter postmarked Line City, 11:45 P.M. last night had been composed. His glance jerked toward the entrance of the hall. Syl and De Verre had come quietly.

"What's happening?" Syl said nervously.

"Never mind. Leave us alone a minute." He looked uncertainly at Measles when they'd gone. He took out the Line City letter, opened it. He held the letter in one hand, the $100 bill in the other, moved to Measles's side.

"Did you write this, and enclose this money?" he said gravely.

Measles peered, reading it. Charles watched his profile, the faint motion of his lips. Measles turned his face, wide-eyed.

"No!" he said hoarsely.

"That letter," Charles said carefully, "is clearly meant to get me out of the state. I'll be a parole violator. And it could look to Grig Proctor as if I was lamming with the dough."

"I see it. I see that, Charley. And my God, they'd nab you. He's probably tipped them off."

"Or you've tipped them off."

"No, no," he protested swiftly. "Why would I?"

"If you killed him and hijacked that game, the why is easy. It clears you in Proctor's eyes. He'd put two and two together, figure I'd cached the money. He'd grab my wife, turn her over to Jack Pake, maybe, if she didn't tell where the loot was. He would never believe she didn't know. Jack Pake would change her face, slowly, with acid, the way he fixed a girl I heard about today. This letter, Measles, is postmarked 11:45 P.M. last night, from Line City. My wife got there around eleven. She could have mailed it. She didn't. Where were you last night?"

"Right here. Keeping De Verre from the sweats . . . keeping

him from breaking and running to the cops and confessing all. You know he's scared and dangerous. . . ."

Charles stepped into the front room. De Verre was in the middle of the room, standing by Syl. "Mr. de Verre, will you come here a moment?"

Charles glanced warily back at Measles, who had made no move, and who looked thoroughly calm. De Verre came, saw their expressions, and drew a long breath. He tried to stand erect.

"What," he said with an effort at dignity, "do you wish?"

"Don't look at him." De Verre faced Charles, firming his features. "Was he here with you last night?"

"He was."

"What time?"

"I should say from eight-thirty on through the night."

Measles put in: "He's not afraid of me. He's afraid of you. He wouldn't lie."

"As God is my witness," De Verre said ponderously, "I told you the truth. He's been here almost continually. He was out a few hours this afternoon, and early last evening. From six till about eight-thirty. Otherwise . . ."

"You can go. Thanks," Charles said. "Six to eight-thirty. You met Nora at six forty-five. Put her on the seven-o'clock bus." His voice was a monotone, a thinking aloud. "From my apartment here is a half-hour, a little less. If you'd left at eight-five . . ."

"I could have got here. Yes. But after all, Charley, I'm not superman. I'd have had to get from downtown at seven o'clock to your place. Half-hour. I'd have had to get Brattsford. I'd have had to get him into your place. Knock him out, put him in the closet. Stab him. Get out by eight or eight-five, in order to get back here by eight-thirty."

Charles's eyes widened. "So you know about the closet. You *know* he's dead. Awhile ago you said you *thought* he might be. But you know . . ."

"Hold it . . . hold that temper, Charley. Sam Keech. I saw him just an hour or so ago. He told me you made him talk. He told me about seeing the stiff, and stealing the wrist watch. The time element, for God's sake. It would be impossible for me to have done it, don't you see? *You* were due any minute. You'd have caught me red-handed. Figure it out, guy, figure it out!"

"Tight it figures. So tight it alibis you! But you mentioned you suspect he was drugged. An autopsy will show he probably was. You had this all set up and timed to the minute. You had him waiting, doped, ready to take him to my place. You had been there, prowled it, knew just what you were going to do. You could even have had him in your car, downtown, drugged, waiting. Then you drive hellbent to my place. Get there by seven-twenty or seven twenty-five. He was just dopey enough to walk. You took him up. Into the closet. Knocked him out right there. Then got the bedclothes, stabbed him through them. Fifteen minutes. You then hid the bedclothes where I wouldn't find them, but the cops would. You remade the bed. You could have done it all by eight o'clock."

"I'm crazy, you think? Crazy. Your train was due in at seven-eighteen. You could've hopped a cab and come home at once and caught me."

"My train was due at seven-five."

Measles flushed. "I know, but it was late."

"Sure you know. Because you checked. And you knew damned well I wouldn't rush out of the station. I'd wait, just as I did, expecting her any minute . . . making phone calls, etc. You could count on it that I wouldn't leave for twenty minutes. From seven-twenty, when I got down into the station, to about seven-forty you knew I'd be in that station. And a cab ride would take half an hour, you could figure. I wouldn't get there before eight in any case, that was almost certain. In fact, I didn't leave the depot till eight. Anyhow, what if I *had* come? You were armed and could have jumped me. But I fouled you on one thing. I moved the body. You thought I'd lam or take a chance reporting to the cops."

"Why didn't I tip Homicide at once?"

"Before the corpse was cold?" Charles said scornfully. "And tip it off that it was a frame? Even Homicide would know I wouldn't be likely to inform on myself."

"You're too imaginative, Charley . . . too much time brooding back there in stir . . . too much suspicion. A friend tries to give you a boost with fifteen grand . . ."

"And then a double-cross so Proctor can find me with all that cash, and good-by, Charley. Oh, no, you son of a—"

Syl's sharp warning cry and the commotion in the front room made Charles spin. He dug for the gun, headed out of the little hall into the front room.

# 18

THE GUN in his hand, the .38 revolver he'd taken from Sam Keech, felt insignificant against the pair of .45 automatics coming down the room toward him. One of them was blued-steel, and in the hand of a foxy-faced, nervous-eyed hood he had never seen; the other was a brownish luster, gunmetal color, carried by Proctor's stony-faced hood Jack Pake. Proctor himself, looking like a sport on the town in black felt hat, black coat with white silk muffler, and patent-leather shoes, balanced on one foot at the other end of the room and kicked the door shut behind him. Unarmed and casual, he watched his boys in action.

"Drop it, Garrell," Jack Pake said, coming fast toward him, off to the right. The other hood moved at Jack's pace, on Charles's left. It was a neat, systematized flanking. Charles remembered the second gun in his pocket, the one he'd taken from Measles. De Verre, terror-stricken in the middle of the room, remembered the gun, too . . . so did Syl. They both stared at Charles, a sort of frozen hysteria in the expressions, knowing the grisly potentialities if he chose to start blasting. Proctor seemed indifferent, crediting him with more brains than the others did. Charles lowered the gun.

Measles moved swiftly, snatched the gun from his hand and yanked the second one out of Charles's pocket. De Verre and Syl resumed breathing.

"Take him, boys," Measles clipped.

"Say, Edwards," Proctor said with dry mockery, starting down the room, "that was a bit of all right, old boy. Disarmed the blighter and saved our hides, you did! What say, lads, a rousing cheer for Our Hero!"

Jack Pake gave Measles a look, very thoughtful, as if he was wondering how a little acid would go with his face. Measles switched lines as Proctor reached them.

"Grig, you're a lifesaver. Literally. This cheap stick-up mug was going to kill me . . . all of us."

Proctor gave Measles a bland look of contempt. "I'll take those guns," he said, holding out his hand. Measles hesitated, then turned them over. Proctor slid them into his side pockets, then looked coolly at Charles.

"Why the gunplay, Garrell?"

"This guy's a tear-off rat and a killer," Charles said tightly.

"Grig," Measles moved urgently to Proctor's side, whispered something. Proctor's brows shot up.

"Well, then," he exploded, "get your ass to that phone and stop her!"

"Who?" Charles demanded.

Measles had gone to the phone.

"He says," Proctor said evenly, "that your lady and . . ." Proctor broke off, looked at De Verre. "Sorry to disturb you, Counsellor, but would you wait for me in the next room?" Proctor winked at him, then took him by the arm, walked to the door with him, talking in a confidential undertone. Coming back without De Verre, he muttered to the foxy-faced hood, "Get in there and keep the savage cool." Charles moved toward Measles at the phone.

"Who's Edwards calling?" Charles insisted.

"He tells me your lady and the two hundred grand are about to emplane from Chi to old May-hee-co. He's having her stopped."

Charles yanked the handset from Measles. "Wait!"

It was a rash move. Both Proctor and Jack Pake started for him.

"Wait! Don't let him call. He's lying, Proctor! He kidnaped my wife . . . put her on the send. Now he wants to have her killed, so she'll never have a chance to spill to you. Don't let him call!"

Proctor stood facing him. "Give him that phone!"

"I'll rip it out of the wall first! He's trying to frame me. He'll kill her."

"Garrell's leveling," Syl cried, running to Proctor. "I saw Edwards put her on a bus last night. He forged notes and tricked her out of town before Garrell's train got him home from prison. Ask Edwards why!"

Measles affected a sneering smile. "She's a good girl, Grig. Loyal to whoever she's sleeping with."

"Filthy liar!" Syl said scornfully.

Charles held onto the phone. Proctor's eyes bored into him. Charles could feel Jack Pake close behind him, waiting for Proctor's signal to slug him. "Ask De Verre," Charles said, "or Syl. I didn't know where my wife was. I forced Edwards to tell me. I phoned her from right here . . . they can tell you."

"For witnesses," Measles said, laughing sourly, "he brings in an Honest John and his sleeping partner."

Proctor ignored him. He pointed to his chest. *"I told you,"* he said, and jabbed Charles's chest, "to give him the phone!" It had became a personal issue with Proctor. Charles was positive Measles would have Nora killed. There was little chance of actually disabling the phone, and that would amount to a small delay at most, while he was getting a beating. Pake and the other hood would love to get into action. That stony-faced hood gave him an idea—a tricky one.

Charles said quietly to Proctor, "Well? Edwards double-crossed you once. Are you going to let him con you again just to show me who's boss?"

There was a hellish moment of silence. Grig Proctor's face turned murderous. Measles looked smug. Proctor laughed abruptly. "Sure, sure. I'm trying to make a big impression on you! I'm childish. So, humor me, huh? Give him the phone. Then I play boss some more and tell Edwards to hang it up."

Charles nodded, gave Measles the phone. "Grig," Measles said, "time's important. Let me contact this buddy in Chi and put him on her tail."

"Humor me, Edwards. Hang it up!" Measles did it. Proctor nodded. "The call waits. If she hops a plane and makes it to old May-hee-co. So? I could use a trip south, amigo. Now, we all sit down . . . you there in that chair, Edwards. You in that one, Garrell. Duchess, you and me'll take the sofa and sit facing them. My friend Jack Pake will stand, the sergeant at arms, eh, Jack?"

Jack regarded Proctor's joviality with mild disgust, said nothing. Charles had noticed Pake's surliness with Proctor last night in the Merry Land Club, and he'd noticed that Pake was nonetheless trusted completely. Now that the touchy moment was past, Charles was glad he'd taken a chance and given Proctor some lip. Charles sat. Measles was in a chair out of his reach on the left. Jack Pake stood to his right. Proctor and Syl were in front of him, with a strip of carpet and a coffee table separating them.

"We'll take it slow," Proctor said. "You first, Edwards. Tell me a tale. It didn't enter my innocent head for a long time that an operator like you would have the guts to double-cross Grig Proctor. Maybe I was overconfident. Now you tell me a tale that'll prove you're just as gutless as I thought."

Measles doubled forward with laughter. "Man, you're priceless!"

"Let's quit running for office. Tell the tale!"

"It's simple. That .38 in your pocket, one of the two you took off of Garrell, belongs to a thief, Sam Keech. Grig, you know Sam?"

"Tell the tale, tell the tale!"

"I happened to see Sam Keech late this afternoon. He put the arm on me. And you know me . . . I kicked through. Jeez, the poor slob has been down on his luck so bad and he was so grateful it was pitiful. He asks me can I help him, because Slugger Garrell here had given him a working over . . . taken his gun and threatened his life . . . and he said Garrell wanted to frame him for a kill! I said to Sam, what the hell's he giving you a bad time about anyway? So Sam spilled . . ." He paused nervously, glanced at Charles, then said to Jack Pake: "Watch him, Jack."

"You can learn Jack his business later," Proctor said, watching Charles.

Charles was reaching into one pocket after the other. He moved slowly, aware of Pake's gun. He put the contents of his pockets out on the coffee table. There was the packet, towel-wrapped, containing Brattsford's wrist watch, and the letters he'd taken from Sam Keech; there was a stack of Nora's letters which he'd got an hour ago from his suitcase. There was the letter from Line City and the $100 bill. He arranged them, his attention concentrated, as if he was unaware that Measles existed.

Measles blurted: "He makes me nervous. Tell him to quit interrupting."

Charles grinned at him, lit a smoke, and sat back. Proctor regarded Measles cynically.

"So Sam Keech spilled to you? Go right on!"

"Sam Keech said that he got a letter three days ago. The very day of the playoff with De Verre. This letter, with ten bucks enclosed, was from Garrell. From Garrell in prison. There was a note enclosed in the letter. Sam was to deliver the note to Garrell's wife. You know, the mail from stir is censored, so this note had to go to her through some other channel. Sam Keech was the channel. Well, that evening Sam Keech went to Garrell's apartment with the note. He's a *gonif* and he prowled the joint, and what the hell does he come across but a man— drugged. Doped unconscious. Sam gives him a frisk, finds it's none other than E. V. Brattsford. Get that, Grig! Right after the playoff, right after Brattsford and the 200Gs vanished, he was in Garrell's apartment, drugged. It's clear what happened. News of the con game got back to stir over the vine. Si Dawson, The Bargain Day Kid, always got scent of anything like that going on. Si liked Garrell and tipped him. Garrell then fixed up a deal with his wife to hijack that game. Garrell's wife lured him to her place and held him . . ."

"How'd it happen," Charles began, "that my wife made contact just when he had the loot on him, and . . ."

"Shut him up!" Measles pleaded. "There's more. It's no mystery how a woman lures a man, and Garrell had found out about the details of the con game and told her. She knew where to be and when . . . she obviously knew Brattsford *intimately* and he trusted her. . . ."

Syl tossed her head contemptuously. "I know that girl, and the idea of her having an affair with *anybody* is ridiculous. . . ."

"She was broke. Furthermore, you may not know it, but Brattsford was in a position to slap Garrell back into prison on an old gun charge. Lieutenant Gobi and Lieutenant Elton are our witnesses on *that* point, as Proctor knows. So shut up. Sam Keech actually saw Brattsford, last night, in the closet of Garrell's apartment. Dead. Stabbed. Last night! Get it. *After* Garrell got home. Sam Keech gave the apartment a prowl because he was sore at Garrell, who was supposed to pay him another yard, and was welching on him. So . . ."—Measles pointed dramatically at the wrist watch on the coffee table— "Sam lifted that watch off the corpse and was going to black-mail Garrell with it. But Garrell stalked him down this after-noon, got the jump on him, and took the evidence away from him. And, furthermore, Garrell made Sam put his fingerprint on the watch, and on some of the letters there, which Sam had heisted while he was about it."

"So," Proctor said, "you figure Garrell's wife held the vic-tim until Garrell could come home and murder him. And the plan now is to head out of the country. Why the delay?"

"The watch!" Measles exclaimed. "God, he had to find Sam Keech and get that watch back. I tried to get you by phone, Grig, and finally I sent that telegram. While I was waiting for you, in comes Syl, and Garrell back of her with a gun, and they got the jump on me. Now, can I contact that buddy in Chi and have that woman stopped?"

"No rush. You've told your tale. Now, Garrell."

"In the first place, why would I trust Sam Keech, with a stake like that involved? He'd have opened the note to my wife and cut himself in right away. He wouldn't have been worried about me paying him a measly yard. A cagey, old-time hot-goods operator like Brattsford wouldn't have let himself be lured with that money by a woman he had forced into an affair. And she certainly wasn't having an affair with him for the big money involved . . . or for *any* reason. Gobi and Elton can tell you what my apartment looks like. Not even front-room furniture."

"They've told me," Proctor said. "What she might do with money I don't know. Maybe she gambles or drinks or has a monkey on her back. But you tell me this, Garrell. Why did you borrow that truck of mine last night?"

Their eyes met. Proctor's blandness had turned cold and

deadly. He added softly, "And be careful to tell it straight."

Proctor knew! That was certain. "I used it to move Brattsford's body. It was, like Edwards claims, in my closet. It was
there when I came home. I had to move it. But I destroyed
the crate and everything that could have implicated you. I
also had to destroy some blood-soaked bedclothes with knife
holes through them which had been hidden in my apartment
. . . for the cops to find. You can't think, if I'm such a cutie
that I can hijack a big game long distance, that I'd be fool
enough to kill anybody in my own home."

"No," Proctor conceded, "it's unlikely, except that I understand you're a hothead—a slugger, a violent guy. *If*— and I
don't say it's so—Brattsford had bought or forced your wife's
favors you might have given way to an insensate rage."

"It's possible," Charles said. "Possible. But I got into the
city, found my wife mysteriously gone, found the body in my
home. As I was moving it in the truck, I saw someone in a
car, watching. I shook him. Today at the restaurant where my
wife works, the Colonial, the hostess there saw a man outside
on the walk. It was Sam Keech, though I didn't know him
then. Two days before she had seen him, too. He was with a
man that couldn't have been anybody but Measles. This was the
day *before* I was due out of stir. Over the phone my wife tells
me that this rat here came into the restaurant in her section—
she's a waitress—and posed as a buddy, and found out when
my train was due in. Meanwhile, Sam Keech, *hired by Measles,*
went to my apartment and opened it. He let Measles in later.
This afternoon when I saw Keech I tricked him, got the jump
on him. Made him talk. I found this watch . . . and these letters." Charles pointed from one to the other. "It's clear that
Measles forged notes from me to trick my wife out of the depot
and out of town . . ."

Syl put in: "I'll swear he put her on a bus, Proctor. He told
me she threatened to spoil the game, he was vague and impatient to get away . . . and snappish."

"Keech will tell you that Measles hired him, and in fact was
welching on fifty dollars he'd promised. . . ."

"Keech is dead," Proctor said bleakly. "Supposedly he fell
out the window and broke his neck. You help him?"

"I?" Charles cried. "Hell, no!" He twisted toward Measles. "So you killed him!"

Measles laughed.

Proctor told him: "Shut up. Now, Garrell, what's all these letters? You say Edwards is framing you. To clear suspicion from himself. I wish you could convince me, because I want that dough, and no crap about it!"

"So help me, this hundred dollars is all I've ever seen of the dough. Read this letter from Line City . . . and look at this postmark. The money was in the letter."

He sat forward, waiting, watching Proctor read. Pake had moved to stand between Measles and Charles. Syl said rapidly: "I was with Garrell when he found that letter, an hour or so ago. It's clear the letter is meant to send him rushing out of town."

Proctor nodded. "You claim, of course, your wife didn't send it . . . but Edwards did."

"He's claimed that before," Measles blurted. "But just note the postmark: 11:45 P.M. last night. I was here, right here, from eight-thirty on through the night."

"Jack," Proctor said, looking at Jack, "what time were you here last night?"

"One-thirty A.M. He was here O. K. Couldn't have made it back from Line City . . ."

"If he was with Garrell's wife at seven, he could've made Line City at ten, mailed it, and got back here by one-thirty."

"Ask De Verre! I was here!"

"If I can have a lamp, I can show you something damned interesting," Charles said.

Proctor nodded. Charles crossed, got a sanding lamp. He removed the shade, replugged it, and lay it on the floor. He focused the light up through the glass of the coffee table. He spread the Line City letter on the glass, with the light shining strongly through it. Then he began to sort through the letters in Nora's hand from which the letter had been composed. With Proctor peering closely, Charles demonstrated how the letter had been put together. He found the lines and sentences of the original letters and lay them carefully on top of the Line City letter. In each case the words fitted exactly. Until he came

to the phrase "The beat of thy heart is the pulse in my veins."
He had to try several letters before he found the one from
which Measles had copied.

"Well, well, well," Proctor said at last. "Perfect copies. Perfect tracework."

Charles said tightly: "I brought these letters home with me.
So he did this copy job today. De Verre says he was out a few
hours this afternoon. Long enough to prowl my place and see
the body he'd planted was gone. So he fixed up this trap and
telegraphed my wife, and probably tipped off the Parole Board.
And killed Sam Keech, too."

"I didn't write the letter," Measles cried. "His wife wrote
it. It's her writing . . . that's proved by the other letters. Naturally her writing looks like her writing."

"Oh, no, you're not so naive as that," Proctor said. "Nobody
can duplicate their own writing *precisely*. No, this is a clear
trace job."

"Anybody, not just a forger, could trace!"

"True . . . partly. But his wife sure as hell didn't go to the
trouble of tracing her own writing. And if she didn't, a guy
with a motive did. And even if Garrell was smooth enough
to trace, he couldn't have done such a sweet forgery on the
postmark and cancellation of the stamp. Oh, your name's all
over this, Edwards. And they've found Brattsford. The autopsy
shows he was slightly drugged at the time of his death. I see
that you're the boy who kept him doped and under cover, and
*you* took him to that apartment. I see you were overconfident,
just like I was overconfident in thinking you wouldn't double-
deal me. You figured Garrell would be frothing around hunting
for his wife and he'd be stuck with the stiff, so there was no
hurry about tipping the cops. Well, where's the dough?"

Measles got to his feet. "Don't get rough, Grig. I'll deal. If
you don't get rough. But if you do, I'll tip off De Verre and
you'll have to kick back."

"We deal, then. Where's the dough?"

"I've got to have guarantees, a getaway, a . . ."

"You never liked 'em pretty," Proctor said to Jack Pake. "He's
yours."

Pake spun him, kneed him, and pistol-whipped his face.

Measles back-pedaled so fast he fell, cowering behind his hands.

"Don't," he begged. "I'll deal. And trust you, Grig. Your word's good. Call him off."

"Get the money, then."

Measles got up. "Blow De Verre out of that room. It's in there."

Ten minutes later Proctor sat at the coffee table counting money, a blissful look on his face. "There's mine," he said smugly. "My fifty grand, plus the twenty-five thousand expenses I've incurred. Which leaves a hundred twenty-five thousand, less a few hundred. Here it is, Mr. de Verre. It's as I had begun to suspect. This Mr. Edwards was attempting to swindle you. And, most outrageous of all, he borrowed money from me to help him dupe you. He's what they call a confidence man, I'm shocked to discover. Tell Mr. de Verre, Edwards."

"Yes, sir," Measles admitted.

"It's much too smelly all the way around to have him arrested, De Verre, so I think you'd just better forget it." Proctor got to his feet, took Charles by the arm, and crossed the room with him. "Now, Garrell, we've got the savage, and we can't let him off as easy as this. We'll take him for that odd twenty-five grand. He'll hold still. This is the play: you can't be cooled. You're hot because he tried to push you around—that job at the warehouse, which he thinks handled slots. You're sore because he was forcing you into that job, handling the hot stuff, and you want to blast him to the Treasury on that cash dough he's got. It's dirty money, and the income boys would stick hell out of him. Now, I'll be the arbitrator. It'll cost you five grand and leave you a clear twenty. You on?"

"Sure. But what about Edwards?"

"Oh, he's dead already, waiting to be told about it. For the killer of Brattsford we can use Sam Keech. He's dead and he ain't got any family or anybody, so he sure as hell won't care. That watch with the fingerprints is enough to build the case around. Now, let's sock De Verre."

They crossed to De Verre, who looked dazed.

"Proctor," De Verre said anxiously, "you don't know it all. I may be an accomplice in a . . ."

"Murder. I know. Think nothing of it. All part of the swindle, I've discovered. I'll explain the whole matter, but at this crucial juncture we have a more ticklish and totally unanticipated problem. Garrell here. You've made an enemy, and he's bent on vengeance."

"I'm going to have it, too," Charles said, looking coldly at De Verre. "I've been intimidated, forced into a job in a crook warehouse, and I'll get even with you." He jabbed a forefinger at the stacks of cash on the coffee table. "The Treasury pays for information about tax evaders. Mr. de Verre."

"Now, now," Proctor said paternally, "that's not the American way—informing. What would Treasury pay? A few thousand. De Verre would do better than that. Hey?"

"Yes, certainly. Not that I couldn't explain this money . . ."

"Crap! Then explain it!"

"Wait, Garrell. I've been your friend, and I'm not the man to mislead you. You'll admit that?"

"Yeah, but . . . *he's* no friend."

"Charles," De Verre said earnestly, "I don't understand your feeling that I intimidated you. I understand you wanted that warehouse job and would get certain generous bonuses."

"How about Gobi and Elton?" Charles said angrily. "Isn't that why they pushed me around? So I'd be docile, and not dare refuse to do what I was told—including working at that warehouse."

"True," Proctor said. "But it was all a part of the swindle. Mr. de Verre was convinced of things that were untrue. He believed that warehouse was actually engaged in illegal shipments of slot machines. He was shown some hardware crates in the Merry Land Club basement and at the warehouse, and I think the foreman out there, Poley, was paid to let him conclude that shady things were going on."

"But you *did* believe," Charles told De Verre, "that I was safe—slapped around till I'd be safe. Didn't you?"

"Yes . . . I . . . but . . . Well, I just went along. I thought you'd be treated well enough. Paid well."

"I want these things," Charles said. "Gobi and Elton take a stretch—I mean that, Proctor. I don't deal on anything till they're fixed and fixed good. Then I want an old gun-theft

charge that they're dangling over my head dismissed. Then
I want a doctor's certificate for the Parole Board, saying I'm
unable to work at any kind of a job for a couple of months.
And twenty-five grand."

De Verre exhaled, said faintly, "That's a lot."

"I mean it! Proctor, will you see to it that those dicks get
a rough ride—nothing less than two to fourteen?"

"I don't know too much about law, but I know some people
of . . . uh . . . resources. Yes, Garrell. I see your position. I
can have them fixed and the gun charge dropped. And the
parole officer will have a medical certificate excusing you. The
rest is up to De Verre."

"Well," De Verre said, "I suppose . . . Well . . . all right.
Would you advise that I do it, Proctor?"

"In your position I'd pay him a hundred grand!"

Syl had gone to one of the windows and opened it wide.
She stood by it, looking moody. Proctor grinned wryly at her,
then glanced at Measles who was snapping his knuckles, watching the others, and most particularly Proctor's hoods who never
took their eyes off him. De Verre shivered, looked at the window and questioningly at Proctor. Proctor went across and
switched off the overhead lights, leaving the room quite dim.
For some seconds Charles didn't sense it. His mind was filled
with the fact of twenty grand in his pocket and with the images of his meeting with Nora at the airport. Another hour,
maybe, and she would be here, safe. Then he began to feel
the dark mood, the quiet, the odd nervous sense of something
—something.

Measles blurted, "Say, what's all this? I've got to get on the
move."

Nobody answered him. He looked frantically at that open
window, then from face to face. The others stared through him.

Syl said: "I want his right arm."

"He's too strong. He might break away," Proctor said quietly.

"You could knock him out, dammit. I've got some right in
this. . . ."

"He wouldn't enjoy it, knocked out." Proctor stared at him,
grinning a little.

"Let's cut the kid crap games, Grig. I got your word. I want to get the hell out of here—clear the *way.* . . ." His voice started out in a normal if anxious tone, but at the end it broke in a high, girlish shrill. . . .

Syl turned on the radio.

"Jack. Freddie!" Proctor snapped. "Throw him face down. . . ." They smacked into Measles, spilled him. He began to kick and twist, fight and squawl. Syl raised the radio volume. "Turn it down . . . gag him. . . ."

When it was done, Proctor said to Syl, "Call the cops. There's a guy up on the roof. Get it? About to jump . . ."

The call was made.

"Take his right arm, Charley."

"I don't like . . ."

"We're all in this. He's dead, no matter. C'mon. He's your meat, too. Don't just stand by . . . you're *in*."

It was nightmarish. Sickening. But it didn't last long.

Syl closed the window and turned on the lights. She was smiling.

"This," Proctor said, "calls for a drink."

It called for several.


Nora came down the steps from the plane, her arms open. He stood there, swaying, a silly smirk on his face.

"Darling!" she cried, wrapping herself around him. He wobbled. He kissed her sloppily and voraciously. She looked at him and began to giggle.

"Why, doll, you're drunk."

He got her into the shadows and bent to her ear and started to whisper. He stood up and looked proud of himself. He tried it again, and she had a very chewable ear, and then he remembered what he had been going to confide. She was kissing him and pouring herself out to him, and he was anxious to get her into a cab and to a hotel, and he never did get around to putting it into words: He wasn't too drunk.

www.ingramcontent.com/pod-product-compliance
Lightning Source LLC
Chambersburg PA
CBHW031127210626
46816CB00015B/983